Somewhere Publishing, LLC, Woodstock, GA.

"Any man who thinks he can be happy and prosperous by letting the government take care of him--- better take a closer look at the American Indian.   Henry Ford

DEDICATION

This work is dedicated to my wife, Barbara, whose love, encouragement and support have made it possible. Thank you, Baby Love.

PIPESTONE

A NOVEL BY ALEX DUNLAP

SOMEWHERE PUBLISHING

A SUBSIDIARY OF SOMEWHERE, INC.

Quarry Painting by George Catlin

PROLOGUE

NORTHERN PLAINS - 1610

A warm autumn sun slanted down on the collection of tepees, erasing the last vestiges of the night's dew, and warming the backs of the women as they rolled the sides of the teepees, opening them to receive the morning rays, and refresh the smoky air within. A short way from the easy activity of the village, two figures sat under the spreading branches of a huge old tree, one was intent on his work while the other watched and listened with rapt attention.

Running Deer loved to hear the familiar stories of their people, and his uncle, One Ear, was known by all who heard him as the greatest teller in the tribe. It was an honor to be a recognized teller of stories, for it was in this way that the history of the people was carried forward. Through the stories, children of the next generation and all the ones that followed would know what it truly meant to be of the Lakota.

The older man had decided to recite, again, the tale of the beginnings of their people. He told of the great battles, and the mighty warriors whose blood had been spilled, and how the Great One had caused the soil to change to a deep red color, the color of their heroic blood......and how he had chosen to fashion them, the Lakota, from the earth of this place. It was a wondrous thing, the story said, to know that the Great One had so loved the Lakota that he had made all the men red like them, and had chosen this special place for the stone of his special people.

One Ear knew he was a very skillful teller of stories, and he had found a like skill in his young nephew. Without saying as much, he had chosen him to carry on the tradition of the telling of the old stories, and was beginning to school him in the more intricate task of weaving a story of new deeds and happenings so they would bear telling, and not be hooted away at the council fires as when tales were clumsily delivered. He took great pride in his skill, and wished his pupil to be as skillful, reflecting the quality of the teacher.

As the tale was being told, One Ear carefully shaped the small, rectangular piece of soft rock he held against the rough hide pad on his thigh. The black stone scraping tool, not unlike the ones women used to clean the hides of deer and buffalo, had been handed down to him by his mentor, and had been shaped from a shard of flint rock uncovered at some long-forgotten winter camp. He worked surely, and with the confidence of the master craftsman; for besides being the tribes most eloquent teller of stories, the one responsible for recalling the history of the people on the holy days, he was the maker of the ceremonial pipes. The soft red rock, of so holy an origin, was the choice material for this purpose, and One Ear the finest maker of the pipes any had ever seen. He understood the character of the stone, and how to find the best veins of material among the many. All marveled at the clarity and simplicity of his designs, and word of his skill had spread among the tribes of the plains, and even back to the despised Ojibwa. Well-made pipes, with the distinctive dark red bowls had becomes a source of commerce for the tribal group, and One Ear was held in the highest esteem because of this; even as high as some of the more accomplished hunters and warriors!

This high regard had not gone without notice by Running Deer, and he was quite proud when his uncle had singled him out as his apprentice. Although accurate with a bow, and a tireless runner,

6

he lacked the bulk and stature of some, and knew that he could not rely solely on his physical ability to achieve prominence. He did not know that his uncle had been faced with that same realization in his youth. He regarded the ragged lump left where an enraged raccoon had torn the left ear from his uncle's head many summers ago. It had given him his name, and one that had earned him great respect, but Running Deer knew that it had also made him unacceptable to the vain maidens, and so his uncle lived alone.

"Watch now carefully, Running Deer. This part of the shaping is very critical, because if the bowl of the pipe is made too thin, it will crack with the heat, and if too thick the pipe will not draw properly. Watch now!"

Running Deer smiled inwardly at the suddenly gruff tone of the oft repeated instruction; he had heard it every time he had been with his uncle for the pipe making.

Cutting the mouth of the bowl with a drill, then reaming with a tapered scraper, One Ear meticulously scraped, smoothed and scraped again. Although working surely, he worked slowly, for he had learned through bitter experience that this was the most critical step in the process, and if hurried would surely end badly. He was secretly pleased that Running Deer had shown the patience needed so early in his training; few youths could restrain themselves. He continued with the story; the dreadful litany of the conflict with the Ojibwa, and the wanderings in the Dark Time, until finally the Great One had seen the plight of his people, and had shown them the buffalo, and the means to hunt them, and then glory that had followed the people since.

The morning wore on, and the two let their blanket-robes fall aside, and focused their entire attention on the pipe bowl. Near the middle of the day, One Ear handed the roughed-out piece to Running Deer. "You finish, Running Deer. You know how to make the *outside of the bowl smooth with the small scraper and rubbing hide. Move quickly before the stone hardens, but be careful not to crack it. When you have finished, we will fit the stem, and you may present this to your father. It is a good pipe, and you have been an important part in its making. Go to work now, and we will be finished in time for the mid-day meal."*

Running Deer accepted the pipe bowl numbly, not having realized that One Ear had not intended to complete it. This was beyond his greatest hope; to be able to actually finish the pipe his father would use when reaching agreements and making treaty with other chiefs. As he worked, One Ear smiled inwardly. The boy had learned well, and when the next summer came, he would be ready to take the raw material from the Holy Quarry, and fashion his own pipe bowls. He had to admit that his skill in making the stems was as good as his already, although this could not be said aloud.

He leaned back against the trunk of the tree, and pondered his good fortune. Although he had no woman, and as a result, no sons, he had been looked upon with favor by the Great One. He had his position in the tribe, well-honored skills, and a talented and willing apprentice who was, after all, of the same blood. It was good. And to be in this Holy place, as he had been for so many summers was also good. He felt the closeness of the spirits of their brave ancestors, and the presence of the Great One, who surely lingered in a place where he had made his finest people. This place must always be remembered so, and kept holy.

With that thought he leaned forward, and quizzed Running Deer on the story he had just told; it must be repeated properly for the benefit of the children to come. They would need to know that the Holy Quarry must be kept as it is, the source of the Lakota.

CHAPTER 1

George Benjamin stared down at the Constitution Avenue traffic from a long window in his office at the Russell Senate Office Building, an angry glare marking his almost-perfect features. His anger was directed more at a situation than a person, and of course he was incapable of being angry with himself. How had things become so uncertain, and in such a short period of time? All he had wanted was to have a long weekend with Laura at his favorite retreat in the Minnesota back country; woods, lake, secluded cabins that allowed resort guests the ultimate in privacy. *"It's a good thing, too"*, he thought. *"That girl calls out when she comes like an opera singer trying to reach the back rows. You could have heard her a block away, even though,"* he admitted to himself, *"I'm not exactly quiet; quite the duet, we are."*

The trip had started well enough, with champagne on the plane, then the scenic drive out to the resort, where he was well known. They had been the recipients of lots of preferential treatment from the time they arrived. Only what he felt his due from the "little people" as the senior senator from the state. After a quick tumble in the bedroom of the cabin and a long shower together, they had a first class dinner at the main lodge, and were on their way back when he received the call. They wanted to meet and discuss the timetable, and there was really nothing he could do about it. "Laura, babe, I need to meet with a couple of guys that are coming down from my campaign office to go over some details of the financial side of the next run. It's complicated and a little confidential, so rather than bother your mind with such things, what about taking a stroll for a few minutes, have a brandy at the Lobby Bar main lodge, and I'll join you a bit later. That OK with you?"

"Sure George. Just don't take too long. I'm a little tired after the trip up here, and I wouldn't want to doze off later", this last with a slight smile. "I'll see you in a little while."   There was an undercurrent of displeasure in her voice, despite the smile, but Benjamin did not sense it. For a man with such finely honed skills in dealing with constituents and his fellow senators, he had no concept of how to relate to another's personal feelings.

"From there on, everything went in the toilet", he recalled. The two men from Iowa showed up as promised, and they met in the living room of his cabin. It was not a contentious meeting, but then not all roses either. *"And God, but those two are a trial. The dweeb couldn't say hello in less than a hundred words, and the other one, the scraggly one, with those hard dark eyes has a stillness about him that always seems terribly sinister, maybe even dangerous."*

After some discussion of the finer points of his role in the plan, they had gotten down to the reason Benjamin was interested in the deal at all; money. He was not accustomed to haggling, and his ire was up by the time they finally agreed to his terms. *"What the hell is the world coming to when people don't fall all over themselves to please a Senator"*, he had thought! Eventually they grudgingly promised the payoff that he demanded, and when they left, he had given them wiring instructions to his Cayman Island account. As he turned to go out the door, he caught a shadow crossing his line of vision from the back hallway. It was gone as quickly as it had appeared, but although no one was there when he checked, he could still make out the faint scent of her perfume.

So now, here he was with the uncertainty of what, if anything she might have heard, and what he should do about it. He was reluctant to break off with her. She was, after all, one of the most enthusiastic bed partners he could remember, and there had been many. But then, what if she had heard the discussion of "his money"? That could be really big trouble if she talked to the wrong people. Wondering what to do about his little nymphet, he eventually decided to let things ride for a time, and see if she brought up anything about that night. *"Yeah, that's what I'll do. She may or may not let the cat out of the bag about what she heard, and I'll deal with her then. She'll likely want some part of the pay-off, but that would be alright. I've enough stashed to take care of one bimbo without making a dent. Yes, that's what to do; play a waiting game, enjoy her for the time being, and see what she comes up with."*

With that decision made, he turned from the window and made his way down to the tunnel for the shuttle that would take him over to the Capital where he knew absolutely how to handle things.

The faint chink of the tiny trowel against the sides of the shallow dish punctuated the pecking of a soft Virginia rain on the roof of the greenhouse. This sound played in turn a kind of counterpoint to the strains of the Mozart symphony from the interior of the house. The man worked systematically, spreading the soil mixture over the carefully positioned roots of the tiny tree. It was held erect with a small stake fastened to the workbench. The only light came from the industrial fixture over the long work area, the remainder of the room was in shadow. As he patted the last of the soil into the dish, he stepped back and looked at the results of his efforts with a critical eye. The slightly asymmetrical shape of the little maple would lend itself well to the windswept, *fukinagashi,* style. It would, of course, require some additional training, but in about two years it would attain the shape he had sensed in its makeup when he had first seen it in the nursery. Satisfied, he mentally approved the effort, moistened the soil, and carefully surrounded the base of the tree with some moss. Later a rounded stone would be selected from the tray he kept for such things to complete the planting; add the last finishing touch.

A tall, slender man, he carried his six decades with ease, testimonial to the regular early morning workouts that he managed even when traveling, as he often did. His dark hair was casually styled, somewhat shorter than present fashion would have dictated, and shot through with silver. He moved purposefully about the room, frowning now and then in concentration as he checked each of the tiny plants, his even, regular features giving no hint of the extraordinary intellect they masked. The pale blue eyes missed little as each of the bonsai was tended; a stray shoot trimmed, a small stone rearranged, a swooping branch bent ever so slightly with the soft wire that was training it.

Absorbed with his tasks, he was startled by the strident electronic warble of the telephone. Tapping the speaker button on the phone, he smiled at the sound of his friend's voice. "Well, hello, Mickey. How are you? And what brings you to call at this time of an evening? Nothing unfortunate like a dead battery and no tow-truck, I hope."

"No, nothing like that; afraid it's a bit more serious. Can you meet me at the Blacksmith Shop in about a half hour? I've just heard something that I don't know how to react to, and certain aspects of it fall in your expertise on Indian related things, and I thought you could maybe help me decide what to do about it."

The normally smooth modulation with which Mickey spoke carried an edge tonight, a tone Kevin knew as an indicator of genuine concern. "Sure thing, happy to, but can you give me a few extra minutes? I'm working with the bonsai, almost finished, and then I'll want to get the dirt off my hands. Say…three-quarters of an hour?

Anything I should bring with me, or begin to think about on the way?"

"Not really. I'll be able to explain things better when I meet you. Blacksmith Shop, forty-five minutes, right? Oh, and thanks!"

"No problem, Mickey. I'll finish here, get cleaned up, and I'm on my way." Switching the phone off, he moved quickly to the last few plants and attended to their care. Next, he pulled off the short apron he used when working in the greenhouse, and hung it on its peg by the house door. Stopping at the deep sink at the end of the workbench, he scrubbed his hands diligently with a surgeon's brush, drying them on a piece of a discarded sweatshirt he kept in the greenhouse for a towel. Pushing the door closed, he turned out the light, paused to switch off the stereo, and went to the garage.

Halfway across the continent, in a brightly lit laboratory, the small cluster of technicians watched as a high-speed printer piled sheet after sheet filled with rows of figures, interspersed with diagrams and chemical symbols. The wire basket on the back of the machine began to fill as the sheets piled into a steadily growing stack. A smallish spectacled man in a long white lab coat turned to one of the others and said, "Johnson, that last formulation was the key, and now we have what we've been looking for! Harry; let's get all this on the way to the Director at once. Maybe the miserable old bastard won't be so prickly the next time we see him, hey?"

Harry Genarro nodded at Dr. Williamson, the laboratory manager, and made his way to the communications console in the next room. Seething inwardly, it was all he could do to keep from shouting at the others that it was *his* formulation, mentioned to Dick Johnson during a luncheon conversation; and now they were, once again, directing all the credit toward someone else. *Some day, some way,* he thought, *all of them will have to finally give me what is my due; acknowledge that without me they would still be struggling with Dickie-boy Johnson's goopy mess; that this entire effort would have been for nothing!* Stabbing furiously at the keyboard, he went through the mechanics of entering the transmission codes in the machine and leaned back while the connection to the Director's console was being made. How very like Williamson to give him this grunt work instead of keeping him at his side to assist in the completion of the analysis of the data. *Johnson can't know what to do, after all, and the rest of these clowns couldn't analyze a cookie recipe! I come up with the single most important compound formulation, the key to the whole thing, talk about it with Dick Johnson, and look at this! I'm in here punching keys, and the rest of them are floundering around, kissing ass, and trying to act as if they knew what they were doing! It's ridiculous, and it's not right! But just wait until they try to do something else; then they'll come running to Harry, trying to bail themselves out again...I'll get some credit then, you can bet your ass! A lot more credit than they want to give me now, much more...Someday...*

Kevin pulled the Land Rover into the space beside Michaela's sleek Audi convertible and switched off the lights. He sat for a moment thinking about the woman he was about to see, with warmth now tempered with concern. She had been among Marybeth's closest friends, had become almost a daughter for them, helping to fill the void when they had not been able to have children of their own. He reflected on his good fortune at their having become good friends as well. He could honestly say that she was among his closest friends, a real confidant, one that in many respects knew him better than almost anyone else. With a smile, he locked the car, and went into the restaurant.

The room was a dim, heavily timbered place, with a rather low ceiling. The large grille which gave the place its name was to the rear, manned by a black giant who surveyed the place with a grim visage, tending his steaks and chops, and hiding a mellow nature only a privileged few had ever seen. A superbly designed hood over the grille silently pulled the smoke out, leaving only the imagination to know the delicious aroma from his efforts. Calvin Macgregor had been the proprietor of the Blacksmith shop for almost seven years, and since buying out its former owner had watched the business grow until it was one of the most successful small restaurants in the Washington area. His careful attention to the quality of service and food had earned the loyalty of hundreds of patrons, among them Michaela Campbell and Kevin Christopher. As Kevin paused in the small corridor before the dining room, Calvin acknowledged him with a smile and a mock salute with his huge fork, and nodded in the direction of a corner table where Kevin saw Michaela, seated with her back to the wall, facing into the room. He strode over, taking a seat across from her. Signaling the head waiter as he sat, he kidded, "This is a fine way to get a free meal from a friend! And suggesting my favorite place so you know I won't..." he stopped in mid-sentence as he took in the creased brow and tension around her mouth. "Hey, just kidding, just kidding. There *is* something wrong, isn't there! Let's hear about it!"

As the waiter arrived, Kevin noticed that Michaela had only a cup of coffee on the table in front of her, and following her cue, asked for the same, and instructed the waiter to give them a few minutes before returning to take the order. "OK, now," he said "from the top."

"You were right, Kev, there is something wrong – not with me," she hurried, noting the concern immediately coming to his face. "But it has to do with a friend of mine, Laura Atkinson. You may remember her; she's a very pretty blonde; works as an information technology specialist in the Administrative division at the FBI. She

15

and I have known each other since high school, and have played tennis together in the Y league for a number of years, among other things."

"Sure," he said, "I remember her, and yes, exceptionally pretty, and she seemed quite bright, too. Is something wrong with her?"

"It's not exactly that," she sighed. "She's gotten herself mixed up with George Benjamin. That's bad enough as it is, but today she called me from home, really upset...No, more concerned than upset. She's happened onto something that has to do with him, and whatever it is, she thinks it involves an Indian, or something to do with Indians, and she's certain that it's no good. That's where you come in, of course, the Indian connection. Whatever the rest is, we'll just have to find out together. She was rather mysterious, sounded... frightened. Oh, and another thing. Whatever this thing is, she emphasizes it has to be altogether confidential. She's going to meet us here in another few minutes, but I wanted to have a chance to talk with you first, lay some ground work. She may not be completely comfortable saying anything in front of you ... I didn't tell her you would be here ... but since this, whatever it is, involves an Indian matter, it only seemed natural to get your input, the Native American perspective. And after all, you're not all that terrifying!"

Kevin had scowled at the mention of Senator George Benjamin, but managed a small grin at the last jibe. "How in the name of conscience did a nice girl...uh, sorry about that, nice *person*, become involved with a self-serving jerk like Benjamin," he growled. "I thought everyone in this town, *especially* women, knew what a sleaze-bag he is. Why..."

"Now don't get up on your soap box," she smiled. "I know how you feel about the 'Good Senator', but it's good to remember that he is not only terribly handsome, in a slightly oily way, but that when he wants to he can be absolutely charming. Admit, it," she said as she sat back, grinning at her friend's frustrated ire.

"Well, alright," he grumbled, "but I still think he's a self serving son of a ..." he stopped as Michaela frowned a signal, and rose with her as a woman approached in the wake of their waiter. Laura Atkinson, he mused, was one of those women who literally turned heads wherever they went, and dressed as she was tonight in a stylish von Furstenberg wrap dress, she was stunning. The dress draped her well-formed figure perfectly, and the soft blue color was exactly the proper compliment to her thick straw-blonde hair.

As Michaela made the introductions, Laura broke in and extended her hand, "Why certainly I remember Mr. Christopher, Mickey! It's nice to see you again."

Kevin entered their drink order; a glass of white wine for Laura and Michaela, and Heineken for himself. They sat and settled into a somewhat awkward silence.

Michaela broke in. "Laura, I asked Kevin here tonight because of your mention that whatever is bothering you had some connection either with an Indian, or an Indian thing. I don't think you know it, but he's a real expert on that particular subject." She shushed Kevin's protest with her hand and continued. "He's completely knowledgeable when it comes to things related to American Indians. Besides that, he is a good friend whose counsel I regard very highly. I know he can be relied upon completely to honor your wishes about confidentiality, no matter what you say here tonight." Looking over at Kevin, they both acknowledged his nodding agreement. "Now is that alright with you?"

There was a pause, and Kevin had the distinct impression that his "character reference" was being carefully weighed. "Michaela," Laura began, "you must know that if anyone, and I mean *anyone* else

17

had said that, I wouldn't have stayed, couldn't have…but with you, well let's just say that it's okay with me."

"Fine, Laura," with an arched brow at Kevin.

"Good enough," he said with an affirmative nod and a smile, and suggested, "If you like, we can relax, have something to eat, and you can begin to let us know what's going on whenever you feel like it."

They made small talk as the meals were being prepared, although an undercurrent of tension remained. Kevin smiled inwardly at the gusto with which Laura attacked a stuffed veal chop, potatoes and salad. She might have been concerned, but for the moment she was able to put that behind her, and concentrate on one of Calvin's specialties. As the table was cleared, and coffee served, she seemed to gather herself, her comely features clouded, and a certain tautness appeared in her manner. "You know I work at the FBI"? She paused, looking at Kevin.

"Yes, Michaela told me, but go on."

"When the Justice Committee was holding hearings on the incidence of computer theft and fraud, the Assistant Director asked me to put together some data for his testimony on the Hill. The report was rather large, lots of charts and things, so he asked since I had helped with the preparation if I would go up with them and help set up the charts and so forth. I thought it would be a good experience, and since there wasn't likely to be any real fireworks, it might even be fun, so I said yes. While we were there, I had to leave at one point to get some other things that were out in the hallway. On the way back in as I came hurrying around a corner, I bumped, I mean *literally* bumped, into George, Senator Benjamin. He was really quite nice about it, and helped me pick up the things I had spilled. We talked for a minute, and he asked me where I worked, and what I did; just small things, and all the while very pleasant. About a week later, there was a group being taken on a tour of the Bureau, some sort of VIP party, and who should be with them but Senator Benjamin. As he walked past my office, he stopped, said hello, and we started to talk some more..."

Kevin watched the girl's face closely as she continued her story. A genuine beauty, Laura had the clear blue eyes and fair skin typically found among those with her hair color. And the hair was special; she had a thick mane of it, and pulled back as it was tonight it accented her delicate features to perfection. He could appreciate the fact that even one so jaded as George Benjamin would be attracted to her. The tale, as she continued, was predictable, and somewhat sad in its predictability; the innocent luncheons, "chance" encounters. Eventually there were political dinners, celebrity-filled social occasions; with it all culminating in an intimate dinner where the charm and glamour of the older man led to a convenient hotel room; the inevitable passionate consummation of the seduction. There was poignancy in Laura's recitation of the beginnings of this relationship; for all her beauty and worldly outlook, she had become putty in his experienced hands. As he listened, an angered Kevin boiled inwardly at the tale. *That miserable, slimy son of a bitch!*

There was a pause, and after taking a sip of her wine, Laura resumed, "It was simply wonderful, being with him. It was almost impossible to think that he cared for me, but it was there in everything he said and did. I began to think that we had something special. I mean, after all, Jack Kennedy met Jacqueline while he was in the Senate; that's at least some sort of precedent...Anyway, we were together all the time! Last week, so we shouldn't have to be apart, I was with him when he went on a trip back to Minnesota. We spent almost the whole time at this resort, way back in the woods somewhere, really remote, and while we were there he had a meeting with couple of men I didn't know. It pissed me off, sort of, to have to be alone, but we were together at night, and that was okay… more than okay…"

Another pause, another sip of wine, and she continued, "I thought it a bit strange that he didn't introduce me, but he said they were just minor players in some political campaign group that supported him; "Peanut players' he called them, and not anyone I would like to know. It was still a little irritating, but I went along, because I didn't want to do anything that would affect our relationship. So, one evening, while they were meeting in our cabin after dinner, I was to take a walk out by the lakeshore. It turned out to be cooler than I thought, and I went back to the cabin for a sweater. Not wanting to disturb the meeting, I went around through the back door, and got the sweater from the closet in the bedroom. Nobody knew I was there or heard me come in, even though I passed the door to the living room. As I passed on the way back out, I heard George talking with the others. He was talking about money, I mean big money, *millions*! I thought at first it had something to do with the campaign coming up in the fall. Then he said that it would have to be handled through either the Cayman Islands or Switzerland. Right then, I knew that it wasn't political money, and these other guys didn't have anything to do with any PAC! I stood in the shadow of the hall to our bedroom and couldn't help but hear, and the more I heard, the more I wanted to run away from there and never see him again! I believed in him! I thought he was truly working for the good of the country and the people. Why that sort of thing would make him nothing but a common crook! I'm no Mother Theresa, but there's a limit to what I'll put up with in anybody…"

The flush this time was anger, and as she paused again, she was reliving, they could see, a personally devastating incident. With an effort, Laura continued. "Of course I couldn't just walk in there, or run out; and if I had, I don't know what might have happened. I made it through the rest of the week, and called Mickey right after I got back. I had to make up my mind what I wanted to do. The funny thing is I think I still care about him. Isn't that a kick? But then, I can't let something like this just go by, can I?" She received the looks of approval she sought. "Can you help me figure out what to do? Deep down I know it's important that something be done to expose him! I'm just not sure what or how... He's an awfully powerful man, you know, and you can't just go throwing allegations around here and there without something to back them up; now can you?" They both smiled at her, understanding the anxiety she felt.

"That's fine, Laura," Michaela said soothingly, "but you need to get into some of the detail for us so we'll be able to understand, to assess what you overheard."

With a small smile, Laura glanced at the two of them, "I guess I ran right past that, didn't I? Well, this is the gist of what was said while I was in the hallway. I'm not sure what it all means, or where the plan leads, but basically these people that George was meeting with seem to have some connection with Interglobal Materials and Mining, IMM. A project they are involved in requires a certain particular material, a mineral of some sort. The source for that, so they say, is found at a place they said really has no meaning to anyone other than a few Indians; that they need to have George's help in opening the place up for mining since it is on National Park Service land...."

Harry glanced at the monitor screen and saw that the cursor was still blinking indicating the data transfer was still active. *Lots of data*, he thought. *I wonder if that old fool will be able to understand what we've done, or if someone will have to translate for him. He might be able to appreciate the significance of the work, but he'll never know that it was only because of my input that there's anything*

other than a lot of inconclusive data and a stack of large cancelled checks.

He mused about how he might correct this injustice until, at long last, the blinking stopped, and a dialogue box reading "TRANSMISSION COMPLETE" flashed on the monitor. He broke the connection with the distant headquarters office, and allowed another sour line of thought. He despised being stuck out here in the sticks while other, far less accomplished men, in his view, moved in the rarified environs of the halls of corporate power. He had never been there, didn't know them, but imagined that these lesser lights were gaining the recognition that *should* have been his, while he languished in Northern Iowa! *It just isn't fair, isn't right!* The pencil he held snapped as he made a fist in his rage.

Kevin leaned back in the old chair in his den, pondering the incredible story he had heard, still amazed at the audacity of it all. Smoke from the Upmann in the ash tray at his elbow curled lazily upward, the panatela forgotten in his concentration. What Laura had told them was, in his mind, almost incomprehensible. That politicians engaged in any number of shady activities he took as a given; it was simply a part of a sleazy game that had been going on for centuries – only something more than two in this country to be sure, but polished to a fine degree by the practitioners. One thing that was a surprise was the lack of subtlety. Generally, books were published and bought by the case, stock tips were received by anonymous staffers from equally anonymous callers, or carefully screened beneficence was bestowed on families, but rarely was there just a block of money. He had initially presumed that it would eventually find its way back in the form of campaign contributions all well within the statutory limits for political gifts, and that Laura's assessment that the individuals were not politically motivated was off the mark. But as her tale spun out he had become less certain. Michaela had seemed equally dubious after they had chatted on Laura's departure, and she had said she would start a discreet investigation into that possibility. Her interest, he knew, stemmed from the time she had spent with a Virginia Attorney General's Task Force that had dug into political corruption in the state. Her passion for ferreting out rotten politicians hadn't dimmed with the passing of time. She had said on numerous occasions that it was almost an evangelical zeal which came over her when confronted with that sort of thing. Even though she was now engaged in her own private practice, she loved the idea of working at uncovering political corruption, even informally.

For his part, the relationship with an Indian concern had come from the comments made about "opening up", and "mining", and "only a few Indians use it". His interest was immediately piqued, as he listened while Laura related what she had overheard. There was only one area where Benjamin had influence that was now used by "only a few Indians" and located on Park Service land, and that was the Pipestone Quarry. Although protected under Park Service agreements, the force of law that existed with formal treaties was not in place there. The agreements had historically been honored, but they would be relatively easy to circumvent with the right application of power at the right levels in the Park Service hierarchy. He had no doubts that some form of lobbying, crude as it seemed to be on the surface, was at work here. What didn't make any sense was that a sensible, and in this case very shrewd, member of any legislative body would expose themselves to what was so clearly blatant bribery. The risk of losing their influence and power wouldn't seem to support the end reward, unless it was truly astonishing and they could wangle a way to avoid prison.

This proposed desecration was not the sort of thing that would be casually considered, much less conspired to actually carry out. Not that it would rank with the pillaging of the Pharaoh's tombs, but there was no way the idea could be condoned. These men were actually planning to annex the Quarry, one of the holiest places of the Lakota, where they reverently took the red stone for use in making fetishes, and ornaments, and their ceremonial pipes. It was the pipes that mattered most. Not only did they form a cornerstone for Indian inter-tribal bonds, to the Lakota they were the centerpiece for their culture. And not just any stone would do for their special pipes; it had to come from the place known now as the Pipestone Quarry.

To do this thing was not just a travesty. It was a real mystery, besides. Why would anyone want to mine in that particular ground in the first place? Since they had stopped using the quartz that overlaid the pipestone for building material back in the late 19th century, there had been no interest in the place except for the Indian craftsmen who received special permits to take small amounts of the stuff for their work. And what part did George Benjamin play in the plot? What motive was so compelling that it could entice corruption of a senior member of the Senate, and in the process heap indignity on a group of Indians?

CHAPTER 2

The Delta shuttle from New York disgorged its typical collection of businessmen, power brokers and bureaucrats that commonly made up its passenger list. Included on this flight were also a couple of diplomats of low rank and a tall, striking man with the classic chiseled features of the Native American Indian. Matthew Little Crow kept his thick raven hair cut longer than the current style, although he eschewed the braids worn by some of his more traditional brethren. Swept back from his high forehead, it framed a high-cheek boned visage that could have been part of a Remington painting. His smooth stride covered the walk from the arrival area to the main terminal quickly, and he scanned the small cluster of people waiting for passengers for his friend. "Hello, Kevin," he called, as he made his way toward the group. "Good of you to meet me; I could just as well have rented a car and come over to your place."

"Nonsense," Kevin smiled, "I need to come here once in a while to remind me why I hate to make the trip. Saarinen's vision has been almost completely obscured by 'improvements', and I don't believe they will ever finish fooling around with the roads! Let's get your bag and get out of here."

" I'm all for that, but tell me, what is it that brought you out here through horrible traffic that couldn't wait a couple of hours for me to get settled in a hotel? I've known you long enough to know you don't make late night calls for advice and assistance on a whim, and then spend an hour in the car just to save a little bit more than that by waiting. And what's all the hush-hush business? Indian matters are important to us, and I think we both agree they deserve a lot more intelligent attention, but they hardly, or at least rarely, require secrecy."

"I'll tell you what; let's get out of here and get you checked into your hotel. On the way we'll talk in the car, bring you up to speed on the situation as I see it. After you hear what I, or rather, *we* are working on, then maybe you'll better understand what all the confidentiality is about. Come on, let's grab your bags and get on the road."

Bags loaded, and on the road, Kevin resumed his response to Matthew's query. "Let me fill you in on what prompted my call..."

Once they hit the main highway, traffic moved much better, and as they turned away from the city and struck off towards the countryside, it thinned steadily. Sweeping along through the lush spring surroundings of Northern Virginia, Kevin related the full story heard from Laura Atkinson. He also shared his puzzlement over the motivation for what was apparently a plan to break the agreement with the Lakota Sioux over use and access to the Quarry.

Matthew listened in silence; brow creased in concentration as he took in all that Kevin said. "You're right," he said when the tale was complete, "there doesn't seem to be a good reason for anyone to mine in the Quarry. Heaven knows, the whites made a killing, no play on words intended, by manufacturing pipes and God knows what-all else back in the bad old days, but Indians are the only ones allowed to work the Quarry now. Even then, it involves a very tedious permitting process, and not all that many go through the effort. And you're right; it's been that way for years, with never a hint that anyone had any designs on changing it."

"That's just it, Matthew," puzzled Kevin. "What with movies like "Dances With Wolves" and "Last of the Mohicans" there was an elevation of interest in things Indian; blankets, crafts, artifacts, and things like that, but that was a passing thing and was several years ago, and besides, there isn't anywhere near enough money in turning out reproductions, for anyone to start talking about feeding offshore bank accounts! It *doesn't* make sense. I worked it over for a few days, but wasn't able to come up with anything I felt I could sink my teeth into, and that's when I called you. You know a lot more people up there, close to the Quarry itself, and have the relationship with them that only another Native American can have. It was absolutely a natural. I was wondering, too, if you thought it might be worthwhile to check with them on the ground up there, see if there is something floating around in the rumor mill, that sort of thing. There's nothing I have been able to find in the literature that I have been able to lay my hands on so far that would entice sophisticated individuals, representing what I *know* to be an extremely sophisticated company, to talk of throwing millions of dollars around. Things like this, that don't make sense but involve a lot of money, make me very nervous. The other aspect of this, and the real reason for the need for secrecy, is that one of the principals, or I suppose I should say *alleged* principals, is a United States Senator! The implications are extraordinary, and we can't just talk up a scandal without some real proof that something went on. I expect to hear from Michaela Campbell later on today. I may have mentioned her at some point; local attorney, friend of Marybeth's, good and valued friend of mine. She's been making a few discreet inquiries regarding the Senator. Did I tell you it's George Benjamin? Anyway, it's possible she may have found something that could give us a place to start on that end of the equation, or at least lend some better insight. She also may have heard more from our source that began all this, a friend of hers named Laura Atkinson. We'll probably not get together with Michaela until later this evening. In the meantime, let's get you settled into the hotel. I made the reservation at the Huntsman; you seemed to like it the time you were here on that Penobscot thing and it'll be the most convenient to both my place and the city, if we ever have to go in for anything."

"You're right, Kevin. It's one of my favorite away-from-home places. I've meant to thank you for introducing me to it."

They turned in at the drive of the Huntsman Inn a few minutes later, both quiet as they pondered the curious situation they confronted. The Inn, so named because in an earlier time the core building had been the stable for one of the local foxhunters, was approached on a tree-lined road that opened on a long, low stone building, still very much reflecting its heritage. What had once been a wide open area for assembling the riders, their mounts and the hounds was now a beautifully landscaped circular drive, with carefully tended formal beds in the center. The covered portion of the drive at the main entrance was paved with smooth stone paving blocks, set so tightly their hairline joints almost looked as if they were a spider web pattern on a flat glazed plate. As they pulled to a stop, a black-coated bellman appeared to take Matthew's luggage, and escort them into the lobby.

The warmth of the room was almost a tangible thing; muted lighting, rich carpets, and bleached-board paneling all lending to the comfort and welcoming feeling reinforced by the smiling clerk at the registration counter. "Good afternoon, Mr. Little Crow, Mr. Christopher! It is a pleasure to see you again."

"Thank you," the two men answered in chorus. Laughing, Matthew, began again, "Yes, thank you. It's a pleasure to be back."

The clerk tendered the small registration card for Matthew's signature, assuring him that all other information had been completed from his file when Kevin had made the reservations. "Will you be with us for very long, Mr. Little Crow? Mr. Christopher left the departure date open when he called."

"I'm not sure," he answered, "but I would expect to be here at least a week, maybe two or so. Will that be a problem for you? If it is, I'm sure we can either set a more specific date, or make other arrangements."

"Not at all, Sir," she replied. "We are more than pleased to work with you on those things, and when you have more definite plans, just let us know. It's a pleasure to accommodate you in any way we can." With another smile, she handed him the old fashioned brass-tagged key, deftly filing the registration card in its slot with her other hand. "We've put you in the Tack Room Suite, so that you can have all the room and privacy you need for your work, and won't have to come and go through the lobby if you don't care to. Once again, welcome back, and please let us know if there is anything we can do to make your stay more comfortable."

The remains of a shared pizza lay on one corner of the large table; half empty glasses close at hand as the two men worked through a large stack of files. Hired by a Security division of IMM, they exuded a mix of toughness and intelligence. It would have been apparent to observers, had there been any, that they had been at their task for many hours, but that much remained to be done. Sitting back in his chair, the larger of the two rubbed his eyes, yawned, and slumped further down. "You know something, Charley? I think this Senator we're supposed to watch must have some special secret to attract so many broads. From what we've got in these files, it looks like he's made a run at half the unmarried women in the District, and a good percentage of the married ones! And a real EEO-fucker, too; if she's between 20 and 45, he's game, no matter what 'race, color, creed, or national origin'. You wonder where he gets the stamina for all that swordsmanship! What is he, fifty-two? Jesus!"

"He's amazing, you're right about that. He must live on oysters, or something, huh? I hear he even made a pass at some ambassador's wife at a state dinner in their embassy; almost had her, too, but was afraid there'd be some sort of international incident, so he backed off. Rumor had it that she was in a state of depression for weeks. He must have all the morals of a goat, that's all I can say."

"Yeah, well let's get through to the most recent ones, and see if there's anything that would cause our folks any heartburn. Most of the files on his women that we've been through so far are at least six months old, and he seems to get tired of them in about six to eight weeks and move on. One thing though, they're all lookers. It's enough to make a guy consider a career in politics!"

Returning to the remaining folders, each took one and scanned the contents. Looking up, the one called Mac paused and looked over at his companion. "Did you ever wonder where these files come from? I mean, here we are, called again by people we've never seen, offered a very big bonus at the end, told to pick up a package at the UPS place, and then given instructions over the phone again. And look at the quality of this stuff; it's great!"

"Yeah, I've wondered about it," admitted Charley. "But then, from the beginning, what, two years ago, this whole setup is strange. Interviewed over the phone after answering an ad in a magazine for private "security personnel", hired without ever actually seeing, or being seen by, anyone, always going somewhere new, getting phone calls and fax instructions. There's a lot of surveillance, and occasionally a wet job. Very strange, but the money is always in the accounts when they say it will be and like you say, the info they get us for background is outstanding; makes our work a lot easier. A guy would have to be just plain stupid not to wonder, but I guess I've just made up my mind to go with it, not question what I'm asked to do, or look this particular gift horse in the mouth; the money's too good. Know what I mean?"

"Yeah, guess you're right about not 'looking the horse in the mouth', but still mighty strange. Well, back to the life and loves of the Senate's busiest lover boy."

An hour later, Mac let out a low whistle. "Maybe we've got something here, Charley. Look at this one – name's Atkinson, and she works at the FBI. I can't imagine that's a group our guys, whoever they are, want to have anything to do with under any circumstances, but especially if this whatever-it-is is as sensitive as we've been led to believe, then that would be a dead certainty. You take a look and if you think it's as promising as I do, then let's raise somebody at that number they've given us for contact. My guess is we'll want to include her in the surveillance, especially since she seems to be this month's playmate."

Kevin and Matthew, after a quick sandwich in the Huntsman's grill room, had gone on to Kevin's nearby residence. Their plan, sketched out over lunch, was to make use of Kevin's extensive library and some of the computer links he had already identified, and try to determine what lure the Pipestone Quarry could have for anyone other than a Lakota pipe-maker. The previous day's rain had given the spring countryside a freshness that was a wonderfully sweet thing, and as they drove through the small woodland that filled the front of the property, they both involuntarily inhaled more deeply to sample that first breath of honeysuckle and wild azalea. Kevin left the car in the circular drive in front of the house, and as they climbed out, they paused for one last deep breath of the spring-scented air.

Of no particular architectural style, it was nonetheless distinctive in its warmth and charm. The deeply recessed entry, flanked by fieldstone columns that supported a second floor bay, was approached past beds of pungent evergreens. Massive stone

31

chimneys stood at each end of the structure, a continuance of the first story's facing. Wide windows lent light and views to each room, and balance to the façade. Broad pine plank floors were evident throughout covered in carefully planned areas by rugs of traditional Southwestern Indian designs. The place had, in its original life, been a farmhouse for one of the oldest families in the area, and when Kevin's wife had first seen it she had wanted no other. Over the years, they had remodeled; improving and updating the large, homey kitchen, adding the greenhouse where Kevin tended his precious bonsai, combining two unused bedrooms to make a studio where Marybeth had painted, sculpted and played her beloved Steinway. Kevin had gently teased her about not being able to make up her mind about her medium; she had put him off by saying that he, like most of his engineering-trained friends, was just too simplistic. With her death, he had given some thought to selling the place, but found that he couldn't live with the idea that someone else would be in *her place*. So he had struggled with his grief, eventually making peace with the loss and with her memory. Now he lived with that fondness, that deep love that they had shared when she was with him. He knew he would never give this house up, and it was a matter of comfort to have that part of his life so well settled.

It was not long before they both realized that for all the generic information available from print and electronic sources, there was nothing immediately apparent that even hinted at a commercial use for catlinite, as pipestone is more properly known.

After a few hours, Matthew looked at Kevin," My friend, this is going to be tougher than I would have thought. There's a lot of information here, mountains of it, and none that I see leading to a get-rich scheme at the Quarry. None, and I mean zero, points in the direction of a use that would interest IMM, or any other industrial user. Since they stopped using the quartz overburden for making building blocks, I haven't been able to find even a *reference* to uses for Quarry material other than artifacts for the Indians. This seems just nutty."

"Same here, and now you can see why I finally sent out my distress call to you. My thought is if we keep digging, it's possible we'll come across some "Eureka moment" or if nothing else we can eliminate a lot of possibilities that have obviously no connection, and maybe allow us to bypass information sources that will have nothing to do with what we're looking for. There is just so much literature, we could be at this for months, without ever finding who or what has started this new commercial interest."

"If what you suspect is true, Kev, we don't have a month, much less multiples of that. Without a break, your "Eureka moment", we're in trouble!"

CHAPTER 3

Kevin looked up from the geological text at the sound of the telephone. "Would you get that, Matthew? I've gotten into this geologic jargon just enough not to want to lose my train of thought."

"Sure thing," Matthew replied, gratefully leaving a treatise on the economic development of the mining industry in the upper Midwest. "Hello, Christopher residence. May I help you?"

"Yes, please. Is Mr. Christopher there?"

"Right here ... for you," Matthew said, turning to Kevin with the phone in his hand, adding, "It's a lady."

"Yes. Kevin Christopher here."

"Kevin, Mickey. Who was that answering your phone? I didn't think you'd brought on a butler."

"Hardly," he laughed. "That was Matthew Little Crow. I think I may have mentioned him in conversation a time or two. We've collaborated before on some studies where Indian rights were an issue, and he's come to lend a hand on this Pipestone Quarry business...what's up?"

"I just heard from Laura Atkinson again, and she asked that I meet her at the picnic area next to the riding academy in Rock Creek Park. We settled on that since she's in the city, and I'm halfway between there and the Fairfax County Courthouse; I'm calling from my car. She'll be on her way back from a dinner engagement she's had with Benjamin, and she wants to pass on some more information.

She called on her cell in a ladies room, and he was waiting for her to come back before they left, so she didn't have time to tell me what it was at the time. I would appreciate it if you could be there too; maybe pick up on something I'd miss. And you could ask any pertinent questions you may come up with from your perspective right then, instead of waiting to hear from me second hand."

"That would be fine, but it will take me a while to get there. If you think it'll be alright, I'll bring Matthew with me. And by the way, is that area safe enough that you two could wait until we arrived? "

"It should be OK on both counts. I checked and there's a lot of activity around the Riding Academy this time of year, and the Park Police keep things pretty well under control. As for Matthew, he'll be with you, and that ought to cover any qualms Laura might have. I'll prep her about him, from what you said, before you arrive. We'll be in the parking area closest to the outdoor riding ring…you'll recognize my car."

"All right then, we'll see you in about an hour. Just be careful, Mickey, this is not the safe city we used to know."

"How well I know! Remember my line of work? I don't always deal with land swaps and estate probate. I'll be careful, and you do the same. I'll see you in an hour."

With the click of the receiver, Kevin hung up and turned back to Matthew, who was once again absorbed in the papers in front of him. "That was Michaela Campbell; you know the local attorney I told you about."

"So I gathered," nodded Matthew.

"It was through her friend that this whole business with the Quarry came up, and I think it will be worthwhile to have you along

35

for a different set of ears, so to speak. For one thing, it'll give you a chance to meet Michaela, and the contact, Laura Atkinson. Laura's very bright, even though we question her taste in men, but she's just not entirely sure what she's stumbled into. All she knows is that it isn't kosher, and it offends her sense of ethics, or at least I think that's what she finds offensive. I believe that Mickey is becoming concerned with Laura's safety; for that matter, I'm a little uneasy myself. There is, to all appearances from what we know now, something very big, and folks involved in large shady deals can become dangerous if they think their scheme is in jeopardy. At any rate, Laura might well say something that would catch your attention while missing mine. After all, this concerns things awfully close to your home territory."

"Good idea. And anyway, I think if I read any more about mining in the upper Midwest, and the money that's been brought out of land my ancestors hunted over, I'd want to re-institute the Indian wars of the eighteenth century! Let me get my jacket, and we can be on our way."

"Okay," said Kevin. "And I think I will take this pot of coffee and put it in a thermos. We're meeting in Rock Creek Park, and it will be chilly there. Grab my jacket out of the closet in the hall, while you're at it, would you, please? I'll lock up."

While the trip into the city was not a hard one at this time of the evening, there was still sufficient traffic that Kevin was forced to slow drastically on a number of occasions where the seemingly interminable road construction created bottlenecks. He and Matthew discussed things they had covered in their reading, and compared opinions on what possible uses there were for catlinite. It was the sort of good conversation that often occurs between men of common interests and comparable intellects, both comfortable with the idea of working together toward the resolution of a knotty problem.

When at last they reached the city, it took another grinding, pot-hole-filled quarter hour to make their way to the Rock Creek Park riding stables. Pulling in to the parking area, easily within the time Kevin had allowed, they immediately saw Michaela's silver Audi convertible parked next to a sleek sports roadster in a surprisingly crowded, brightly lit area. With the abundant light, they could easily make out the silhouettes of two women in the car, apparently engaged in conversation. Kevin pulled in one of the few spaces available, and the two of them got out and approached Michaela's car. Rapping on the window of the driver's side, the two occupants started, and then smiled in recognition. After greetings and introductions were exchanged, they settled on one of the pairs of benches overlooking the paddocks, and Kevin asked Laura to bring them up to date, apologizing for asking her to repeat what might have been said to Mickey before they arrived.

"The most significant bit of new information," said Laura, "is that George has been talking some more with the representatives of IMM. I still don't have any names, but I should soon. We're going out in the country to an inn that's one of George's favorites over the weekend, and I'll almost certainly find out then. He said tonight that he'd be going away after our weekend to meet with them, so it will be a natural thing for us to discuss the trip, and the people he's going to be with. He likes to think it impresses people to know who he rubs elbows with. And can you believe that someone who is a US Senator, and with his standing, still believes he has to be a name dropper to be appreciated? It's probably the only thing he's uncertain about; his being accepted for what he is, and not who he knows!"

"Good, Laura," said Kevin. "If you can learn some names it would be almost perfect. The point, now though, is to make the most of the information we already have, as this new meeting would indicate to me that possibly things are moving to some conclusion.

We need to concentrate on how IMM is involved, why they're involved, and who got them into the mix in the first place."

Pausing, he looked directly at Laura from under the brim of his hat, his expression grim. "I don't know exactly how to say this, Laura, but you must know that when the stakes are very high, many of the accepted rules of ordered society go right out the window. You've already done a great service in bringing this to our attention, and it's not the kind of thing that you must feel is your personal concern, your own little crusade. We're prepared to carry forward with this from here, and you can fade away from it knowing that it won't be allowed to just die and go away. What I'm saying in a nutshell is that we have come to believe there is genuine danger, and we don't want to compromise your safety. You understand that, don't you?"

"Of course, and I appreciate your concern, all of you. But the fact is, I've become very much interested in seeing that Mr. Benjamin gets his come-uppance. I've done a lot of thinking over the past few days, and have come to realize that he has all the depth and sincerity of a flat stone, and if my latter day Mata Hari act can at least put him in his place, then in some measure it'll help me feel a bit better about having made a fool of myself."

"All right, then," said Kevin, "but remember that if for any reason you want to back away, for any reason at all but particularly if you sense a threat, all you have to do is do it, and it'll be fine with us. OK?"

"OK, I'll let you know, but I don't think you'll hear me 'cry uncle' until this is taken as far as it can go. Speaking of which, I really must go, but I'll keep in touch with Mickey if or when I come across anything more."

"Thanks again for calling, and don't forget what Kevin said about backing off if things look as if they could put you in any kind of jeopardy," Michaela said as she touched her friend's shoulder.

The three of them watched thoughtfully as Laura's little sports car flashed off in the direction of the Interstate. Reaching for the thermos on the bench beside him, Kevin broke the silence. "How about a cup of coffee? Anyone? I have some foam cups here, if I haven't managed to squash them in their travels." Filling two, he handed them to his friends and then poured another for himself. "Mickey, I want to tell you I think your chum Laura is showing us remarkable strength of character. It takes a lot to admit you've made an error in judgment, but to be willing to put yourself possibly in harm's way for the sake of a principle that has been compromised by that poor judgment is extra special. My hat's off to her," he said, toasting the air with his cup.

"Speaking of hats," said Michaela, "Where in the world did you get this latest? You look like an off-his-luck Indiana Jones!"

"Why this is a wonderful chapeau," huffed Kevin, in mock indignation. "It's actually an exact copy of Harrison Ford's, and came with a little certificate that says so. I think I look rather dashing!"

"Well, I still think old 'Indy' Christopher looks as if he's seen better days," she kidded. So what do you think we ought to do now?" Michaela looked inquisitively at the two men.

"I think it would be a good idea if we went somewhere other than this riding ring, and talked it over," Kevin replied. "It continues to concern me that a corporate giant like IMM is involved. The clout those people have in almost any quarter is enormous, and if we have any hope of saving the Quarry, we need to know what motivating force is behind this whole affair. What do you say we adjourn to my house, brew another pot of coffee, and see if we can sketch out some sort of plan of action?"

Harry Genarro looked quickly through the dingy window into the small, nearly deserted restaurant, a feeling of unease deepening. The crumbling industrial neighborhood was once the site of hustle and bustle from humming factories, but the succession of recessions and the decline of US heavy industries were gradually choking the life out of the remaining businesses, this grimy place one of them. He wondered if the need for revenge that had burned so fiercely in the relative comfort of his apartment was strong enough to support him through the next step.

He had spent considerable time and effort to find this group, the last vestiges of the once-thriving campus radical movement of the sixties and seventies. Despite his efforts, it had been a chance encounter with a college-days acquaintance that had ultimately led to arrangements for this meeting. In the course of their reminiscing, his friend had happened to mention that while looking for distressed real estate with renovation potential, he had seen someone he thought was one of the campus leaders of the Weathermen. Following up on that conversation, Harry had, with growing frustration, managed to locate someone who passed him on to someone else, who ultimately arranged the introduction to Jake Monroe.

Monroe, a long-time fugitive, was still angry with the "establishment", or so he proclaimed. While the makeup of his current group was not well defined, and its size completely indeterminate, Henry wanted to gain a sense of whether there was any depth to the hate supposedly carried by the man, and if it was there, then that suited him perfectly. If he could persuade Monroe to join him in discrediting Interglobal Materials and Mining, and especially the research group, then he could once more feel like a man.

The air in the restaurant was stale and smelled of old grease and sour beer. It was an apt reflection of its surroundings, and the few customers, although closed within themselves, were suspicious of the newcomer. Harry looked around the room, and finally spotted Jake Monroe at a table in a far corner. *How ironic*, thought Genarro, *that he sits in such close proximity to a door, with his back to the wall, like some sort of Old West desperado.*

Making his way between the tables, he approached Jake and the three others seated with him. "Hello, I am Harry Genarro; you're Jake Monroe, right?"

"Sit down, Mr. Genarro. I understand you think you may have something that would be of interest to us," Monroe said, gesturing slightly to the other men at the table. "Tell us what makes you think we have anything to discuss."

Somewhat put off by the man's abruptness, Harry hesitated, then began, "I work for a large multi-national company that is engaged in business that I know you once were violently opposed to…"

"We have used violence only when it was necessary to make the stupid public understand that there was, and is, a greater rationale they should acknowledge other than money and power!" Monroe spoke the oddly outdated phrases with a fervor apparently not dimmed by the passage of time. Harry knew at that moment that Monroe and his colleagues would forever find themselves at odds with the mainstream, and would never yield to the norms of society. Although chilled by the thought that such people were still around, he felt they would, indeed, be of assistance to him.

41

"I didn't mean to infer that you were inherently violent; it was just a figure of speech." Harry was relieved at the grudging nod he received in return for his explanation, and went on to describe the activities of the research group in terms he felt would do the most to arouse the passions of his listeners. "I work in a unit at IMM that's devoted entirely to the development of various means for mass destruction. We are also perfecting devices that will allow for ever more detailed information to be gathered about people from long range and satellite systems. Right now we're focused on the development of weapons made of exotic materials. As it happens, the weapons from these materials could be especially useful to those who wish to move through detection devices while still retaining their arms." He paused, reflecting that his choice of words was almost as stilted as Monroe's. He went on to elaborate on the activities of the corporation's arms and chemical manufacturing projects, hoping that the picture he painted would be enough to convince them that IMM was a threat to the world order they believed in, and an entity that should be hampered, at least, in its goals. That some public opinion could be aroused against it would be the obvious objective. When he paused, he looked around the table to see if he could determine the impact this was having. As he viewed the men more closely, he noticed that two appeared to be American Indians, one seated in shadow so deep few of his features were visible; the other's bronzed face ravaged and pock marked by some past brush with disease, his coarse black hair arranged in a pony tail tied with colored strings. The other was a stolid man of middle-European descent, his broad face partly covered with a thick beard. None of these three had spoken, or for that matter given any sign they either approved or disapproved of what he said.

"Let me discuss this with others of our group," said Monroe, after a minute. "IMM, although it represents a great deal of the evil that makes the realization of our goals more difficult, would be a formidable adversary, and in these difficult times we must be more pragmatic in our outlook and choice of adversaries. You must let us ponder the things you say, and decide whether our resources would be best utilized in taking action against them."

"Very well," said Harry, "but how will I know when you have reached some sort of decision?"

"Meet me here again in two days, at this same place. Come at three in the afternoon, and I will tell you then."

"At three on Thursday, then," said Harry, rising. "I will be here and will bring some additional information, if you think that would be a good time."

"No, not then. I will let you know when more specifics will be required. Good-bye, Mr. Genarro."

Bridling at the curt dismissal, Harry turned and left. *These people are nearly as arrogant as those toads at the lab! Just tools, though. Just tools and a means to accomplish the proper downfall of those who have so carelessly used and dismissed me. Just tools...*

When the door had scraped closed behind Genarro, Monroe nodded to the bearded man who stood up, and pulling a greasy cap low over his eyes slouched out the door to follow Genarro. There was silence at the table for several minutes, broken at last by Monroe, "Well, what do you think of that, my friends! Just walks in off the street and asks if we want to take on one of the largest conglomerates on the planet. Got to give him credit for giant balls, though. You guys got any slant on what this Mr. Harry Genarro had to say?"

The pock-faced Indian spoke, "We need to keep our minds on what we have to do now, and not what this stranger might have us help him do in the future. You said that South Dakota National Guard sergeant was going to let you know when a truckload of weapons was being transported, and you had an idea how we might hit them. What's the latest? That's really why we're here in the first place."

"Why, John Wolf, I thought you guys were supposedly famous for your stoic patience." Monroe scoffed. "I've never known you to be so anxious before; something going on in the world of the Red Man that I need to know about?" This last carried an edge to it, accented by a scowl creeping across his face.

Wolf's voice was hard as he met Monroe's suspicious gaze. "Don't give me any of that 'world of the Red Man' shit, Jake. You know damned well we don't like to get involved in your bullshit anti-establishment politics; we're here because you told us there was something in the hit we could use. So let's get down to it...What's the story on this Guard sergeant? Why's he so willing to help out with something like this?"

As Wolf's tone had grown sharper as he had spoken, his companion had moved silently out of the shadows to stand at his shoulder. Monroe was not intimidated, was inherently incapable of being intimidated, but he understood the implied violence he faced with these two. Softening his expression, he made a placating gesture and said, "Hey, John, Andrew, cool it! No problem here, we just need to all be together, ya' know? Here's the skinny...This Sarge, he's got a taste for the good life. Ran some dope during the first Gulf War, felt the heat and quit, but not before he found out that money can make a big difference in the way a man lives. So he kept in touch with his sources in the Middle East after he got out. Moved around some, gotta give him credit for that, kept away from big population centers where there are lots of narcs, and settled down in South Dakota. He got in the Guard, more to have a way to spend the odd weekend than anything else. Then he wound up assigned to that part of the outfit that keeps track of the weapons for the unit. It's not anything more than a straight infantry outfit, so the stuff isn't very sophisticated, but it's our kind of stuff. Anyway," pausing for a sip of the beer at his elbow, he saw that he had the attention of his audience, "This guy, he begins to think he could improve his way of life by selling a few of those weapons. He's got not only a streak of larceny - he's got a couple of hobbies that take cash, plenty of cash. Seems our boy spends a lot of time playing poker; badly I must add. At the same time, he's taken up with a young lady with a rather unsavory reputation, but shall I say, a vivid imagination? Our Sergeant has managed to get himself into debt to some very nasty people, and at the same time his little nymphet has him running around with his tongue and his dick hanging out. The poor fellow is beside himself."

"How'd you get to know all this stuff, Jake? It's not like you're in big with the Dakota Guard!"

"Well, ya' see, it's like this." Monroe leaned back, clutching the beer bottle against his chest. "Ole Jake, here, has a stake in some gambling places that are not within the law, and I also have some contacts in the Middle East. As it turns out, some of the same contacts that the good Sergeant knows; only they've been doing business with me a lot more than with him. So when I heard that he was around and looking to maybe get back in the business, I worked it so we could bring him into a couple of the games out there; nothing big at first, but as things went along, all of a sudden our man is winning a few thou, thinking he's on a major roll. Enter dear Jennifer…I arranged for her to meet up with him after I heard from my overseas friends that he had an inclination for younger women. Sweet child, twenty-four but looks sixteen, face of an angel, big tits, amazing energy, and an unfortunately habitual need for cocaine." Our girl's habit, for the time being, is a habit that our Sergeant Bellows, that's his name, is feeding. Poor guy has himself in deep. After the man got up a few thousand, the stakes of the games went up, and now he's in way over his head."

45

Although his expression remained as impassive as ever, Wolf was reminded again of the disgusting duplicity in whites. There seemed to be no depth to which the whites would sink to achieve whatever devious end they had in mind. Silently he waited for Monroe to continue. When he seemed lost in satisfaction with his plan, Wolf spoke again. "So what does all this mean to us? This Sergeant Bellows owes money and is mixed up with a junkie; so what?"

Feeling magnanimous now, Jake smiled up at the frowning face across from him. "What it means, my friend," he said making a sweeping gesture with the beer bottle, "is that Sergeant Bellows is desperate for money, and will do a lot more than he ever had in mind to get it. He is going to sell us a whole truckload of small arms in order to meet his payment to the gamblers and to keep his girlfriend's habit fed. Ya' see? And the beauty part of it is that he'll be able to doctor the books so that it won't look as if anything's missing. We'll have a truck full of high-grade, if slightly out of date, weaponry that nobody will know about! These weapons will be just what we need to fill the needs of some people I know here and there, for a premium price, of course. I'm told there are even some shoulder-fired rockets, and that'll really excite some gents I know overseas. Why those things can open up an armored limousine or cop riot vehicle like a can of beans. And of course, after those *transactions* are done we'll have all the money we'll need for almost anything that comes to mind in advancing our causes. All we have to do is keep track of Bellows, and when he takes that truck out." Looking from one to the other of his companions, he smiled with satisfaction at the thought of his plan. What especially pleased him, but not shared with them, was the considerable extra payment he expected from his customers in several Middle Eastern countries. Ones who would reward him handsomely for the weapons, but mostly for the turned soldier that could keep them supplied with arms and information. That connection was sure to fatten the off-shore accounts much more than what he might realize from the thefts he managed with the Indians on an irregular basis.

CHAPTER 4

The drive back to Kevin's house took less time than the trip into the City, and he, Matthew and Michaela were comfortably settled around the eating bar in his kitchen within an hour after leaving the Park. After Kevin had made the coffee, they started to review the information they had gathered earlier.

"From what Kevin and I have so far," Matthew began, "there is no commercial use for the catlinite, or pipestone as it's more widely known, or for the quartzite found in the Pipestone Quarry, and there isn't any indication that there is some underlying strata that would excite industrial interest. There's simply nothing there that isn't available from any number of other sources. The Quarry *is* unique in that it is entirely on Government-controlled, Park Service land. Its importance in Indian culture lies in the color of the mineral as it is found there; and this significance is especially important to the Lakota, a branch of the Sioux Nation. The Lakota legend has it that the tribe originated from there, and that the red coloring of the stone represents the flesh and blood of their forefathers.

My ancestors, the Chippewa, had some interest in the pipe making that went on there, and so did many others, but the real cultural value lies with the Lakota. The roots of their tribal heritage rest there and violation of the place would be viewed, by them anyway, as a genuine tragedy. Pipes were, and to some extent still are an integral part of many Indian societies, used symbolically in spiritual rituals and to complete agreements and treaties. White men found that the quartz that's found with the stuff made a good, durable building material, and for a time mined it and used it in the construction of buildings near there. Everything else aside, the place is considered one of the more important single sites to modern Indians, Native Americans to the politically correct."

"Catlinite occurs in other places, but varies in color from the red Quarry material to shades of yellow, pink, black and grey," Kevin added, "but there isn't any physical or chemical difference other than color that we've been able to identify so far. What *is* special is Matthew's point that this deposit of catlinite is on government controlled land, and someone at IMM has apparently found a use for it. Lacking anything to the contrary, we have to deduce that the Southwestern Minnesota location mentioned in the conversation that Laura overheard, and government control of the site is almost certainly the tie back to our friend, 'The *Honorable* Senator'." Michaela and Matthew laughed at the expression on Kevin's face, and his cynical reference to George Benjamin.

"I have to admit that I've never heard of any ties between him and IMM, but I can't think of any other reason for a clandestine meeting such as Laura described if there wasn't something to hide. And Mickey, did you pick up on the total lack of respect he has for her, in that he didn't feel she was either bright or important enough to have made sure she wouldn't overhear what went on at his meeting? He just didn't seem to care if she heard what was going on or not. "

"Well, no, I didn't think about that. I am concerned, though, that if we focus all our attention on him, we may miss something important that's going on somewhere else."

"My feeling," Matthew broke in, "is that for now he is the best and only genuine lead we have. We've found a lot of technical information about catlinite, and there is likely some more if and when we crack the books again, but Benjamin's presence in the mix changes the dynamic. It's not the mineral itself that's significant it's what someone's found out to do with it. That, and why that whatever it is could be important to a company as big as IMM. I have a friend at the Department of Interior that might be willing to tell us something that's not on the web sites or in their printed pieces. You guys?"

"I've already called a few people that I know, including some at Interior," offered Kevin. "Your person there wouldn't be Irving Acosta would it?"

"No, I spoke with Jim Martinson. He's in the Deputy Secretary's office, and has been around awhile. His office title might be enough to shake some of the more reluctant bureaucrats into helping out."

Michaela followed the conversation, watching this new man curiously. She wanted to like him, since Kevin obviously had a great deal of respect for him, but there was something aloof, almost arrogant about him that grated on her sensibilities. *He certainly isn't talkative, but when he speaks, it's as if he were talking down to those without his level of knowledge; actually, with borderline condescension. Maybe it was his striking good looks that had added that touch of egotism, since a lot of people would have reminded him of that all his life, most likely* all *the female people!*

It seemed they all knew someone who was connected in some fashion with various agencies of the government, and they made a list of those that would be contacted in priority order. Matthew said he would check the personnel roster at the National Monument up in Minnesota. There might be an acquaintance there with leads to information, and there would almost certainly be rumors. It was agreed they would meet again at Kevin's house the next evening, unless one of them came upon a revealing piece of information in the interim, in which case they would call. At a lag in the conversation, Michaela said, "I really must be getting home, if I'm going to be in the office early tomorrow. Can I offer you a lift back to your hotel, Matthew, or are you and Kevin going to keep at it a while longer?"

"I think I'll accept your offer. Between the conference I was attending, and the day we've had so far, I could use some sleep. I'll arrange for a car through the Huntsman's concierge so I'll be able to get around, and then guess I'll see you tomorrow evening. Right, Kevin?"

"Right. I think you're both being smart. I'm going to go over a few more of these books, and get my questions straight for my calls tomorrow; then I think I'll turn in too. It's not too much trouble for you to drop Matthew off at the Huntsman, Mickey?"

"Not at all. It's really only a little bit out of the way, and generally in the same direction. It's no trouble at all." With that Matthew and Michaela went out to the car and were gone.

Kevin went back through the kitchen, gathering cups to put in the dishwasher, and after starting the thing, continued on into the greenhouse. He often found clarity in his thinking as he tended the collection of small plants, and they had not been cared for today. He went from one to the other, checking the moisture in the soil, carefully clipping an unwanted shoot, turning and positioning another, feeling the comfort he found here settling over him. As he made his way down the rows of benches, he began to ponder again the primary question, the center of this puzzling situation, *why the Pipestone Quarry?*

The noise of the gathering continued as a happy din, many of the normally staid researchers grinning widely, toasting each other and the apparent success of the project again and again. Genarro smiled at the antics of his colleagues, careful as always to sustain the image they had of him as a friendly sort, easy-going and generally passive. It was a source of great amazement to him that these otherwise intelligent people could have so little perception of the real person that boiled beneath that bland surface.

"Come, Harry", called one, "join in the fun! It isn't often we can claim a genuine breakthrough like this. Have another glass of champagne!"

"Thanks, George, but I think I'll be taking it a little slower; I've a longer drive home than most of you, and I wouldn't want to wind up in a ditch! But let me get you another, okay?" *The clod had been of no use on the project, and now he's carrying on as if it were his original thought, instead of mine.* He picked up the small plastic glass of champagne and handed it over to the widely smiling scientist. "There you are...have you had any of those little sandwiches? They're great and the ones with the cucumber especially! They're a real burden on the ole digestion, but if you can chug-a-lug enough Pepto, it works out..."

"God, Harry, but you're a stitch; 'chug-a-lug Pepto', really! Can't imagine how we dreary lab-rats managed until you came along with that sense of humor or yours!" With a slightly inebriated guffaw the man wandered off in the direction of another group.

What would you have done, indeed, you buffoon! For one thing, you'd never have made this project successful...not without Harry Genarro! And you'll remember that name, so help me!

Although Matthew had known Kevin for a number of years, and felt considerable comfort in their friendship, he knew almost nothing about the beginning of Kevin's deep interest in Indians and the preservation of their culture. He listened attentively as they drove through the night while Michaela, in answer to his question, related how what had begun as mild curiosity had grown to become a central factor in Kevin's life. The interest in Indian lore that had been with him most of his life began to flower during Kevin's third year with the Oklahoma-based exploration unit of one of the major oil companies. The company sent him to meet with a group from one of the Tribal Councils to gain their permission for additional exploration on their land. It was a process that had been repeated several times, and had brought considerable wealth to the tribe, so there seemed no reason to expect there would be any reluctance to continue an activity that had brought such benefit. Kevin, along with his superiors in the company, had thought the trip would be more a formality than anything. As it turned out, it was anything but! There had been rumors for some time about discontent among the reservation's population over distribution of proceeds from the various Tribal Council ventures, and indications had been that Bureau of Indian Affairs-supported cliques were more and more being held accountable. More damaging, however was the flat statement from the Council Chairman that there would be no extension of the leases, no new ones awarded. Consequently, as a business effort, the meeting was a catastrophe.

It seemed that company-sponsored drilling crews had recklessly disregarded the terms of earlier agreements, failing to care for the land, or restore ruined grazing and streams. The resultant attitude of the new Council, now comprised of more traditionally-minded men, was not at all impressed with the fact that much wealth lay beneath their farms. With characteristic courtesy, the exploration proposals were dismissed, and he was given a proviso that within a reasonable period of time the Council expected to be presented with a program of specifics dealing with restoration of damaged areas, as well as a proposal for compensation for past transgressions.

Following a tour of the ravaged countryside, Kevin had sent a blistering report to his manager and up the ladder of the company to the corporate headquarters in Houston. The report almost cost him his job, but the copies that had arrived at corporate headquarters also found their way to the Tribal Council, elevating him in their regard. A harsh reprimand of the regional management had hurtled down from the headquarters in Houston, and the local Resident Manager had been moved out of operational oversight of field operations. A Senior Vice President had come up to take personal charge of the restoration effort, and by means of diligent attention to the task had turned the Council's ire to a guarded level of cooperation. The field eventually had been re-opened with full Council approval, and Kevin had been lauded for his effort, and had subsequently been assigned areas of greater responsibility in dealing with the Indian holdings. He never forgot that first meeting with the Council, and made it his personal goal to learn as much as he possibly could about the American Indians' culture, and to make as many friends among the various bands as possible. Mathew was left deep in thought after Michaela's recitation, and did not notice her inquiring glances as they drove through the cool spring night. "What's on your mind, Matthew?" she asked. "Still trying to make some sense out of nonsense?"

Matthew frowned, and replied, "Not exactly 'nonsense' is it? This is very serious business, and although we're beginning to accumulate a lot of information; we're not anywhere close to putting it into a proper order, a structure that will form the direction of our future effort."

Put off by his manner and negative outlook, Micheala pushed to another subject. With more than a touch of frost in her voice, she inquired "What is it you do, Matthew, when you are not participating in Native American Rights seminars or testifying before Congress?"

"Actually, lecturing at the University of Minnesota in their Fine Arts Department."

"University? You mean college students? You're a professor?"

At her look of surprise, he went on, "I'm professor of Fine Arts, and I lecture almost entirely in English Literature; specializing in Shakespeare. We Indians *do* read, you know... Maybe some time when the day hasn't been so long, if you're interested..."

"If you think you can stand to tell it again, I'd love to hear it then", she replied, a little too blandly to indicate real interest. A short while later she dropped him off at the Tack Room's outside entrance, and drove away, without any further conversation.

She is quite stunning, Matthew mused, as he made unpacked and made ready for bed. *Nice even features, great figure... Awfully reserved though, standoffish really, a real Ice Princess. It's going to be tough to generate much enthusiasm about working with that. I can't imagine what she could contribute to what Kevin and I have laid out for us. Kevin seems to have confidence in whatever it is she could bring to the table though, so guess we'll wait and see...*

CHAPTER 5

Laura Atkinson studied the face across the table as she sipped the excellent wine he had chosen. George Harmon Benjamin, Senior Senator from the State of Minnesota, was arguably the handsomest man she had ever personally known, and certainly the best looking man on Capitol Hill. The broad, intelligent face, with those incredible pale blue eyes and perfect smile, was almost Hollywood quality. Topped by a head of thick sandy hair, he looked every bit the accomplished pinnacle of the Nordic dream in the New World, and his constituents loved him as few politicians had been loved since the passing of Hubert Humphrey. He worked very hard to polish that Nordic image, although his ancestry was questionably Scandinavian. Like so many things about him, it was somewhat true, but not quite. He appeared and sounded intelligent far beyond his capabilities, and was able to pull off the illusion because he was extremely good at absorbing the facts of a briefing by staffers, and holding the facts for a short period. With an easy shrewdness, he never allowed himself to be pushed into speaking about things on which he had not been briefed. The press often was frustrated by his glib sidestepping of thorny questions, but he was essentially unassailable in his home state, and they had learned to accept that. He was as cunning as he was good looking, and Laura knew it. There was little doubt in her mind that he would negotiate well with anyone who chose to make personal deals with him. Even though the technical facts may have been beyond him, any advantage for him of a situation would be quickly discerned.

He was speaking now, and she roused from her reverie with a start. "I'm so sorry, George, I didn't hear you...Doing some wool gathering, I'm afraid. Would you please..."

"Just as I thought!" he laughed. "Hardly through with dinner, and already you're bored."

"Now you know that's not true! I'm not in the least bored, but sometimes my mind wanders...just like a woman, wouldn't you say?" She thought he would rise to that and as his smile widened, knew it had been the proper tack to take. His public pronouncements on the equality of women did not in the slightest way coincide with his personal outlook.

"Remember, now, that you said it!" The smile was quite wide now, with all the mega-watt charm that had become a famous trademark. "What I said was that on Friday, I will be leaving town for a few days. Going back to Minnesota to take care of some things, and deal with an issue that has come before the Select Committee on Indian Affairs. I won't be gone very long, but too long for you to come with me, I'm afraid. And it also means I'll need to meet with the staff almost constantly before then, so we will have to cut our evening a bit shorter than I had, rather *we* had originally planned." His eyebrow arched suggestively as he paused. "Do you think it possible we could spend a little *quality* time together before it gets to be too late?"

"Well, I suppose it might be possible," she smiled at the carefully phrased euphemism. "Some *quality* time could be simply the very best way to conclude the evening. It's much better than brandy and espresso, or even one of those wonderful napoleons. But while you're handling the check, would you excuse me for a visit to the ladies' room; it won't take a minute." She rose while speaking, turning away as he motioned to the waiter.

The Inn, as it was simply called, a remodeled Colonial-era coach stop inn, was a favorite of those "in-the-know" in the Washington area. Located in the rolling Virginia countryside, it was close enough to the City for a fashionably late dinner, but in a setting that seemed to be thousands of miles from the hustle and bustle. Renowned for the quality of its fine food and wine cellar, it had earned a near-permanent position on all the lists of "Best Restaurants". What wasn't widely known was that a limited number of guest rooms were located on the upper floors, available by prior arrangement only, and not to the general public. In catering to his ultra-sophisticated and conspicuous clientele, the owner had quickly realized that the rooms could have considerable appeal for those seeking a discreet setting for their indiscretions; and over the years George Benjamin had become one of the more frequent users of those facilities.

Laura glanced quickly about to be sure she was the only one in the small rest room, then dialed Michaela Campbell's number. "Mickey," she said as her friend came on the line, "I can't talk now, seems I'm calling from the "john" again, but GB is going to Minnesota later this week. Something about Select Committee business. It's the Indian thing again, Michaela, and I still don't know what it's all about."

"Don't worry about it, Laura. I'll pass the word along to Kevin, and we'll see if our little brain trust can make anything more out of it. Did he say anything about further meetings with IMM?"

"Not a word, but I'll keep my ears open. Got to run now, before he begins to wonder where I've been besides the Ladies Room. I'll get back to you as soon as I can."

Outside the Inn, in the shadows of the loosely defined parking area, the man lowered the long gun-like device and looked over at his companion. "Charley, I don't know who that was on the other end of that phone call, but that broad has been in touch with them before, and has somehow connected the dots between IMM, Benjamin and this Quarry place."

"That spells real trouble in my book, Mac. Put that together with the fact that he's been seeing her regularly for the past couple of months. Why, hell, we've seen them, what, six, maybe eight times now, and who knows how many times there were before that. Assume pillow talk, and it makes that bug we planted even more important."

"You're right about that, for sure, but what do you think we ought to pass on to the Director? Just what we know now, or wait until we get an ID on whoever 'Michaela' is…either way the big guys are not going to be happy. You know damn well they are going to want to be sure Benjamin isn't leaving anything physical around that could tie them together. If you really want to know, I'm not keen on this whole idea of surveillance of a Senator, much less trying to find out what's in his files. I'm still grateful they went along with us about not trying to put a bug on *his* phone. That was a big relief. Let's get back to the truck, and decide what to do about what we know now. I don't want to have to explain what I'm doing out here in the dark with a high-resolution laser mike. We could really get our asses in a crack if somebody happened on to us." Silently they made their way back through the hedges, and after stowing their gear climbed into the dusty Suburban and went over the situation again.

"It's one thing for us to find out about this girl and her friends, but another altogether when the Senator is brought into the picture. If she's trying to pass on information that could somehow queer the deal they've brokered with the guy, then we need to let the guys up north know about it, and pronto."

"That's my take too. Not sure what their deal is up there or what they have cooking, but I damn sure don't think they've put us down here to count the Senator's broads!"

Later, the scrambled telephone conversation was shorter than either Charley or Mac had anticipated. After deciding that it was best to keep their superior completely up-to-date, even with incomplete information, the call had been put through on the specially designed phone. It had been surprising to them that the call was so well received. From now on, they had been told, they were to continue with even closer surveillance of the woman, report daily on meetings with people other than her normal workplace contact, and supply photographs of any others with as much information on them as they could. In addition, they were to dig deeper into the other individuals that she or the Michaela- person was talking to; find a string of connections that led from Atkinson to anyone else with an interest in the "project", and find the end of that string.

"Kevin, it's Mickey. I heard from Laura, and she said that Benjamin will be going to Minnesota later this week on Select Committee business. He didn't mention IMM, but she thinks the trip has something to do with the Indians. She was hurrying, so we couldn't talk long, but it could be there is more to the trip than meets the eye."

"Could be, and I certainly trust your instincts. Did you get any sense that she felt danger at all, or is she still avoiding that subject, even in her mind? Let's discuss it when we get together to share what we uncovered with our various contacts in the government. I have to run a few errands so won't be back until late this afternoon. What about meeting at the Blacksmith Shop, and we can have dinner while we talk."

"That sounds fine with me; seven o'clock alright? I was supposed to meet with Matthew up at Interior after lunch, but he left a message with my admin that he couldn't make it. No explanation, so I don't have a clue what's going on with him. Not much of a communicator, your friend. Anyway, I've located some things that might eventually be interesting from some friends at Defense and the GAO. Will you be able to get in touch with Matthew to let him know about dinner?" "That will be fine Mickey. I'll take care of passing the word to Matthew." As he hung up the phone, he wondered at the casual way Mickey had dismissed Matthew's mission to Interior. He had thought, without really thinking about it, that the two would develop at least a mutual professional regard. That it wasn't happening was a disappointment, and he wondered if it would work against their efforts in the long run. Still pondering the question, he gathered his papers into his briefcase and left for his meetings.

NORTHERN PLAINS - 1610

One Ear examined his work carefully, and picked up the knife again to continue the pattern he was carving into the stem of the pipe. This was a special ceremonial pipe for use by the shaman, Black Cloud, and he had to be sure that all the carvings were correct. The light was becoming almost too dim to do the finer work with which he was engaged now, and it would soon be time for his evening meal. He had intended to walk to the nearby river and watch the sunset, but he'd become too engrossed in his work and now the sun was almost gone. He checked the pattern once again, then laid the unfinished stem aside. Tomorrow he would complete it, and prepare it for the medicine ceremony, as prescribed by custom. Rummaging in a small bag, he came up with some dried buffalo meat, cut a thick slice from the nearly black chunk and set it aside as he pulled some fresh berries from another sack. The berries had been plentiful this season, and he found them the perfect complement to the strong-tasting meat. Cool water from a hanging skin sack completed the simple meal.

After he finished eating, he seated himself outside the entrance to the tepee and watched the activity in the camp. It gave him great pleasure, at the end of the day, to see all the calm activity of the camp; of a people in tune with the Earth, and the Spirits. A feeling of great comfort came over him, and as he reflected on this, a small group of young men approached It was not unusual, with his standing as a storyteller, for people to come to him and ask about the history of the People, or of some legend from the long-ago. He smiled inwardly, although his expression remained unmarked and serene. This was something he enjoyed, and he looked forward to what he would say, mentally reviewing the most commonly requested stories.

"Greetings, One ear," said the youth in the lead. "We have come to see if you will tell us something about our People and the People of the long-ago."

"And what is it you would hear, Grey Wolf? A tale of battles with the Ojibwa; the bringing of the buffalo?"

"Tell us one of the stories of the long-long-ago when the Spirits were with the People."

Screwing his face into a thoughtful scowl, One Ear pretended to be puzzled by the request, forming his thoughts as he frowned at the ground in front of him. "That is not an easy thing," he said, and gesturing to the open space in from of him "Sit, while I think about what you should know." As the small group settled themselves in front of him, he loosened the blanket around his shoulders and shifted his weight on his lean haunches.

"In the long-ago, there came a time when food in the camp was very scarce, and game could not be found. The people had become very hungry. Two young men were sent away from the camp to hunt for game. They hunted for a long time, but still could find nothing to feed the people in the camp. As they hunted, they went to the top of a hill, and looked all around to see if there were any animals further away. When they looked to the west, they saw something coming toward them. 'What is that?' the first young man asked. The second young man could not tell either, and they watched as the shape came closer to them. Soon they were able to tell that it was a woman, a very beautiful young woman walking so lightly over the ground that she appeared to float. As she came even closer they saw that although she appeared to be wearing a black robe, she was without any clothes; it was her long hair that flowed about her

63

body!" One Ear enjoyed telling this part of the tale. The inherent modesty of the Lakota always generated a chorus of shocked gasps.

In a very serious voice he went on, "As the woman came nearer the first young man said that he would go to her and embrace her, and if he found her good, he would hold her in his tepee. His friend was worried and asked his companion, "What if she is a Buffalo woman? She could enchant you, and take you away to her people, and hold you there forever. But the first young man's mind was filled with bad thoughts, and he left his companion on the hill and went to the young woman. When he came close to her, he grabbed for her, and at that moment the sky became dark and the two were surrounded by a cloud; a cloud so thick the man that had remained on the hill could not see anything through it. And there was wind and lightning, and when the cloud cleared away, the young woman stood alone on the prairie. She called out to the young man, and asked him to come to her. She spoke in the language of the Lakota, so he thought she was one of his people, and he went over to where she stood." Although he knew that his listeners had heard the story before, he always paused at this point, and made a fuss over preparing his pipe. Judging the mind of the group, he began again just before they could become restless.

"There on the ground at the woman's feet was all that was left of his companion; a pile of bare bones! As he stood there the woman told him that the Crazy Buffalo had caused his friend to try to do her harm, and that she had destroyed him, and cleaned his bones of all their flesh. This made the young man very much afraid, and he drew his bow and arrow to shoot the woman. 'Do not be afraid,' she said. 'If you do as I ask, no harm will come to you. You can not hurt me with your arrow, for I am wakan, *holy, the White Buffalo Calf Woman. I bring to your people a holy thing, and a message from My People. Go to your camp, and tell the council to prepare a medicine lodge for me, and I will come there in a short time. As she said these things, she held up a bundle, 'Tell your people this is a good thing.*

64

And if you do these things then you may have any girl you wish for your woman, but if you do not do as I say, then you will be destroyed as he was, and she looked down at the pile of bones on the ground. The young man did as she asked. When he arrived at the camp, he told the council all as he had been instructed by the White Buffalo Calf Woman. A crier was sent through the camp, telling the people that something good was to happen, and that all should be made ready for a holy visitor. Then a medicine lodge was prepared, and an alter facing to the west. After all the preparations were completed, the people waited. For four days they waited, and at the middle of the last day, they saw something coming towards them. As it came closer, they saw it was the White Buffalo Calf Woman. She came into the camp, dressed now in the softest deerskin, with fringes and decorations more beautiful than any Lakota woman had ever worked. She carried a bunch of the sacred sage, and a bundle that the young man had seen before. The People welcomed her to the lodge, and gave her a place of honor. She had food, and she served it to all the people, starting first with the little children, then the women, and lastly the men of the tribe. When the food was gone, she took up the bundle, and unwrapped it showing then what was inside. 'This is the Chanunpa, *the Sacred Pipe.' She walked around the circle in the lodge, holding out the pipe and telling them what it meant."*

One Ear fished a coal from the fire, and held it to the bowl of his pipe, lighting the well-tamped mixture carefully, habitually following the ritualistic methods, even though this was not a ceremonial occasion. Drawing smoke slowly through the long stem, he watched the attentive young faces. "Come again tomorrow at this time, and I will tell you more of the White Buffalo Calf Woman, the Wohpe, *some say. Go now, and attend to the chores your families have for you." Obediently, the youngsters went off to their evening tasks, leaving the old man hunched in the gathering darkness, his grey head wreathed in aromatic smoke.*

65

CHAPTER 6

When John Wolf entered the house, he knew that the others would have arrived some time before. He had been particularly careful on the way to the meeting, using every ruse he knew to assure himself that no one was following, or had an inordinate interest in his movements. On this day, he was seeking to avoid not only the authorities, but also anyone who may have been allied with Jake Monroe's group as well, for today he carried information that was of a unique nature, and it was not to be shared with anyone outside this small circle. With one last, careful check of the street near the old dwelling, he mounted the steps to the porch and quickly entered the place.

Inside, to the right of the small entry foyer, what had once been the parlor had been set up for the meeting. Chairs had been removed, and the dozen men sat cross-legged on the floor, waiting in stoic silence. The latecomer glanced about to be certain that all the others were there, and took his place against the peeling wallpapered interior wall. For some moments the silence continued, almost as if the others were in some trance, and had to rouse themselves.

Finally, the eldest of them spoke. "You are late. Does that mean that the information you claimed to be so important has proven otherwise, or that you were followed?" His voice, though calm, carried a quality that bespoke authority, and everyone looked at him with respect.

"No, neither is the case," said Wolf. "I was being extremely careful, and waited outside in case one of you had been followed. That would have been unlikely," he added hastily at the murmurs and frowns, "but with so many brought together in one place, I felt the need for additional precautions. I have been moving, after all, in circles more widely known to law enforcement than this council." He had risen, and gestured around the room to include all those gathered. "I regret that you have been kept waiting. The news is of great concern, and could mark the beginning of a new direction for our cause."

"We accept your apology, and credit you with taking the extra precautions to make sure that we were not all seen to be in this place together. Since the incidents at Wounded Knee and the persecution of our brothers among the Lakota, no degree of caution can be considered too extreme. Since we are all known to you and you to us, we will ask you to continue and share with the council this new information." The older man's stilted speech brought to mind a time past, when he would have been known as a Chief, and the others his Council of Warriors. As he spoke a sense of union among the assembled men became an almost tangible thing, a feeling of purpose. They, in fact, represented the most radical elements of the American Indian Movement, and were of several of the recognized tribes. Their group had long since been cast out by the mainstream organization as it regained respectability in its representation of Indian causes and needs. But as in days gone by, there were renegades, and this little gathering represented the last of their persuasion; those who felt that the only way for Indians to regain the pride and stature they felt they should have would be with the taking of lives, with the shedding of the blood of whites to avenge the deaths of so many of their brothers and sisters. They felt that in no other way could they ever hold their heads up again.

"There was a meeting with Monroe and another white who wishes to bring discredit to the organization for which he works," Wolf resumed. There was a disgusted murmur at the mention of the white man's betrayal of his employer; they had no loyalty! "During this meeting the man, who called himself Genarro, spoke of weapons he had helped make that are invisible to detection devices. The weapons are made of a composite material that relies on catlinite as one of its ingredients. Neither Genarro nor Monroe understands that catlinite is another name for pipestone, and that the red catlinite Genarro used comes from one place, the Pipestone Quarry. He does not know, or care, about the source of the mineral as best we could tell from his conversation with Monroe. I am unsure of the importance of the color of the catlinite in the compound used for the weapons, and Genarro did not say, but if it has significance, the Quarry is in danger." He paused to look around the room. Some of these men were of the Lakota, and he knew that this was shocking news to them, although their demeanor seemed not to change.

After a short pause, Wolf continued, "Monroe has been very useful to us in the past as a source for what weapons we need and money. He did not seek this man Genarro, and is unsure of the degree of aid he will lend him in meeting his dishonorable goals, but the idea of weapons that cannot be detected by normal means has great appeal for him. I believe that he will help Genarro, at least to the point where he can gain access to the weapons. At that time, we may wish to consider the value of these weapons to our cause, as weighed against the value of our continued relationship with Monroe. The other consideration is that if these weapons are found to be useful to the government, or to others, the Quarry's sanctity, the *Quarry itself*, could well be lost."

In the silence that followed these pronouncements, an air of tension began to grow, and then, as he returned to his seat, one after another, the various members of the group stood to make their opinion known. Some felt a cautious, wait-and-see approach would be best; others that Genarro's workplace be found and somehow destroyed; still others that Genarro, Monroe and everyone known to have a connection with the weapons be located and killed. The opinions were strongly stated, and counter arguments made, always with courteous regard for the other speakers, but as often as not in contradiction one to the other. The debate went on for some time, only the older man remaining silent through it all. As the hour neared midnight, he finally spoke, "All the discussion has made me think that although all would stop the white man's raid on the sacred land of our Lakota brothers at the Quarry, there is no one who can say for sure that this is going to happen. To react very strongly now would reveal our group to all who would wish to see, including the Federal and State authorities. That would not be good, if there was no real threat to that holy place. When we know that this desecration is what the white men intend, then it would be in our best interest to come from the shadows and proclaim our rights; to shout for the whole world to hear of this betrayal of yet one more treaty. You, Wolf, were right to bring this thing to us. You must now go back and join with Monroe. Appear to support his action with Genarro, but you must always be alert to find out what the real meaning of your information is." He paused for a moment, and then said, "Go, now, all of you as you came, and beware of those who may be following. We will meet again when I have heard more from John Wolf about Monroe." As he finished he rose, and made his way towards the rear of the house. The council was over.

"George, this is Laura. I got your message and am delighted to hear that your trip has been postponed. I hope that means we'll be able to see each other again soon!"

"I'm not sure how soon I can make it happen, but if I can arrange the schedule, you know how much I want to be with you. The hearings that caused the postponement in the first place will have to take priority, but I'm sure we will be able to manage a couple of evenings. I'm rescheduled for late next week in Minneapolis, so maybe we can work out something for the weekend...

69

"Oh, George! Another whole weekend? That would be almost too much!" Laura hoped that her gushing reaction wasn't overplayed, but the weekend would allow much more relaxed time together, and when relaxed George often talked about what he was doing; not just how great he was, but the actual things going on. At first it had been fascinating, but had lately become grating; and now that the IMM thing had come out, with all the implications that came with it, she was beginning to feel the edge of anxiety. She had begun to recognize that this was serious business, not just satisfaction of her curiosity.

"Hold on, now," he protested mildly. "I know it would be a treat, but let me see what the staff has going for me, and I will be back in touch with you. In the meantime, think about a place you might like to go, if I'm able to get away."

"All right, but don't let some dry old briefing keep us apart. It wouldn't be fair to get my hopes up and then cancel out, now would it?"

He smiled to himself, and then said, "It would be a shame. Let me get the staff working, and you begin to think about where we'll go, OK?"

"That's fine, George, but let me know as soon as you can. I'll need to make some excuses for being away again, and not being able to take the normal weekend rotation here. I don't want to use up any good will that I don't have to; after all, I'm just a working girl, you know," smiling wryly at the double meaning of the phrase in this situation. After she hung up, she waited thoughtfully for a few minutes, and then put in a call to Michaela Campbell.

"Mickey," she began after her friend came on the line, "George has put off his trip and we will probably go away together for the weekend. He's asked me to suggest a place, and I wanted to ask you if you thought it would be better to stay close, or to go a long way to give some sense of being isolated…maybe encouraging him to talk more. What do you think?"

"Well, Laura, you certainly know him better than I. For what it's worth, I would feel more comfortable knowing you were fairly close by, but you may have a point about distancing himself from DC. "

Laughing ironically, Laura said, "There's absolutely no doubt that I know him better; better, I'm afraid, than I want to at this point. I'm just so anxious to find out what he's doing and put all this behind me! Hope you don't mind my using you for a sounding board, it's just that I'm starting to get a little uneasy about the duplicity; afraid he'll notice something…"

"Don't be silly, Laura. As we and I mean all of us involved in this thing, have said before, we're counting on you to tell us when you've had enough, and we will approach the situation from a different direction, using your information as a base. You know you can come to me like this any time, and I'll give you an honest opinion of what I think. Don't worry about that anymore, just keep me posted as to what you decide."

"Thanks, Mickey, I will. And I really appreciate all you guys are trying to do to help keep me out of a fix. I'll let you know what we decide to do, and where we will be. So long; I'll be in touch."

George Benjamin was in a fine humor as he drove out of the city and into the Virginia countryside. He had managed to deliver a couple of well-rehearsed jibes in the hearing room, and had learned that they were already being broadcast on the networks. His pleasure was enhanced by the fact that the hearings had been continued, without weekend testimony and within the limits of his previous staff briefings, so the entire weekend could be his. That the staff would be putting in long hours preparing for the next week's hearings did not concern him at all. That was their job, and as long as they did it well, and kept him supplied with quotable phrases that would keep his name and face in the news, then he could relax. He did not worry about their loyalty or ability, he simply accepted it as a fact, and used it to his advantage. Now, all he had to think about was the next three nights and two days with Laura.

As he turned into the parking area at the Guest House, making his way around to a subtly screened space at the rear, he was already in a heightened state of anticipation. He spotted her little Crossfire , parked beside it, pulled the small case from the back seat, and went in the side entrance; unaware of the older Suburban that had parked in the lot next door. Laura met him at the doorway to their suite, negligee-clad, with open arms, a lingering kiss, and, later, a glass of champagne.

Harry felt much better. *It's all going to work out just as I have wanted*, he thought as he drove towards his apartment from the latest meeting with Jake Monroe. *They seem, at last, to have gotten past their concerns over IMM's size, and into the real business at hand. When I show them some of the weapons, we'll be able to do the detail plan on how this entire business can be made to embarrass those assholes! It will be so great to see the looks on their faces!* He was so encouraged, he pulled into a liquor store and bought a small bottle of Chianti to have the with the frozen lasagna dinner he had selected this morning before leaving for work; it was always good to know what you were going to do with the day, as his mother had always said.

Jake Monroe was also feeling good, but Harry would have been shocked had he overheard the conversation among the men at the grimy table. "You see how easy it is, my comrades? This idiot actually thinks we will make some sort of action against IMM! Doesn't he realize that anything we would do to that company would simply lead to our annihilation? The man is our tool now, and he will never realize it. When we get our hands on those weapons, we will be in a position to make a significant statement, much as our Palestinian and Al Queada brothers have time after time.

"And what would our target be," John Wolf asked casually. "These mysterious weapons he keeps talking about are possibly of interest to us, but we will need to know more before we will commit to some unknown objective. I would not wish to meet my ancestors before I gathered some honor for my tribe; and I am sure that I speak for all like me as well.

"That has not been determined, my Red Brother, but it would be best, I think, if we can select a small, but prominent objective, possibly even an individual. Come here tomorrow for more discussion. This may be our best chance for a meaningful demonstration of the worth of our causes since the 70's. We don't want it squandered." Jake resisted his temper, remaining silent as the others left. These men had provided skilled people on more than one occasion, and could again, but they were entirely too parochial for his tastes. They only wanted to address Indian matters, not realizing that the greater good to be served was the disruption of the entire society, leading to its replacement by a revolutionary council that would express the true will of the people. It was a constant source of amazement to him that so few could see the vision he held for the future.

CHAPTER 7

Kevin looked up from the report he was writing at the sound of the phone, bringing his thoughts sharply back to focus. Picking up on the third ring, he growled a greeting into the receiver.

"Well, and a good day to you too, Mister Grouch," Michaela replied. "And what was the occasion that got you up on the wrong side of the bed today?"

"Sorry, Mickey," Kevin responded. "I didn't mean to come across so much like a crab, I was just in the middle of a report for one of the Senate Committees, and was struggling a bit when you called. Blame it on the politicians, it certainly isn't you! Good to hear a friendly voice. What's up?"

"I've heard from several of the people I know in the various agencies, and although they obviously can't give out anything that's classified, I *have* learned that IMM has a nominally secret laboratory out in the middle of nowhere in Iowa that has done a lot of work for Government agencies in recent years. I say 'nominally secret' because although they do lots of sensitive work that *is* classified to one degree or another, and the company doesn't talk about the place or its work at all, its existence has been known generally almost since it opened. They like to say that the people there are doing pure research, but anyone connected with IMM knows that they really specialize in hush-hush stuff on contract. I believe I'll have an idea of some of the past, de-classified projects when I have a chance to sit down with some of those guys later on, but I don't have anything now that's any more specific. They're all very sensitive to what is in writing, either literal or electronic, so a lot of this type of investigation is going to rely on the verbal; yields deniability for them. This could very well be just another blind alley, but I still have some other calls to come back to me. How's it going on your end?"

"This report has me stymied for the time being. It's turned into a real bitch, if you'll pardon my French, and I don't think I'll be able to do any more with Pipestone until late tomorrow, or probably Monday. This weekend is going to be shot, I'm sure. I even had to call the secretarial service for a special weekend standby so that I can have the thing ready for review by the various staffs early in the week. Do you have time to spend with Matthew on it? I hate that he's come down here and now I'm tied up."

"It's no problem at all, as long as I can get a call back from him! We had already made arrangements to meet later on today, but haven't heard a peep about when or where; *very* aggravating, not to mention just plain rude. Afraid I don't have very good vibes about your Mr. Little Crow! Maybe we can carry on from this end, and sort some of the wheat from the chaff, so to speak, so long as he takes the trouble to make it known where he is and what he's up to. I'll keep trying to get in touch with him, and if you hear from him, would you ask him to call me at the office? When we next hear from Laura, her weekend with GB will likely have yielded something too, and it would be good to have someone familiar with the subject to bounce things off of. You keep on with your report, and let me know if you want to take a break, or if you hear from your missing Native American cohort." I can meet you then."

"We'll keep in touch Mickey, but at the moment I don't see any hope for the weekend. If you find something big, yell, and I'll make time."

After goodbyes, and with a fresh Uppman smoldering in the fired-clay dish at his side, he was soon buried once again in the study on success rates of various educational programs that had been tried on the reservations.

Michaela's administrative assistant put the call through, saying it was from a gentleman, "I think he said his name was something Crow?"

"Thanks, and since it's nearly noon, why don't you go ahead and take an early lunch, I'll deal with 'Mr. Crow', and then I may be out for the afternoon. You know how to reach me on the cell."

"I do, and if that's all you need, then I'll take you up on it, and have a good afternoon."

Tamping down her irritation, Mickey punched in the blinking button, took a deep breath, and with a neutral tone, "Hello, Michaela Campbell here. May I help you?"

"Why certainly, Mickey. This is Matthew Little Crow. I thought I'd passed my name on to your secretary. I spoke with Kevin, and he said that you wanted me to call?"

Flabbergasted at his cavalier dismissal of the appointment with her that he had silently missed, she hissed her response, "Yes, I did ask Kevin to pass on that message…that in absence of any sort of word from you. I was not sure if you had abandoned the project, or if you had suddenly gone off on some tangent on your own. Where have you been and what the *hell* have you been doing that you couldn't at least let anyone know where you were? Are you still part of this, or not?"

Taken aback, Matthew started to reply, and then bit off the strong retort that had half formed on his lips. "It was not my intent to give anyone the idea that I was not continuing in this… just trying to dig into some information that's not available here. If my actions have caused you concern, then I apologize, but I did not understand,

and have no intention of ever being tied to some sort of reporting apparatus, or that I had to clear my movements with anyone."

The hollow sound of the silent phone connection was the only indication that neither had hung up, but that silence lingered. Finally Mickey spoke, "Let's begin this again.. I had thought we were to meet after your session at Interior, and there was no indication from you to the contrary. I wound up cooling my heels in the restaurant where we were to have had a luncheon meeting, with no sense that you were still interested in the information we were trying to gather. Not to put too fine a point on it, but didn't it occur to you that others are involved here, looking to you for input, and that this is a team effort?"

Taking a deep breath, he responded with a coolness he did not feel, "I apologize again for any inconvenience I may have caused you, and will be pleased to cover the cost of your lunch, but I have been exploring a source of information, and would like to pass that along to the *'Team'*," he said with some cynicism. "If you like, we can meet at the Huntsman, I'm on my way there now, and we can share thoughts as to what my contribution to the project might be."

Still deeply annoyed, Mickey agreed, hung up rather more forcefully than necessary, and gathered her things to leave the office.

Michaela Campbell had always admired the way in which the management of the Huntsman had achieved a level of elegance and country charm that blended so perfectly one was never aware of the intensity of the effort required to sustain it. She knew more about the running of the place than most; her summers having been spent working in the housekeeping and later, administrative areas of the place. She looked back on those times with fondness. Entering the lobby, she waved a greeting to her friend from those summer days, now the day manager. "Janice, how good to see you! I can't remember the last time. How have you been?"

"Well, look who's here! You look simply terrific, Mickey! And I'm fine; you?"

"I couldn't be better, and busy as a bee, which is good, since I hung out my own shingle."

"You did? How wonderful! We all knew you'd do well. But what brings you out here?"

"I'm meeting a guest of yours, Matthew Little Crow. We're to meet for lunch in the dining room. I may be a bit ahead of time, though, so why don't we grab a cup of coffee, and you can catch me up on how all the 'Gang' are doing. If you have time, of course," she added quickly.

"Sure I have time," Janice smiled. "Give me a minute to let my office know where I will be *'in conference'*. You go on ahead to the dining room, and I'll be right there."

Michaela mused as she waited for her friend to appear. Although she had a sense of relief at finally making contact with Matthew, she remained displeased with his attitude and lack of communication. *He should know that anyone involved in this sort of endeavor should constantly communicate with others engaged in the same effort. How else are we supposed to coordinate our efforts in uncovering just what's going on! Despite the fact that he's an annoying, inconsiderate jerk, I can't wait to see just what it was that has kept him out of touch. It surely better be something significant that can lead us to some motivation for this travesty. Well, here I am, anyway, working toward what could become a national-scale scandal, analyzing information on an obscure culture with a man of that culture I really don't know , and not entirely sure I'll care for when I know him any better!*

"Now where were we," Janice said as she seated herself in the chair opposite. "I'm sure you remember…"

The two women fell easily into conversation as they reminisced about the good, and not so good times, and people both had known; the grumpy managers, the "dreamy" waiters, the gay cook, and the madcap times they had enjoyed as they had worked their summer jobs. They were still laughing about a party night when Matthew came into the sunny room, and paused at the Maitre'd stand. Michaela rose and gestured to him to come over. "Hi! I think you know Janice Bigelow. We were co-workers here during summer break 'lo those many years ago', and were catching up on things."

"Yes," Matthew said, "Janice and I have met several times. Turning to Janice he asked if she could join them for lunch. Noticing the air of tension that had risen with his appearance, she declined, and left the two of them standing by the table.

"They sat, and studied the menus offered by their waiter in chilly silence. When the waiter returned, they looked up, and spoke simultaneously. Smiling at the small gaffe, Matthew gestured to Michaela. "Please, ladies first."

"Isn't it funny how those things happen?" Mickey said. *We* have *to get beyond this monosyllabic nonsense, and engage in conversation! We'll never conclude anything unless we can talk; exchange ideas.*" Do you think there is anything to a theory I heard once about ESP causing it?"

"Maybe there is something to your ESP theory. I am always a bit reluctant to lean in that direction for concern that there will be whispers about the "superstitious red man" behind people's hands." *Where the hell did that come from? I don't feel that way at all...Just trying to get her goat for some reason, or what? Let me try to get some civility back in the conversation, or there is going to be a genuine breakdown in our efforts here. Can't have the group not speaking to one another, can we?* "I'm sorry...didn't mean for that to come out the way it did! It's just that for the past couple of days,

I've been too immersed in the past and the prejudice that was so widespread then, and still lingers, I'm afraid. Okay for a 'do-over'?" He looked inquiringly across the table, and was relieved to see a small smile on Mickey's face.

"Of course," she said, "a 'do-over' is always acceptable. Wish it worked in court sometimes! But in the spirit of 'do-over', I would like to apologize for my attitude when we spoke on the phone this morning. That was really not called for."

"Good! Apology accepted, and let's hope we don't have to do that so much in the future. Now, what do you think about lunch?"

From that point on, the conversation was relaxed, and congenial. As they were finishing, Mickey steered the light conversation back to more serious, "I talked with Kevin this morning. He was completely bogged down in some report that's due on Monday so we'll be on our own for the next couple of days, unless we come up with something absolutely earth-shattering. Then he insisted we call. "

"I think that's okay, but I am not at all sure we're doing this in a way that's going to produce revelations of motive, objective, and so forth in the short time I know we're all concerned about." As they had talked, it became more and more apparent that Matthew was not comfortable with the clean, academic approach they were taking. *I'm sure Kevin's ability to glean good information from seemingly unrelated documents, and put the information together in a coherent narrative can't be surpassed, and Mickey will probably find some tidbits from her contacts that will flesh out Kevin's work, but that's going to take forever!. We don't have that much time, not at all...* "We don't know nearly enough about what's going on in Minnesota, and until we do, all the rest is just data, meaningless without some context." He paused for some coffee then he looked up at her, "I hate to think that all this is taking you away from your clients, as much as your input is appreciated. Don't you have things you need to do to meet your obligations to them?"

Stiffening at the inference that she would neglect those depending on her, Michaela responded with a quick "Don't worry about it; my practice, my clients. I'll be sure they are served well and properly."

"I'm sorry, Michaela! And I find myself apologizing again! I didn't mean to say that you weren't meeting your duties to your clients, it just seems as if this is taking a lot of time on something unrelated to your law practice." He laughed, a little awkwardly, and changed the subject to the quality of the Huntsman's lunch.

Following their after-lunch coffee, they adjourned to Michaela's office for more study of Pipestone, re-hashing what they had been able to find thus far, and comparing the several sets of data. The more they talked, the more Matthew became convinced that researching from an office environment in Northern Virginia was only going to get them so far. They were both uncomfortable with the situation as it was unfolding, and making sense of the sheer number of loose unconnected facts seemed a ridiculously daunting task. Their major underlying concern, the real stone wall they saw in front of them, was that they still had no idea why there was suddenly a commercial or industrial interest in the Quarry.

"I believe that there is one critical factor missing from this whole investigation," said Matthew after they had settled in Mickey's offices. "We don't know the first thing about the situation on the ground in Pipestone County. Before we can draw meaningful conclusions about what the literature and various people at the agencies have to say, we need to find out if there is anything in the wind up there that could point us in a more fruitful direction…"

"Hello? Is there anyone here?" Kevin's voice surprised them as he called down the corridor.

"We're back here in the conference room," Michaela responded. "What brings you down here? Did you hear something really terrific? I surely hope so, 'cause all we have to show for several hours analysis and discussion is a handful of loose ends that get looser by the minute, and Matthew's firm belief that we're missing the crux of the matter struggling away down here in Virginia, when the real insights could be better found in Minnesota. Right, Matthew?"

"Well, maybe I have come onto something," Kevin said as he entered the well-appointed room, "but first let me answer your first question. I came to a stopping place in my report, noted the hour, and decided that since I had nothing available for dinner that appealed to me, I would find you guys, and see if you had any ideas about food."

"You came to the right place as far as I'm concerned," said Matthew. "That was a fine seafood salad I had for lunch, but that seems a long time ago! How about you, Mickey, aren't you about ready for a recess?"

"You bet! But tell us about your news, Kev. Then we can get down to the more basic aspects of subsistence."

"Don't you just love it when she veers off into that legalese, Matthew? I mean, to refer to a good meal as "the more basic aspects of subsistence' sounds as if it came from some congressional staffer, not a good country lawyer!" Kevin chuckled as he kidded Michaela, knowing she took no offense, and appreciated his chiding about becoming too stuffy in her speech. "Anyway, my early contribution to your efforts is that I think the connection between IMM and the Quarry may be related to their weapons research programs. One of my calls was to a contact who works as a research analyst at Defense. He mentioned in the course of our conversation that rumor has it that IMM is in delivery trouble on a couple of their research projects. When they were pushed, so my guy says, the response was that a recent breakthrough utilizing an unnamed material showed such great promise that no additional deadline extensions would be required. What caught my attention, though, was an offhand remark that this material was readily available from a source in Southern Minnesota. Does that light any bulbs over your heads, eh?"

Michaela and Matthew looked at each other and started to smile broadly. "You talk about a break!" Matthew exclaimed. "That's the link we've been trying to find. Did your guy know which program, or where it was being worked?"

"No he didn't. But he did say that a listing from another office there was being sent to a Ms. Campbell, whom he understood was with the Washington Post..."

"Well, I had to tell them I was with an organization, and my cousin Jane *does* work at Post, so..."

"So you just stretched things a bit, in the interest of a good cause. Suppose we can overlook that, Matthew?"

"I suppose." Matthew said nodding blandly. That's a great break, Kevin. Maybe when we put the list Mickey finagled together with your information, we'll have something to go on. I still believe that there is much to be learned up there, something that's been happening under the radar. Otherwise, I believe that this calls for a small celebration, such as Calvin's Porterhouse Lafayette. Sound good to anyone else?" he asked looking from one to the other.

At that moment the phone rang, all three starting at the sudden noise. "Hello, Law Office," Michaela spoke into the receiver.

"Hi, Mickey, it's Laura. I have just a second, but wanted you to know our boy's on his way out of town, he thinks now, on Thursday. I probably won't see him again, but I'll keep trying with what's left of the weekend."

"Thanks, Laura. Call me when you get back to town and we can really talk; and be careful!" Hanging up, she turned to the two men. "She sounded OK, but I can't shake the feeling that she's in some kind of danger, actually *real* danger. Is that silly of me?"

"Under the circumstances," Kevin replied, "I think your concern is very well placed. I just wish she would steer clear of that guy at least until we know some more about his involvement, don't you, Matthew?"

"She doesn't seem to me to be as concerned over her own safety as she should be, but then I've only met her that once, so I don't have a good feel for how she might be reacting. My first impression is that she's a pretty strong lady, but that doesn't take away the concern I would have with her moving in some awfully elevated shady circles. People at that level seem to have a way of skirting the law, both moral and legal."

"I hadn't thought of her that way, Matthew," said Kevin, "and I hope to God you're right. As it is there's nothing we can do but keep in contact, and try to steer her away from any trouble that we can see coming."

"I still think she's got more trouble than she, or we, know," insisted Michaela.

"Well, that may be," said Matthew," and as I said, I know her hardly at all. Kevin's right, though. We are, of necessity in the background, and what we need to do is stay in touch with her, and to try to help her avoid the real trouble, whatever that might be."

"That's right, Mickey," said Kevin gently. "I know how close you feel to Laura, and really do understand your anxiety. Is there anything you can think of that we *should* be doing? I can't."

"You're both right, of course, and I know I sound overly worried, but she's a good friend, and I just hate the idea of her with Benjamin, how she's faking, and how vulnerable that makes her, and... I don't know, - I'm just worried." Pausing, she shook her head and began to gather papers back into their files. "Now let's get things put into some kind of order, and didn't I hear some talk about food? About a Blacksmith Shop steak? Come on guys, let's get going!"

It had taken a longer time than usual to reach the Director, and when the Washington detachment finally reached him, it was obvious that he was not pleased to have the intrusion. The report from Washington was lengthy, though, and by the time the information from the various eavesdropping devices had been passed on, the man's mood was considerably altered. Business of their sort really knew no regular schedule, and he found himself commending the crew for their diligence, while earlier he had groused at a seemingly trivial interruption. "That the woman has made a connection and is passing along information to others is bad, but she seems to have gone beyond being just another power-broker-fucker and has gotten into the industrial espionage business. Is there any indication how much the others are involved or how much this Campbell woman and her associates actually know? And do any of them have enough juice to do anything of significance?"

"We don't have anything, really, on what Atkinson may have heard or told Campbell before we began the detailed surveillance, and the conclusions we can reach from what's been overheard is that she has told them something, or they wouldn't remain involved, but for right now, they don't have information that takes them anywhere. There are only three, as far as we know, that are involved. The Campbell woman, who's a local attorney, small time, but with lots of friends around here; she's lived here most of her life. Then there's a guy named Christopher and another guy, an Indian by the way, named Little Crow, who showed up here about ten days, two weeks ago. Christopher is *very* well connected. Does a lot of special interest testimony on the Hill on Indian affairs; a lobbyist really. He knows almost everybody who has had anything to do with the BIA in both houses of Congress, and on both sides of the aisle. Wealthy, independently, and well thought of in the community, as well. Little Crow is from Minnesota, teaches at U of M, and does a lot of the same things that Christopher does, but much less frequently, sort of a spare time thing. And since he doesn't live here, he doesn't have the connections the others do, although he is not without some. From what we have pieced together these three have focused on what the Atkinson woman has fed them, and are trying to sort through to the root of the project. "

There was a pause, and then the Director, almost as if thinking out loud, said, "So the Atkinson connection has had an undetermined negative impact, but remains a conduit for information from a seemingly careless, if not willing source. If we close that conduit, the sources of real trouble for us are left only with what they have at present. I think we can extrapolate that they have insufficient information to act, or we would have heard they were making plans to either take their case either up to the Hill, or public. Yes, that's the way it shakes out. We need to bear down on all three of those people, find out just how much they really do know, and what they plan to do with it. Do whatever is necessary to gain that data, and focus on Christopher, at least for a time, since he's the one that seems to have the influence. As for our 'conduit', it must be permanently closed, and within the week. That action will need to be done carefully, but make your plans. It will look like an accident, of course, and we can't compromise our man. I'll be back in touch within the hour if I come up with some reason not to proceed, however I don't believe that will be the case. If you don't hear from me, then it's a go." He then broke the connection without waiting to hear their reaction.

Back in Washington, Charley and Mac looked at one another, blank expressions on their faces. It was the first time in years that neutralization inside the States had been considered, and the first time ever they could recall one with such a short planning schedule. They were expected to come up with an accident scenario in a day or so, and one that would in no way lead back to them. This whole business was a bit curious, but they had known the Director for a long time, and in these matters, his judgment had always been sound.

CHAPTER 8

George Benjamin rolled lazily back in the bed, and rested with his arm behind his head. He felt completely sated. The food at the restaurant had been predictably excellent, the wine perfect. As for the events which followed, he could only smile in remembrance. Turning to the door to the bath, the sound of the shower made him smile more broadly, and he slid out of the bed.

As he entered the spacious room, steam from the shower curled around his head, faintly scented from the expensive European soap used in the place, and he quietly closed the door behind him. The outline of her body could be seen through the frosted glass of the enclosure, contrasting to the deep blue tiles on the walls. As he came closer, he paused a moment to admire what was an almost impressionistic result from the combination of steam and figured glass. "You should have awakened me," he said as he pulled the door open, grinning as she started

"Jesus, George! You scared me to death!" She had instinctively folded her arms across her chest, as she half-turned toward the intrusion.

"I'm sorry," he said, without conviction, "but the thought of you in here all alone was just too much, and I felt this urgent need…"

"You can't be serious! After last night, and what we did? How could you possibly feel *any* sort of need. Are you sure?"

Closing the room off behind him, he reached for her and held her by the shoulders at arm's length. *Of all the women I've known, this one has to be the finest piece ass of the whole lot. What a body! And what an appetite for sex! It doesn't even matter she won't go for group stuff, she's a group all by herself – in a class by herself.*

She accepted his ogling stare, knowing he must be thinking about the night just past. *What the hell. Let him look, and giving the devil his due, he is inventive and ardent. No denying he's a son of a bitch and a philandering rake, but not all this has been bad, Laura-girl, and you need to admit that to yourself. The man knows his way around a bed or whatever. Do you suppose...*

No words and few thoughts followed as he folded her into his arms and caressed her back and buttocks. She felt the warmth rising in her again, and lifted her face to his. Slowly moving their hands over the other's body, they easily reached a level of arousal more quickly than either would have thought possible. With increasing urgency, as the water cascaded over them, their bodies moved, sliding against each other in an easy rhythm. He moved slightly away from her and ran his hands over her; high full breasts with the pink nipples now erect, smooth waist and back and hips, thighs slightly parted and opening for his probing fingers in the nest of tightly curled hair. She shifted her stance to better allow his stroking there, and she reached down for him, finding him hard and ready. Lips parted, eyes hooded, they moved easily together to the small ledge at the back of the shower enclosure. As he lifted her up, she pushed her weight onto the ledge, wrapped her legs around his hips. He stood for a moment with her arms loosely around his neck and then moved into her with a smooth, deep thrust, eliciting a soft moan from low in her throat.

He was finishing dressing, humming tunelessly to himself, Laura drying her hair in the bathroom, when the phone rang. Frowning at the thought his staff had ignored his instructions of "no-calls" he answered with a gruff "Hullo."

There was the faintly hollow sound of a secure phone on the other end, and a familiar voice said simply, "Benjamin, can you talk?"

He glanced over his shoulder reflexively, seeing Laura in the mirror with the dryer still going. "Yes for the moment. Why did you call me here, and how did you know I *was* here?"

Ignoring the questions, the voice continued, "Our situation has gone critical, and you need to be aware of the scenario, as we see it developing…"

"What do you mean, 'gone critical'?" Benjamin interrupted.

"There is every reason to believe the catlinite source is known to others and that a leak exists which could jeopardize the project."

"What leak? And how is the project jeopardized? Say what you mean, dammit, and quit the spy novel dialogue, OK?"

"As you wish," the voice continued, "but hear me out before you start complaining about how and what I tell you. The information on the trips you take, and who you meet is being passed on to individuals who have an interest in the catlinite site, we believe their goal is the preservation of its current National Monument status. That information is coming from the woman you are with now."

"What are you talking about? How do you know there is any information?"

"I said hear me out! With the information and suspicions she has passed on, these others are planning to take steps to make it very difficult, if not impossible for us to utilize that catlinite source. And you know if that source is not available, costs for another source to provide what we need for completing the project will go far beyond the allocated resources that we have available, and the whole thing goes down the drain. Along with the project, of course, go the 'contributions', shall we say, that are being made to a certain Cayman bank account that you know about. Are things clearer now?"

Benjamin had sunk into a chair as the monologue of the other had continued, and now felt cold sweat on his brow. "Go on," he croaked.

"The catlinite source *must* be protected for our use. It has become the only variable on the critical path to successful accomplishment of the project, and that is the only thing you need keep in mind. As long as your end of the bargain is kept, there will be additional funding forthcoming, and your account will be credited with the two million as agreed. To that end, it has been decided that no further information must reach those opposed to our plan, and that will be accomplished by ending the leak from your lady-friend."

"That's simple enough, then," Benjamin broke in, "I'll just stop seeing her until this is finished After that, I can handle her as I have others; it's amazing what a 'Retirement Account' can do to some memories." He spoke with more assurance on this familiar ground.

"No, that will *not* be the way this will be handled. A final decision for termination has been reached and confirmed. It will be done soon."

"Termination? Do you mean, uh, mur…"

"Don't say that! This is merely an action to assure success of the project, and your input was not considered essential to that decision."

"My God," he breathed. "You can't be serious! For this *rock* you would go to that extreme? Call it off! There must be another way!

"That is not a decision you have any say in, *Senator*." Emphasis on the title was almost a sneer. "You should have had those thoughts before indulging in pillow talk about our business. Try and refrain from any more until the field has again been made clear. Consider yourself advised. Is there anything you wish to ask?"

After a pause, while he adjusted his thinking to what he now saw as inevitable, he asked when and where the action would be taken.

"You know I can't tell you about that," the man said flatly.

"You don't understand. I just don't want to be anywhere near. That we have been seeing each other is rather widely known, and I know that any such association would be damaging, dangerous actually, in a political sense. There can't be any hint that I could have been involved. You know how the tabloid press loves things like that." His voice became steadily stronger and persuasive; this was now a matter of politics, and he knew politics well.

"I see," was the reply. Thoughtfully the man continued. "Make some excuse and leave for Minnesota early. That will provide ample distance when the termination occurs, and the extra day or two of exposure shouldn't make too much difference now. But be careful while you are with her." With that the connection was broken, and George heard the buzz of the dial tone for a full minute before he roused himself and hung up. Laura had finished with her hair, and was putting the finishing touches on her makeup as he rose and stood staring bleakly at her reflection in the bureau mirror.

"How do you know, Kevin, if the Select Committee even cares about what happens at the Pipestone Quarry? I'll grant they've worked very hard to come up with assistance in education and job training on and off the reservations, even the damned casinos. And to some extent they've even shown some support in treaty violation issues, but this is simply a matter of an Indian tribe's right to its heritage. There isn't a single thing that will have a tangible result in the whole business, and I for one don't think they'll pay any attention unless there is some kind of financial impact."

Smoke curled around Kevin's head from the cigar clamped in his teeth, and he regarded Michaela's frown. Their discussion had gone on for hours, and both were tired. They had settled, for the moment, in the greenhouse. Theirs was simply a disagreement regarding what the best means would be to stop exploitation of the Quarry. Kevin had pressed for an approach that would involve the stature and power of the Senate Select Committee on Indian Affairs. Michaela, on the other hand, felt the time involved in such an effort would be too long, and would not allow for the necessary pronouncements to be made that would delay IMM"s use of the Quarry.

As they talked, Kevin had started to work with the bonsai, readying them for the seasonal placement in the shade-house beyond the terrace. The words exchanged had often been strong, but the feelings of both were so firmly committed to rectifying what they considered a potentially damaging situation they stopped short of outright acrimony.

"Have you heard anything from Matthew since he went tearing off to Minnesota?" Mickey asked. "Maybe he has been able to uncover some information up there that could give us a new angle to work from."

"No, but that doesn't surprise me. He would have to work through the local Lakota Council, and those kinds of contacts and discussions can become pretty convoluted and time consuming. I would have hoped to hear from him today, but have been in those circumstances myself, and you wind up working altogether to their pace, not yours."

"Did he say anything about looking for any information around Benjamin's home area? That could provide a whole new avenue we could dig into."

"He didn't mention it before he left, but from my experience he's pretty thorough, and I can't imagine he'd go that far without turning over a few rocks around Benjamin's stomping grounds. The whole area of timing has become more and more troublesome to me. This whole thing could be on its way to happening, whatever it is, and we don't have a clue as to their schedule!"

As the day had worn on into mid-afternoon, it had become clear that no simple solution to the impasse would present itself. Kevin, concurring with Mickey, was aware of the inherent danger of delay in his conservative method, but was convinced that the Committee's endorsement would lend immeasurable stature to any action taken in this situation, helping in others like it that could arise in the future. A glum silence hung in the air following that pronouncement, as they both pondered the tangled situation they confronted.

"You said 'from your experience' working with Matthew, Kevin. What is that? Other than being your friend, and associate occasionally, I don't know anything about him, and it's unusual, to say the least, to find an English professor that hales from an American Indian background."

Wiping his hands on a towel to rid them of the soil that had clung to them during his cultivation efforts, Kevin motioned for Mickey to precede him out of the greenhouse. "Matthew's history is an interesting story; his association with me rewarding but *not* all that interesting. Let's get some of that lemonade we made earlier, and I'll fill you in on the Little Crow story."

Settled shortly in the comfortable chairs on the patio, drinks at hand, Kevin related Matthew's story, as he had been told. "Matthew was born up in the northern part of Minnesota near Lake Superior, an only child in a very close, but gruesomely poor, family. He was raised in his early years in a generally traditional home, and his parents went to some lengths to instill in him a love and respect for the Ojibwa-Chippewa Way."

Continuing his narrative, Kevin told how Matthew had gone to one of the first really progressive schools on the reservation. "At this school they actively incorporated Indian culture in the curriculum, balancing the basic "three R's" on a foundation of traditional Chippewa culture. Matthew found refuge from the hardships of 'life on the Res' in the books he found in school. He soon established himself as a star pupil, loved by parents and teachers. When he was in the third year, though, everything was turned upside down. He and his family were on their way back from visiting with another member of the family when they hit a patch of ice on the road, slammed into the back of a log carrier, and both his parents were instantly killed. Matthew wasn't, but was trapped against the floorboard of the pickup for almost two hours before the emergency crew was able to get there and cut him out of the wreck. After that, he was passed from relative to relative until finally the tribal authorities and the Child Welfare Agency arranged for him to go to the Episcopalian orphanage in Duluth."

"My Lord, I had no idea he had come up from that sort of beginning. Was there any residual injury from the wreck? This certainly sheds some light on his reserved ways, but where did the English professor part come in?" Mickey asked.

"I've never heard him say much about it, but I know he does have a problem with claustrophobia, to some extent; all that time trapped in the wreck almost certainly. Well, anyway, it's as if his life has been a series of very sharp turns. He was settled in at the orphanage, when one of the ladies on the volunteer Board spotted him and inquired about him, noticing that he was so withdrawn. Seems she took quite a liking to him, and great sympathy for his tragic circumstances. She persuaded her husband to become acquainted with him, see if he could draw him out of his shell. The two became fast friends, and the couple eventually asked him to become a part of their family. I understand Matthew was reluctant at first, but agreed after a time.

"The relationship between the orphaned Ojibway and the childless couple, Ralph and Georgiana Webster, blossomed into a wonderfully close family group; the Webster's making sure that Matthew had all the books he wanted, and at the same time, arranging for him to remain connected with his roots. Lacking a genuine grandparent, Ralph had talked the Council into appointing a 'Grandfather' to assist Matthew in continuing the cultural relationship his parents had begun.

"So Matthew was brought up with a foot in both cultures, and somehow managed to successfully integrate his thinking into both. The depth of his knowledge of the Ojibway is phenomenal, and 'Poppa Ralph' and 'Momma Georgie' took great care to expose him to the best opportunities in 'our culture'; theatre, arts, literature. He came to love English literature, and eventually finished his degrees in that field and ultimately became a Prof at U of M; actually is Doctor Little Crow."

"That's quite a story but I still wish he'd somehow picked up a little about communications and team relationships. These periods of silence are ridiculous!"

The sound of a car in the front drive interrupted their conversation, followed shortly by the sound of Matthew's voice as he rounded the corner of the house and approached over the terrace. "Hello! Were you able to find out anything further in all that paper, or develop a new strategy while I was up North? I had some interesting visits with people up there. Actually might have pushed a few buttons…Anyway, I realized the time of day as I was coming from the airport, so stopped at a market and picked up some stuff for dinner, if there's any interest along those lines. If you are of a mind, I can fill you in on what I did while in Minnesota, and you can let me know how you folks did, OK?"

"What a good idea, Matthew," Mickey said coolly, "and it might have been even nicer if you'd kept us informed while you were away. We *are* all in this together, aren't we?"

Taken aback by the tone of her voice, and the disagreeable expression on her face, Matthew's good humor evaporated, and he stopped short of the patio, gathering his thoughts. "I see. Well, maybe I should just dump the groceries and go somewhere to prepare an annotated written report, properly tabbed, of course…"

"Now cut it out, you two! There's nothing to be gained by sniping, and I, for one, would really like to hear what transpired up in Minnesota, without a lot of undercurrents! Now let's get these groceries, talk about the weather, or the Nationals chances this season, or damn near anything but catlinite, and when we've deflated the tension level, we can circle back to Minnesota."

There was a moment of total silence, then Kevin continued, "Mickey, if you would please see what I might have in the fridge for

97

snacking, maybe some cheese that isn't too old, and Matthew and I will bring in the rest of the stuff and get the dinner going."

Kevin's strategy worked, if slowly, and after a stiff start, the small-talk conversation gradually eased the tension that had risen. Although far from convivial, the three settled into comfortable conversation; weather changes, the Nationals looking at little improvement over last year, Mickey's practice growing.

After dinner, with a couple of glasses of wine, they settled in with their after-dinner coffee near the patio's shade house where Kevin continued arranging the bonsai in their warm weather places. "Okay, Matthew. If you'll hand me that plant just to your left, I'll get on with my chore, and you can fill us in on what transpired up in Minnesota." With continuing kibitzing from the others, Kevin placed the bonsai, arranging them on the slatted shelves in the irregularly configured redwood-framed shelter. When all the plants had been placed, they stood back and admired the display. "So now, let's get into what you found, how it went up there, Matthew. Okay, Mickey?"

"Absolutely. I'm anxious to know what information from up there, if any, will fill in some of the blanks in what we've gathered from our resources here."

There was a moment of tense silence, then Matthew began, "This was one of those instances where getting there was definitely a part of the adventure, but not a part of the fun. I wound up flying out of Dulles, but as you might have imagined, Pipestone, Minnesota doesn't show up in any of the airline hub and spoke business plans, so what should have taken the better part of a day to get there, including the hour's drive from Sioux Falls turned into something else entirely. There was one of those rapidly-developing spring snow storms..." He paused for moment, reliving the hours in the rental car.

The snow was blowing almost horizontally, and I felt like I was moving inside a white bag, the road unwinding like a black ribbon in an otherwise featureless landscape. There was that feeling of deep anxiety, calling back again that night so long ago; the wind-blown snow, the thumping rhythm of the wipers as they vainly fought against the wet, heavy flakes. He could almost smell the dusty warmth of his father's old pickup, and hear the quiet conversation between his parents as they drove through the blustery white night, his head pillowed on his mother's lap. Then Mother's sharp intake of breath, Father's muttered curse as he worked brakes and steering to straighten the swerving path of the old vehicle, caught in the traction-less sweep of black ice. There was the shriek of tearing metal, the butt-end of a huge log seen through the shattering windshield...

With a shake of his head, he went on, "At any rate, I was able, after some difficulties with the weather, to make it to Pipestone, and locate an acquaintance who works with the Indian committee that awards permits for taking pipestone. They usually only give out a few a year, and the season for extracting the stuff is pretty short, so there isn't much traffic, either literal or in the form of communications. This winter, though, there had been a rather sharp up-tick. They had an application rate almost four times the norm for the single-month permits. My friend thought there was something fishy, but it's a pretty closed community, and even he couldn't find anyone who could account for that kind of increased activity."

"Kevin and I haven't even heard about that aspect of this," said Mickey, "and there wasn't anything I could see on the Internet that would have pointed in that direction either. I suppose there wasn't a commonality among all those applications?"

"Not a thing that we could see in the review I did with him up there. It was just the standard array of Zuni fetish makers, several pipe carvers, and a number of general Native American artists. If

99

there was anything unusual, it was that there seemed more than the normal number of apps from South Dakota and Iowa, and virtually all those were for the monthly permits. That *could* infer that those applicants did not want to wait the half-dozen years for one of the annual permits, and you can extrapolate from that that they wanted the catlinite quickly. There is something there to focus on, I think."

"You're sure there was nothing else?" This from Kevin as he leaned forward, elbows on knees, concern etched on his face. "That's a pretty thin thread!"

"Unless there's something you guys have come up with inside the agencies, or from the Hill contacts and I haven't heard that's the case. I agree that it's not much, but it does indicate there is at least a geographic focus. I'd be inclined to dig into that deeper if for no other reason that there's no place else to dig." He frowned across the patio table at the other two, noting the skepticism in Mickey's expression, the puzzlement in Kevin's. "Look folks, I've spent the last four days either in the clutches of the airline industry or working the Park Service guys for any information they could generate without telling them what I'm up to; a kind of deceit, by the way, that I *really* hate. I'm beat, and would have thought that to bring back a suspicious avenue for investigation would have warranted a bit more in the way of a positive reception. I'm going to get a good night's sleep without the gaiety of the Pipestone Hotel's cocktail lounge in the background, and talk to you tomorrow. Thanks for your hospitality, Kev." With that he pushed his coffee cup back to the center of the table and strode off to his waiting car.

"A bit touchy tonight," mused Michaela. "Is he always so sensitive to someone's contrary opinion?"

CHAPTER 9

The Suburban line of vehicles manufactured by the General Motors Corporation were derived from their line of light trucks, adapted to provide a measure of creature comforts not available in more utilitarian models. Air conditioning, power accessories, and interior finish options in the bewildering arrays that mark American automotive products were made available. Both two- and four-wheel drive models are produced, with engine and trailer towing packages in the line of options that can meet virtually any customer's wants and needs. Directed at the market their name would imply, the quasi-gentlemen farmers of America have embraced the Suburban as their own. This generally well-to-do group had allowed their desire for perfection in landscaping to outstrip the capabilities of the old reliable family station wagon, forcing them to seek a vehicle that was tacitly a truck. But naturally it couldn't actually *look* like or *be* a truck, and besides, it needed to carry the family in comfort as well. It wouldn't do to have the future head of Father's brokerage firm sitting out in the back of a pick-up like some Southern, red-neck, *real* farmer. No such vehicle existed until the Suburbans, sold both under the GMC and Chevrolet nameplates, and they were eagerly received by the latter-day planters outside America's great cities. A substantial number of the four-wheel drive version also made their way into the construction, and, yes, the agricultural industries, but these more practical uses were reflected in more Spartan fittings and lack of such comforts found in the "civilian" models as carpeting and stereo systems. The roomy cargo space and towing capability make the Suburban especially attractive to those involved not only with landscape chores, but with horses as well. To the horsey set, the Suburban is as common a mode of transportation as the traditional sedan, and as ubiquitous in those particular suburban areas where horses are kept.

One such area is the rolling Virginia countryside outside Washington, DC; famous for its breeding farms, fox hunts and horse shows. A sturdy Suburban towing a horse trailer, a load of hay, or simply taking the groceries home from the supermarket is a common sight. Knowledge of this had influenced the IMM security group's choice of a Suburban for their surveillance in this instance. Laura Atkinson's home in the village of Purcellville, a typical example of horse-related living, had made the choice obvious.

Charles Dolan O'Brien, Charley, particularly liked the Suburban for their purposes. Not only was there adequate room for his bulky frame, but for once there was ample space for the various electronic components and devices that were the tools of the covert surveillance trade, close at hand instead of in the trunk as they had to do when they were in a sedan. This particular vehicle had apparently even been fitted for hunting or fishing, with racks and compartments throughout the interior that yielded even more orderly use of the cargo space. It was better, in his mind, than a van. You couldn't always rationalize a van, but around here these things were simply everywhere and when the occasion called for it, they just melted into the crowd.

At the moment, he and Mac were taking advantage of their vehicular anonymity as they made their way along the highway between Purcellville and Washington. This was the route they knew Laura Atkinson travelled as she commuted to and from the city, and it was somewhere along here they had decided to precipitate a "traffic accident", thereby eliminating Headquarters' cause for concern. It would be best, they knew, if the thing could be done without any witnesses, and they were prepared to be patient. Once the location was selected, there was, in fact, not much to do but wait.

"Hold it Charley. Swing a U as soon as you can. I think I saw a good place back there about a hundred, hundred-fifty yards after that big gateway. Ya' know where I mean?"

Charley grunted in reply, and swung the big car around in the next side road and headed back the way they had come. Mac didn't have a lot to say, usually, but Charley knew that when on the job he spoke only when it made sense. Charlie had always felt that for all his professional skill, Mac, or Nathan J. MacDonald as his drivers' license read, had left something in the Central America jungles; that something in his makeup was missing. He hadn't been able to put a finger on it, but he knew something wasn't right with him. He glanced sideways at his companion as they retraced the route, noting once again the expressionless look that came over the man when he worked.

Slowing as he approached the spot he thought Mac had meant, he said, "This is it? The wide space there beside the big tree?"

"That's it. Pull in, and let's take a look around."

They pulled off the shoulder into the shadow of a huge old poplar. Stretching in front of them was an abandoned drive of some sort, partially overgrown. It faded, and then reappeared in a meandering route across a weed-choked meadow. A dilapidated shed sagged on the far side of the meadow, close against the edge of a heavy patch of woods. "Whadda ya' think, Charley? It looks pretty good to me."

Charley considered the scene carefully. "That shed, if it isn't too crapped up with old junk would be a good place to hide in the car during the day. You think this old road will be OK if it rains? It looks like it hasn't been used for months, maybe years."

"Not a problem, Charley. Look at the base they put in for the thing. That's good crushed limestone. Doesn't look like much now

103

with all the weeds growing through it and all, but for us it'll be OK. Wouldn't want to put a big rig on it, but what we're driving will be fine, and what the hell, we got four-wheel anyway. Does the main road setup suit you? That's really the key to this op anyway. Looked OK to me..."

"Let's check it out from this side," Charley broke in. He liked the concealment, but wanted another look at the way the main road approached and departed. It was important for them to be able to see someone coming without being obvious from the roadway, and of course there needed to be a suitable "accident" site not too far away. They stood beside the poplar, screened from casual observers by some straggly brush along the fence line. The road curved gently past the property, on a slope down toward the river crossing just visible somewhat more than a half-mile away.

"It might be a little far from the river, but that would give us a chance to scope out any other traffic, and the river's really the thing, don't ya' think?" Mac's assessment was, as usual in such matters, correct.

"Couldn't be a better place within several miles, and out in the middle of nowhere like this, the traffic probably won't be too much of a deal. You're right. This will be just about perfect. Let's check out the shed and then head back to the motel. I could use some shut-eye and bet you could too." Turning, the two men started off across the field.

Work in the laboratory had settled into a routine of long days of observation, the kind of activity that Henry Genarro despised. The researchers had to wait now for the armorers and gunsmiths to do their work, fabricating weapons from the material they had produced after the expenditure of so much time and mental effort. Henry knew that the material was perfect for their needs. He had even thought of a name for it, Hengenite, a clever acronym in the fashion of science these days, he had thought. After all, hadn't he provided the key to the compounding himself? No one would admit that, of course, but he knew it, and he would show them all!

"Henry, would you help me here just for a few minutes? We're a couple of guys short today." His resentful reverie was broken by a call from one of the armorers, working at a bench on the far side of the lab.

"Right, Bill. I'll be right there," was the audible reply, but muttering under his breath, *you cretin! These men were simple working men, with no right to be in a scientific laboratory! It was a wonder they hadn't spit on the floor, or pissed in the lab sinks.* It was beyond Henry's comprehension how management could have allowed such a thing. This situation certainly would not have arisen had he been in the charge, as he should have been. Putting on what the thought was a pleasant expression, he approached an enclosure with a bench where the man named Bill was working with one of the weapons. "What can I do for you?" he inquired.

"If you would, please, just tighten those two clamps while I hold the weapon upright. We want to set it up in this stand for test firing, and I don't have enough hands, it seems."

Henry was certain this was yet another example of the man's crude humor, for he was, in fact, missing one hand. It had been preplaced by an operable hook-like prosthesis, and he had grudgingly admired the skill with which Bill had used it in some rather delicate operations, but he clearly could use some help now. This was the largest of the weapons, roughly three feet long when fully assembled, and relatively heavy; the compound weighing more than conventional plastics, although still much lighter than the metal it

105

was replacing. It had a grenade launching tube affixed under the barrel of the heavy caliber machine gun. Bill had inserted the ammunition magazine in the receiver, and was holding the thing balanced in the hook, with his right hand positioning the collapsible stock over the clamp of the firing stand.

"Now if you'll just crank this back clamp closed when I say, and the one over the barrel, we'll see if this sucker works!" Bill smiled at Henry, although he, along with the rest of the weapons crew had quickly come to loathe him. He was obviously an intellectual snob, and even with virtually no knowledge of what they had been doing for two weeks, he'd stuck his nose into every step of the process, offering worthless suggestions at every turn, then showing increasing disdain for their lack of perception when they ignored him. *A complete jerk, but all I need now is an extra pair of hands, an event his asshole can't screw it up.* "That's it, Henry. Just another half-turn…that's it. Now for the front, and we're done. Thanks, Man. Wanna hang around and watch this baby run?"

"No. Thank you," Genarro replied tersely as he turned on his heel and stalked back to his former position of observation. *Watch this baby run, indeed! What did these idiots think of him that they could be so casual and rude in the face of a genuine scientific breakthrough? Most of them had never even been to college, for God's sake! Why, they were products of the armed forces, and everyone knew how base that was. "Watch this baby run"!*

A temporary testing range had been set up in the far end of the laboratory, another mistake in Henry's eyes. Partitioned off with sound-deadening materials, and lined with two rows of sand bags and a draping of Kevlar, the enclosure was being used to "hot test" the various weapons as their fabrication was completed. Starting from blocks of the catlinite-laced compound formed in the lab, the gunsmiths had crafted each part, even down to the smallest bolts. Their work had required little from the permanent staff, but they had

106

been retained in the lab to accumulate the scrap material and reform it into smaller blocks for future use. After the initial discovery of its properties, the production process had proven to be relatively simple, and the laboratory crew had been able to provide sufficient quantities without having to call on the manufacturing group. Some testing had already been completed on smaller guns, but the larger-caliber weapon now in the stand would be the real proof. If the material could stand up to the added stresses from the heavier shells, then the material could be called a genuine success. Only a few problems had come up in the testing; one 9-millemeter machine pistol had abruptly disintegrated for reasons not yet clear, and there was an air of achievement among the craftsmen. The technicians that had been at work for the last fortnight had been deeply screened from various divisions of the company. They were given little information about the work, other than it was highly classified, and that they would follow existing weapon designs, so as to make ammunition readily available.

Bill, as task leader for the high-caliber assault rifle, checked the video cameras ranged around the test stand enclosure. Shielded by double thicknesses of shatterproof, bulletproof glass, they would capture every aspect of the test firing in standard, slow and super slow motion speed. Sure that the tape magazines were full and the cameras set for the proper speed, he took up a position in the observation booth. Starting through the abbreviated check list, he turned on the range lights, verified that no one was in the space, and rang the alarm bell three times. "Ready on the range!" he declared through the PA system. And with a slight pause, he pushed a relay button that activated a small electric motor, which in turn pulled a short steel rod against the trigger of the fixed weapon. Set for single shot operation, the carefully crafted mechanisms chambered one round and fired. The heavy report was greatly muffled, and could not be heard beyond the lab's walls, but the target showed a large jagged hole, and the stand bucked slightly. "So far, so good," muttered Bill, as he went back through the enclosure to reset the weapon at full automatic. "Now, my beauty, we'll see if you have the right stuff."

Back in the booth, he checked the range again, and pushed the "Fire" button. With a deep roar, the dull red weapon sprayed the target area, shredding the cardboard of the target, and shifting the heavy firing stand as spent shells flew from the ejector. Although his view was somewhat obscured by the smoke of the firing, Bill could see that the weapon was intact and seemingly unaffected. Switching off the cameras, he shed his ear protectors, and walked back to the test stand. Tapping the weapon gently with his hook, he smiled down at it, almost as if it were a precocious child that had performed well for relatives. "That's it, darlin'. You showed us all. Nobody wanted the heavy cal job, and I was stuck with it, but you came through. Good girl!" He studied the thing carefully, noting the slight curl of smoke from the barrel and the oily sheen that all the new guns had shown after firing. *Must be some sort of heat-induced reaction in the stuff they had us make these things out of. Don't really know what it is, but it doesn't seem to affect the performance. . I'd like to see how much of that sweat the other guys noticed. Jerry and Sam both commented on it. I'll check it out with them when they get over whatever kind of flu has gotten so many guys down. Maybe next week in time for the final reports...* He continued to muse and unconsciously register small details as he deftly lifted the heavy weapon from its cradle with his hook and carried it back to his bench for cleaning.

Henry Genarro had surreptitiously watched the whole procedure from his place at the other end of the room, pondering the results of the test. Monroe would like that gun. Not at all subtle, but the damage it could inflict would be very much to his liking, and the folding stock and demountable barrel would allow easy concealment. Already Genarro had selected three types of arms from the collection that had been made in the lab, and over the past few days with so

108

many of the technicians out sick, had been able to smuggle them out in his gym bag. His knowledge was slight, but he had listened carefully to the characteristics Monroe had described, and he was sure he had come up with the right choices. It was a shame about the little machine pistol; that would have been another good choice, but then, there was no use worrying about something you could do nothing about. This last would more than make up for the loss of that one. He would make excuses to be the last out tonight, and take the last of the chosen pieces out with him. It would be a pleasure to leave this place once and for all, and to watch from afar the fall of those who had merely used him to further their own ends. His meeting with Jake Monroe was for eleven that night, and it would be hard to make it on time if he wasn't able to push these people out of here faster. So many had become ill over the past few days productivity of the effort had fallen drastically. He only hoped whatever particular strain of flu it was wouldn't strike him as well.

NORTHERN PLAINS - 1610

Seated in his accustomed place, he awaited the arrival of the youngsters.

"Greetings, One Ear," Grey Wolf spoke courteously. "As you said we could, we have come again to hear more of the story of the White Buffalo Calf Woman."

"It is good to know that you care to hear more," One Ear said, including the whole audience. "I will tell you more, and I hope that you will think of what I say, for it is because of these stories that our people know the proper way to continue their relationship with the Spirits." He paused for effect, the continued. "When the White Buffalo Calf Woman opened her bundle, and showed the people of the camp the Chanunpa, she told them she would also tell them what it meant and how to use it.

'The bowl of the pipe is of the red stone. It represents the flesh and blood of the Buffalo People," and looking around the circle, she smiled at the people. 'It also represents the flesh and blood of those that have come before you, the Earth People, the Lakota. The wooden stem of the pipe is to remind you of the growing things on the Earth; trees and grass and all growing things.' Then she took willow bark and tobacco from her pouch, and filled the pipe and lighted it with a coal from the fire. And she took a draw on the pipe and passed to each, until all had smoked. 'The smoke of the Sacred Pipe is as the sacred wind, and carries your prayers to the Creator, Wakan Tanka. I will serve you always, when you follow the Good Red Road. As you saw me first in smoke, you will always see me in smoke.'"

One Ear paused, caught up in his own story, filled with emotion as he pictured the beautiful Wohpe *speaking to the people, instructing them in the Way. With a low cough, he cleared his throat, took a sip from the bark cup at his side, and went on. "After all these things were told to the people, White Buffalo Calf Woman told the shaman how to gather the bark and the tobacco, and how to prepare and care for it. Then she told the people how to hold the pipe, and offer it to the Flour Sacred Directions. When this was done, she remained with the people in the camp for many days. All the time she was there the people were happy, for she was so beautiful, and she went from tepee to tepee and spoke kind words to all."*

One Ear was interrupted at this point by the noisy arrival of a hunting party that had been away from the camp for several days. Anxious to avoid discourtesy, the youngsters fidgeted, and with a smile the old teller waved them on their way. He knew they would return, and he knew the joy that comes with the return of the hunter; perhaps_if their luck had been good, there would be a feast, with much to eat, and offerings to the gods who had blessed them in their search for food. He leaned back against the tepee poles, and watched the joyous greetings for the returning hunters.

CHAPTER 10

It was unseasonably warm in the city, and sweat stained his shirt as he walked swiftly up the street. John Wolf had left the restaurant/meeting place a man perplexed. Jake Monroe was difficult at all times, but he had been especially so for the past few days. John knew it had something to do with the man known as Genarro, but he was sure that wasn't the complete story. Normally given to talk, *preaching really*, Jake had become quieter and more tense than he had ever been in Wolf's memory. He had tried discussing this with his friend Andrew Moore, but had given up. Moore, recently preoccupied with his father's accelerating descent into alcoholism, had become almost useless.

Lacking Moore's feedback, Wolf determined that he must go alone to the Council. They should know of Monroe's shift in attitude and demeanor, and he could not seek advice elsewhere. It bothered him to come again without solid proof of the suspicions that had begun to boil in his mind; that Monroe was leading them to a disaster. *If only I could only persuade Jake to tell us what the plan, what the objective of all this with the Genarro man is!* In this strange world of hiding and subterfuge he was frequently uneasy; there should be more direct ways of dealing with things, more straightforward answers to the needs of his people, and the lack of specific action frustrated him, as it did many of the younger braves. He had no way of knowing that it had always been so, and in all societies, but his determination to call attention to the misdeeds of the whites and the avenging of so many slights and actions on their part knew no bounds. *Something must be done!* No solid information as to what was happening with Monroe was available, but he sensed that the Council would have an answer as to how he should react. He slowed, and then casually leaned against a light pole. Seemingly relaxed, his eyes darted over the mix of pedestrians and vehicles that passed, searching for tell-tale signs of surveillance, signs he had learned to recognize through years of dodging FBI warrants. After several minutes he made his way, unobserved, to the back door of a house midway down the block.

It took another half hour before the members of the council were all there, and in that time, Wolf began to feel as if maybe he had made too much of what was being said by Monroe. He had almost decided to avoid the issue, and make a cursory interim report, when he caught the eye of Sam Walking Hare. With a slight gesture of his head, Walking Hare indicated that he should move out into the hallway in the center of the house.

Meeting his questioning gaze straight on, Walking Hare spoke quietly, "I am aware of the confusion you suffer, John Wolf. The ways of the man Monroe are a puzzlement to many of us, and your close contact with him could not but help add to the uneasiness that has been with you for some time. Do not hide your concern when you speak with the Council. This is a bad man, and I know he has no sympathy with *our* goals, only those in *his* mind. What he wants will not serve us well, no matter what that turns out to be! Your words will add weight to mine, and possibly the council will wish to reconsider where we go, and with whom we make that journey. Tell them what you feel"

When they returned to the room, there wasn't doubt in John's mind any longer; he would say what he had come to say, and listen to the advice from the elders. That would be the proper way, and with all the information at their disposal, he had every confidence there would be a more definite course of action for him when the meeting was over.

It took much longer than Wolf had anticipated. Following the recitation of his observations and concerns, each of the Council members asked questions, carefully cross examining him about every aspect of the relationship, and his specific feelings regarding them. Old Harry Chosa was particularly interested in what John felt was the ultimate demand that Monroe would place on The Movement, and bore down on him hard when he replied that he was not sure. "You are the eyes and ears of this Council, John Wolf. It is from the information you bring to us that we must decide who will be our ally, and who will be numbered with our enemies. I do not ask you to tell us what you know for fact, now. We have heard that. I ask you what you think is in the heart of the man Monroe; what his true feelings are towards us, and to what end you *think* he is heading. Tell us these things, and let *us* consider the consequences of continuing to deal with him."

"He is, I *think*, a man with much hate in his heart." As he spoke, John hoped the emphasis on the word would not be thought disrespectful. He was uneasy, again. He did not feel comfortable in this role. The things in men's hearts were difficult to understand with any degree of certainty, even for those wise men skilled in such things. Nonetheless, he plowed ahead. "When he speaks about what he refers to as "the system", he talks of bringing it down, and of the hurtful things he has had to endure because "the system" would not listen to him, and his friends, many years ago. He says these things often, but somehow it does not seem as if he actually believes what he is saying." He paused and looked around at the others, the question obvious in the perplexed expression on his face. Had they known men who said one thing but meant another? The nods and an unknotting of furrowed brows told him they had, and he continued. "I am as sure as I can be that Monroe's feelings toward "the system" are nothing more than talk, a smokescreen to hide his actual objectives. He has other goals, possibly objects of hatred, possibly something else. The hatred is pure; its object is unclear, and may likely have nothing to do with this business with the Genarro man. This is what makes the big question in my mind."

There was a courteous period of silence, and then Standing Bear, the genuine leader of them all, began to speak for the first time. "I have heard the things John Wolf has said about Jake Monroe. I have heard the questions raised by you all," as he gestured to the circle of men, "and John Wolf's response to those questions. There is one possibility that has not been discussed. Hate changes the man who harbors it for a long time without being able to rid himself of it. It brings *aksiwin,* sickness, to the mind. Jake Monroe has hated for nearly forty years without being able to see any of the things he hates changed as he would have them. He wants, *must have*, some way to get rid of the hate he has carried with him; that he has nurtured as one would a monster child. That is the danger in Jake Monroe. The need to get rid of the hate will now be very strong and there is little hope of knowing what way he will choose to do that. But in many ways he is like the wolverine; when we can see him we know what he is about, and can maneuver to avoid his fangs. It is when we do not know where he is that the danger becomes ever greater. You have done well, John Wolf, to come here with your worries; they are good. But now we must ask you to be, still, the one who watches the wolverine. Do not wait to bring news of any change, or any action that will tell which direction he will take. We have put ourselves in this position, and now must not only find a way out, but one which will allow us to do so without being killed by the one we watch." He stopped talking, and after the group had acknowledged his words, he drew out the pipe, and with appropriate ceremony filled and lighted it. It was passed about the circle, including John Wolf, and when finished, the ashes offered again to *Wakan Tanka*. Carefully returning the pipe to its deerskin pouch, Standing Bear rose and left the room. The sound of a door closing somewhere in the back of the house caused to interrupt the spell of mysticism that had come over the group, and they each congratulated Wolf on his elevated role, then left the house.

Matthew reflected on the course of the previous evening, recalling a rhetorical question Michaela had raised about an unholy alliance between IMM and Benjamin; *"You know something that seems funny to me about this whole business? It's the alliance between IMM, a citadel of the big business conservative mindset, and George Benjamin, absolutely the country's most outspoken champion of all things liberal. What is so special...I mean, what kind of thing could possibly have brought them together? The Quarry obviously fills some short-term need to IMM, but what could Benjamin possibly hope to gain? This can't be just about money. It just doesn't make sense if you look at the face of the matter, does it?"* That had evoked a spirited discussion for a time about what Kevin had dubbed "The Connection". *That abrupt departure I decided on had certainly put a stop to anything productive,* he thought. *Need to mend some fences there! Kevin was going to call some agency people, Michaela checking some political connections for Benjamin background, I'm to check out a connection at the BIA with a guy Kevin didn't know...*

Rolling over in the Inn's wide bed, he checked the time on the bedside table's alarm clock. *Six Fifteen. Good. All those years of early rising haven't been lost after all. Thank you Grandfather. I could have been a real slug- a -bed if it had not been for your teaching. Good, and thank you!*

Coming out of the shower, he noticed the message light on the phone and called the desk. Clamping the receiver against his shoulder with his chin, he rummaged through his suitcase for clean clothes while listening to the faint whirs of the system as the front desk connection was made. "Yes," he replied to the operator," this is

Matthew Little Crow. I have a message light. I was here, but didn't hear the phone ring; maybe while I was in the shower…" He stopped in mid-sentence. *Why am I finding it necessary to explain to a desk clerk why I didn't pick up the telephone? Must be some remnant of an etiquette lesson in…*

"Why yes, Mr. Little Crow. You have a message from a Ms. Campbell. She asked that you call, and indicated that you had the number. Is that correct?"

"Yes, thank you." Hanging up, he quickly dressed, then dialed Michaela's office number.

"Law office," sing-songed the service operator.

"Miss Campbell, please. Matthew Little Crow."

A click, a short silence then Michaela's soft "Yes, Michaela Campbell speaking. May I help you?"

Matthew smiled. *That sounds nice… Yes, very nice.* "Good morning! And what has you out at such an early hour, Counselor? I thought all you city lawyers began your days at a more civilized hour, like maybe ten or ten-thirty. You'll ruin your image!"

"The image was ruined the first time I realized there was no associate to complete the brief for a court case," she laughed, "and in any event, it only makes good sense to take advantage of a time when the damned phone isn't ringing off the hook. But thank you for returning my call so promptly. I have to be out toward the Inn, and thought I'd pick you up and take you over to Kevin's rather than have all three of us with cars over there; if that's OK with you, of course."

"That would be fine, and I'll buy you breakfast, if you haven't already had yours."

117

"I have, but would love to have some coffee while you eat. Is half an hour good for you?"

"Very good. See you then." He mused as he finished dressing. *Not nearly the starchiness I've become accustomed to this morning... wonder why? At any rate that's a fence I definitely need to mend.*

This is the kind of weather they had in mind when the convertible was invented, thought Laura, as she drove along the narrow road toward the city. *And this is the kind of weather, and road, and drive I had in mind when I moved way the hell and gone out here in the country. No one can imagine the feeling of renewal I find in this commute every day.* All her friends had said she was crazy to go so far into the Virginia countryside, leaving the more cosmopolitan, if somewhat sleazy, life in the city. She had found the small cottage while antiquing with Michaela Campbell, and had fallen in love with it right away. The town was quaint to the point of looking similar to a movie set, but the people were friendly and open, and somewhat bemused by the excitement she displayed. It took a month to reach agreement with the owner, a widowed teacher who had left for an extended stay with friends in Florida, but from the day she had moved in, she had never regretted the choice. Driving was a pleasure to her, and on bright late spring mornings such as this, the trek into the city was perfect for ridding the mind of cobwebs. Besides, she enjoyed the mere act of maneuvering the well-tuned little car through the curves and rolling hills. Her contentment was complete as she passed the big stone gates and headed toward the old bridge over the Potomac tributary. Laura was only peripherally aware of the other vehicle pulling out of the drive, and realizing it would not interfere as she passed, returned her concentration to the curve in the road ahead.

As had been the custom in early road-building and design, routes had followed traditional, old paths from the days of ferries and fords. This practice usually resulted in simply replacing the ferry / ford with a bridge. Since the old methods of river crossing were to minimize the time in water, they tended to be essentially perpendicular to the banks, regardless of the angle of the road's approach. This design philosophy sometimes necessitated putting rather sharp curves in roadways as they cut through the countryside at angles to rivers. Such was the case with the Purcellville Bridge. Its short, and thus less expensive, span had been situated nearly perpendicular to the stream, with a sharp turn just before the crossing, and another near-right-angle turn occurring just after.

Slowing, Laura smiled. This part of the drive was really her favorite. Laura down- shifted in anticipation of acceleration out of the turn, already hearing in her mind the wonderful rattle-thump as the car would race through the aging truss, across the planked decking. She was not aware of the rapid approach of the other vehicle, focusing instead on the bend immediately in front of her. When the collision came, fractional seconds registered jerky still-frame images and sensations in her horrified mind; the loss of control, the onrushing guard rail, the sense of emptiness as the roadway vanished in front of her, the starred, shattered windshield, a feeling of helpless flight as the mangled little car slowly turned end over, revealing the rocky stream bed below, excruciating, blinding pain, blackness...

With an instinct from long experience, Charley had timed the exit from the gateway perfectly. The huge vehicle, more than twice the weight of the little roadster, was accelerating smoothly, powerfully as the other began to brake for the turn onto the bridge. It took only a small adjustment to strike the other car squarely from behind, joining the momentum of the two and forcing the convertible across the road and into the woefully inadequate wooden guard rail. It wasn't necessary to push the other completely off the edge of the

119

ravine; the blow struck in the collision had been more than enough. Braking to a stop in front of the hole in the railing, Charley nodded to Mac, who vaulted out the door and peered over the edge. It was a matter of precaution, of course. Black, oily smoke was already riding from below.

"Done deal," Mac stated bluntly as he climbed back into the right seat of the car. "The thing landed upside down on some rocks, broke the gas tank and started to burn. No one lived through that, that's certain. And not a mark on us, except for maybe a little scratch on the bumper, and I'm not sure that hasn't been there all along."

"Then we're gone. As soon as we clear the area, call HQ on the scrambler, let 'em know and we'll get back to watching the girl lawyer and the other two guys." Charley was backing and turning the car as he spoke and they were quickly on the road back the way they had come, the black smoke cloud growing, billowing behind them.

CHAPTER 11

Senator George Benjamin stared blankly at the thick stacks of papers cluttering the desk. The small office he maintained in his home district in Minnesota was maintained for the purpose of meeting with constituents during the requisite visits to the state. The actual office was only a small portion of a rather large suite of rooms. Located in a renovated warehouse complex, and essentially donated by a developer who had received advance information on the selection of a site for a large Federal administrative installation, the huge profit on otherwise undesirable acreage more than made up for the loss of rental from the offices. In addition to his receiving office, the suite included space for the local staff, a state-of-the-art mailing center for his communiqués to the people of the state, and on the second floor, a loft apartment for his use while in the area. The same warehouse complex held a nice selection of expensive specialty shops and a good restaurant overlooked the river. It was a perfect setup for him and Benjamin rarely left the comfort of the enclave except for various ceremonial appearances.

Little of meaning actually was done here, but keeping the appearance of a "home district" working office was something he had learned long ago from a colleague and had come to realize was an absolute political necessity. People wanted to believe that you actually worked for them, even when you were back here in the hustings. He took it almost as a point of personal ethics to try to do something while he was here, but today had been different. The complaints and concerns of the constituency he courted so carefully were of no interest. His thoughts were focused on the telephone, and the call he expected on his private line. They had said it would be soon, but it had been four days since the hastily arranged departure from Washington, and only silence. *What's the problem; can't they just get it over with?*

His ruminations were interrupted by a soft knock on the office door. "Senator, could I have a moment of your time?" The question was from Evelyn Johannsen, a fairly new staffer.

"Why yes, Evelyn. Come in, will you?" His return from reverie, and to character, was instantaneous; a reaction born of many years on the stump. He half rose, gesturing to a side chair, nodding and smiling as the woman timidly entered the room. "What can I do for you?"

"Senator Benjamin...I don't know how to say this exactly..." She paused, looking at her hands as she made halting steps toward the chair.

"What is it, my dear," he asked, with the smarmy charm he'd found so effective in dealing with his feminine constituents. He truly didn't care, but knew it was important to constantly reassure these inside people that they worked with a compassionate, heroic personage. It amazed him how gullible they were; how willing to believe almost anything he told them.

Seated finally on the edge of the chair, Evelyn looked up at him, a shy blush glowing in her pale face. "Sir, I would like to ask if you could see fit for me to transfer to your Washington office?" The words had spilled out quickly, and she ended abruptly with a look of anxiety that reminded him of a cocker spaniel.

"And why would you want to do that, Evelyn, when you are so effective here?"

"Well, sir, you see, my mother lives in Baltimore, and I just heard from my brother that she's had another heart attack, and she was calling for me during the night. See, my Dad died several years ago, and except for my brother, I'm all she has left, and he's got a shift job at the rail yards there, and he's gone a lot at night, and...", breathless she paused again.

"Yes, I understand," he broke in. "But you understand that such a transfer might take a little time to arrange. Staff positions in Washington are not always open, and when they are, many would like the opportunity to work at the seat of government." He used the arcane term only when he wished to be obscure. There was something about the omnipotence and vastness of "seat of government" that intimidated the yokels, and it gave him pleasure to intimidate them. *This girl would no more fit in with the high-energy group he had there...But what about that; soon there would be no Washington office, although no one knows that yet...could tell her anything she wanted to hear...that's a wonderful bust...Scandinavian, so possibly a true blonde...this could be strung into something worthwhile...*

Kevin watched the bluebirds come and go from the small box he had fastened to the old gum tree so long ago, and wondered idly how many of the tiny creatures hatched in the coziness of that nest still frequented the woods hereabout. Taking a sip of coffee form the steaming mug, he set it aside on a small wrought iron table, and picked up the quadrille sheets at his elbow. Diagrammed on the papers was an outline of the corporate structure of IMM. The complexities of the organization were extraordinary, and he wondered at the rationale for creating such a tangle of extremely diverse companies. Even given the fact that this chart was made up from published articles and reports, and lacked detail about interlocking levels of responsibility, it was a maze. As advanced as management systems and reporting procedures were, he knew instinctively that it would not be possible to account for all the activities of every group in every division should someone with a modicum of authority wish it not to be so. Selected things would simply not come to the notice of corporate level management. The opportunity for a maverick operation certainly existed. The question was whether or not it did, and if so, could it be found.

He studied the pages of notes accompanying the diagrams, he winnowing out the obviously unrelated entities, concentrating on ones that could possibly have a need for, or be involved with, technical research. Even after dropping all the extraneous divisions; hotels, cruise line, dry cleaning equipment, there were still more than a dozen distinct divisions that could at least be presumed to have interest in some form of scientific research. The problem was in finding the common link that would allow some sort of investigation of the whole without going to the effort to go over each one. After another hour of study, Kevin set the files aside in frustration, and walked out to the benches off the patio, seeking the soothing effect the bonsai always had on him. The thought came to him as he trimmed an errant shoot from a gnarled *moyogi* pine.

Modern management demands some thread of continuity, and it's found in the networks of their computer systems. Aside from individual work stations in some design groups, almost every system has a wide area network that allowed various branches of the company to transmit data and other information freely. Because of the large number of users and myriad uses, network managers would be placed to act as overseers; maintaining the hardware and the software libraries, checking the compatibility of new applications, and monitoring the accumulation of data and text information. A network manager, by virtue of his position would have access to all the levels of files and applications, and would be able to tap into remote computers from a central point. Certainly the stuff of privacy advocates' nightmares, but in reality those guys are the real computer experts who keep the company's information systems

124

running. Now what I have to do is locate a network manager at a high-enough level inside IMM's information systems group, and find out how the routing of research documentation from the Iowa location is done. Mind racing, he left the shade house and the grooming of the plants, and returned to his study, where he ran down the list of departments within IMM, searching for one that could provide the inside opening which he sought. He left a message with Mickey's service, saying he would be down in Atlanta for a couple of days, and said he'd call when he got back, but thought he had a lead worth following. Then he called his travel agent and checked on flight schedules between Washington and Atlanta.

Matthew Little Crow faced a dilemma. He had rigorously adhered to a philosophy that one did not become personally involved with those connected in career and business. And he extended that feeling to interim projects of the sort he did with Kevin. Michaela Campbell for all her cool reserve and mannerisms, had found her way into his thoughts, and was testing his resolve in that regard, not, he thought, that she realized it. Matthew found himself musing over something she had said, or a particular gesture that had somehow intrigued him. Only an inborn sense of responsibility, and the discipline to appear impassive had restrained a new desire to reach out to her, literally or figuratively. He wondered when, or if, he had reached the point where he was not sure he *wanted* to be so disciplined. They had been together daily for almost two weeks now, and there had been some real clashes, but with each passing day he became more…interested. Again today they would be together, and he found himself looking forward to her arrival.

When she entered the Huntsman's dining room, he was surprised to see that instead of the tailored professional clothing in which she normally dressed that she wore a brightly colored tennis warm-up outfit. Rising as she approached, he inquired about the change in apparel.

"Well, right after I spoke with you, I received two calls in quick succession. One, from my service was a message from Kevin. He said he was going down to Atlanta for a couple of days to pursue an idea, not sure what he's going to *find* in Atlanta, but that's where he's headed. The second call was from a member of my tennis group, who desperately needed a substitute for her match this morning. I had a cancellation in my schedule, so I told her I'd play. Aannnywaaay," she said, dragging out the word, "I thought if you don't mind, maybe you could watch us play for about an hour? Presuming you can stand the thought of being the lone spectator, and male, among a group of suburban women. And since the brainstorming session with Kevin would be off until he returns, I thought we could spend some time looking at this corner of the world, my own personal favorite corner. What do you say?"

Accepting with a grin, Matthew dug into the platter of waffles, sausage and eggs in front of him as she poured coffee from the carafe on the table. "That sounds like fun. As for the tennis, if your group of 'suburban women', don't mind my being there, then I'm all for it. And the tour I really look forward to. It seems I am always in airports, taxis and meetings, and the countryside I've only seen out of airplane windows and in pictures in some office or other. I'd very much like to see it at ground level, and hear how a real native feels about their "favorite corner'."

"Well, good," Michaela replied, and after a short pause, "How in the world can you eat a breakfast like that and not weigh about five hundred pounds?"

"It's really quite easy, if you have a supersonic metabolism, and a propensity to miss lunch or dinner or both. Would you like something? "

126

"Thanks, but no. I don't want to eat anything this close to playing. Take your time, though. We have ample time to get to the courts. They are only about a mile from here."

The small talk through the rest of his meal was comfortable, and Matthew noted little of the deep reserve he'd always sensed in her before. The light heartedness continued on the short drive to the courts, located in a pleasant little park tucked into a wooded area nearby. Michaela introduced him as an out-of-town business associate to the collection of athletic-looking women volleying on the courts when they arrived. Then, shedding the trousers of the warm-up, she took to the court with her group, and he settled on a bench under a small gazebo between the pairs of courts.

Matthew was familiar with tennis, and although not an aficionado, he sensed as he watched that this was really quite good. The women were obviously intent on the competition, and the jocularity that had prevailed during the warming up gave way to serious if not grim determination as the matches wore on. He watched with pleasure as Michaela and her partner, a stocky little woman with a powerful stroke, rallied from several points down to win the first set. Taking a drink from the fountain attached to one of the gazebo's posts, Michaela winked at him and said, "It won't be much longer now. Marilyn's hit her stride, and when she's on like this, she can be just devastating. Watch the serves this set!"

With that, she whirled back through the gate and took her position at the net. Matthew found himself paying much more attention to her figure, revealed now after she had shed her jacket early in the match, than to the level of play. *Nice thing about tennis clothes,* he thought, *is how they show off the legs...*

True to her prediction, Michaela's match went rapidly in the second set as her partner seemed to gain strength and accuracy with each shot. Michaela, who had maintained the team's competitive position in the first set with uncannily accurate passing shots, was seldom called upon as shot after shot was pounded with rifle-shot power and accuracy by her diminutive partner. At Michaela's service, Marilyn was a virtual wall at the net, volleying strongly when service returns were within her reach. Smiling broadly, the victorious two-some shook hands with their opponents, and swung easily off the court. Their relaxed manner made it clear they were accustomed to winning, enjoyed it, and felt confident they would continue in those ways.

Still chatting animatedly with her friends, Michaela donned her jacket and trousers, took Matthew by the arm, and started off toward the parking lot. She called farewells over her shoulder as they reached the car, and, still bubbling with enthusiasm from the match, almost literally jumped into the car. "All right, now, how was that for a morning's entertainment?"

"It was exactly what the doctor ordered as the start to a day of relaxation. It was a pleasure watching you guys play, and have such a good time competing. I liked that, although the two on the other side of the net probably didn't find the same level of enjoyment! What's next, Tour-Guide, ma'am?"

"To tell you the truth, I need to take a few minutes out to check with my office, then a shower. Do you mind waiting a bit more? We can run by the office, go to my place, I'll take a quick rinse and change, and then we can take a nice drive out through the country. Sound OK?

"Good with me! Let's do it!"

Then, backing out, she maneuvered the car through the others in the lot, and turned onto the main road toward her office, neither noticing a light blue Suburban loitering along several cars behind them.

Mathew Little Crow sat in the sunny kitchen of Michaela's carriage-house apartment, and watched the old cat. This was an animal, he thought, that would have pleased Grandfather. Upon their arrival at the apartment after Michaela's tennis match, the cat, after eyeing him suspiciously, had allowed her mistress to scratch her behind the ears, and then had stalked off. Michaela had gone into another part of the place to shower and change, and Matthew had seated himself in the kitchen, waiting for the offered pot of coffee to finish its cycle, enjoying the warm room and the rich smell of the brewing Kona blend.

He felt, rather than saw the cat's gaze. Turning in his chair, he saw her mottled shape seated carefully at the edge of the carpet between kitchen and living room. No motion was noticeable as she regarded this stranger in her domain. The seven or eight feet separating them was apparently as close as she felt necessary for her inspection, and she watched him with unblinking topaz eyes.

"Hello, Old Cat," he said in a respectful voice, as he had been coached by Grandfather. This elicited a slight nod of her head, and she resumed her consideration. "Would you like to come in here, or do you find my presence disturbing?" Another slight head bob. The coffee had finished and he rose, poured a mug full, and resumed his place at the small table. He had found a container of cream in the refrigerator, and added it to the mug until its contents turned a rich tan. The Cat did not move through this, continuing her watch, carefully observing all movement for some sign of threat. He relaxed again at the table, watching her surreptitiously out of the corner of his eye. After a moment she rose, stretching luxuriously in the rhombic-shaped patch of sunlight that slanted through the window. Tail switching, she ambled into the room, and settled again just in front of him, resuming her observation at closer range. And so it was for several minutes. *Grandfather, this is a white man's cat with proper Ojibwas manners. Taking the time to be noticed, not*

129

intruding on another's place. She would have been welcome in your lodge.

He heard the sound of a hair dryer, as did his companion. Glancing over her shoulder, she noted the noise, identified it, and then relaxed into a slumping posture that allowed her to groom her back legs and paws. At some sound only she heard, she abruptly stopped, looked agitatedly around, and with a bound leapt to the window sill to check something outside. Satisfied with what she saw, she yawned, and looked back at him expectantly. For a minute he didn't realize what she wanted, then noticed that her gaze went from his face to the cream container and back. Chuckling, he fetched a saucer from a cupboard and poured a small amount of cream in it. After he placed it on the floor below the window, he sat back and waited to see the reaction to this offering. For a time, there was a studied ignoring of the milk. Lucille watched things out the window, cleaned her front paws, and occasionally looked over her shoulder at the man seated at her table. Eventually, she dropped heavily to the floor, sat for a moment to regain her dignity, and walked stiffly to the saucer. Shivering with pleasure at the first taste, she then greedily lapped at it.

Michaela's entry from the back spaces interrupted the little tableau, Matthew rising to greet her, the cat rising quickly and placing herself between her mistress' feet. She had dressed in well-fitted hiking clothes; soft, loose shirt, multi-pocket rip-stop pants, and lightweight boots that had seen no small degree of off-pavement wear. Her rich auburn hair was pulled back in a jaunty pony tail secured by a green ribbon. *She looks* great…*could model for REI in that outfit…looks as if she would know her way around when she's in the woods…something of a surprise to see, where I have thought dyed in the wool City girl…interesting…would not have expected this at all…*

130

"I see you two have managed to make your acquaintance and you sir, used shameless bribery! Imagine that! Taking advantage of a poor feline's weakness. Shame on you!"

Her smile belying her words, they looked at each other, recognizing the beginning of a shift in the relationship. For a moment their eyes locked, then she broke the moment with a busied flurry of activity, shooing the cat into the other room, retrieving the saucer, rinsing it and placing it in the dishwasher, wiping at countertops already clean. "All set?" she asked. "As soon as you're through with your coffee we can be on our way."

Still adjusting his thinking toward her, Matthew raised the mug in a half toast, drank the last of the coffee, and rinsed the empty mug at the sink. "I'm ready when you are. Does the cat need to be let out, or anything?"

"Heavens, no. She wouldn't know what to do out there. She's been a house cat all her life, and very content with that lot. I'll check to be sure she has water and food, and that she can get to her litter box, and we'll be on our way." The hint of awkwardness that had been there moments before was gone.

"If you don't mind a small detour, I would like to stop by the Huntsman and get my hiking boots. Your outfit suggests we might wind up walking in the woods, and these TopSiders wouldn't do very well for that. OK?"

"Sure. I had originally thought we'd make a kind of driving tour, but on second thought there is a very special place that I'd like to show you. It's a bit out of the way, and we'd be driving around on some pretty narrow, curvy country roads for a while. That wouldn't be a problem for you would it?"

"Not in the least! Curvier the better with a car like yours. What do you say we put the top down and really take advantage of the day?"

"That's what I was hoping you'd say. This place we'll go belongs to an old friend of my parents, and is what he calls his Cottage. It's a really, really nice place, much more than what 'cottage' would make you think, but he uses it only rarely anymore; really bad arthritis that keeps him confined to his City house. I check on the place once in awhile for him just to make sure the hired agency he has is doing their job looking after the place. He's always encouraged me to make use of the place if I want, and there are two reasons I like to go out there; gorgeous woods with one of the most beautiful overlooks of the river, and it has a bathroom. I never got the knack to peeing in the woods without getting my shoes wet!" She colored at this last, and glanced sideways at him to see if he was shocked, or offended. Instead, to her relief, she saw a broad grin.

After a short stop at the Huntsman for Matthew's boots and a change of shirts, (*"It'll be cooler in the evening out that close to the river, and you'll appreciate long sleeves."*) they pulled away, top down, smiles all around. It *was* a splendid day, and as they drove through the blooming countryside, the sheer beauty of it was infectious and they became closer with their mutual appreciation of the surroundings. Absorbed in their conversation and the countryside, they once again didn't take notice of the big SUV a few cars back.

After a short while, they came upon a small collection of buildings at a crossroads. "This is Chamber's Crossing," stated Michaela. "It dates back to the very early days, maybe even pre-Revolutionary time, and has lasted without growing much at all. The real reason we came this way is for the General Store, over there. The people that run that store have caught on to the idea that gourmet food will bring folks a long way. They've put together a sort of carry-out and catering operation that you'd be hard to pressed to equal anywhere in the country. I asked them one time why they didn't set up somewhere like DC or Baltimore, where they could easily triple their business, and they just said, 'Why would we want to do that? We've got plenty-enough business here, and we don't have to live in those places.'"

"I can't say I blame them. It might be a little remote for some people's taste, but this area is absolutely beautiful, and there's a limit to what anyone should be expected, or willing, to pay for success. This would be ideal for a lot of people, I would expect, if they took a true look at their lifestyle," said Matthew as he regarded the weathered exterior of the old building, and reflected on what he thought was the wisdom of the people who made their business there.

Gathering up their purchases, and acknowledging the good wishes of the proprietor, they set out again, mutually enjoying the way the fine German car wound around what was, indeed, a curvy road. After a time, Michaela turned off the main road onto a narrow lane that meandered through a grove of tall pines. Breaking out of the woodland, they crossed a small meadow and pulled up in front of a rambling stone and clapboard house.

"Good Lord, Mickey! If this is a cottage, I would be amazed at what your friend would call a real house! This is beautiful, and easily as big as Kevin's place, maybe bigger!"

"And better yet," she smiled, "it has a fully operable bathroom, which I believe I will make use of now. If you'll get that blanket out of the trunk, and the picnic basket out of the back seat, I'll turn on the well pump and bring back a cooler with some ice for the wine."

Following her up a shallow slope away from the house and drive, they stopped at the edge of a fringe of trees and admired the view, a sweeping vista of tumbled hills, and dense green woods punctuated with the blooms of redbud and dogwoods, and the twisted river course below. A shelf of meadowland led to the edge of a shallow bluff, cut into the face of the hill eons ago by the stream. This was where Michaela spread the blanket and gestured for him to set the basket. "What do you think about this as a scenic view, Mr. Little Crow?" She cocked her head to one side, smiling as she awaited his reply.

"This is quite something…" Pausing, he looked directly at her, "This is truly, absolutely beautiful, Michaela…truly beautiful."

Silence followed his words, and they broke off their gaze simultaneously, and busied themselves with smoothing the blanket and emptying the basket.

Charley pulled the truck off on the shoulder of the road, and looked across at his companion. "Whadda ya think, Mac? I'm all for offing these two. Wouldn't be too tough to get near them with all these woods; knock 'em in the head and drop 'em off that bluff down to the river. Might be one of the easier jobs we'd ever have".

"I don't think so, man. The Director said to just watch 'em. He'd be pissed big time if he thought we were going off on our own, without clearing it with him first. We dealt with the blonde woman, and that was good and clean. We need to keep things that way. Ya' know, I say we figure out how to get turned around and see what the older guy is up to. These two aren't going anywhere for a while from the looks of all that picnic gear, and even when they leave here, there're only a couple places they'd go, and we can check those out later. What do you think?"

"Not a bad idea at all. Between the place the Indian guy's staying, the lawyer's office and house, I can't think anyplace they'd go after they do whatever they have in mind here. The only risk is that we lose them for a few hours, but really don't think there's that much risk. I say let's go back and see what the old guy is up to.

CHAPTER 12

Since their Georgia Tech student days, John Washington and Kevin had been friends. Both had entered the school on special scholarships set aside for especially gifted applicants of poor economic background. Kevin haled from the "hollers" of West Virginia, John from the depths of the Atlanta ghetto. Lacking the means to become part of the social whirl, they labored over the books, worked at odd jobs, and at graduation were in the upper percentile of their class. Following graduation they had remained in touch, even from the distance of jobs in different states. Now, as business partners, their regard for each other had become solid as each came to appreciate the character of the other. They were both now quite wealthy as a result of their collaboration on the development of Kevin's metering valve idea; an idea that had evolved during a hectic, non-stop week together in an Atlanta machine shop and John's garage-office CAD design station. When the patented device made it to the oil field market, it had become a benchmark development only surpassed by the Hughes drill bit in its virtually universal acceptance. The Christopher Valve Company now managed and monitored the licensing agreements for the valve manufacture, and constantly put forth engineered improvements and modifications as the petroleum industry's needs changed. The frequent telephone conversations between the two men concerning their business were always interspersed with personal subjects; the happenings in John's large family, Kevin's travels and Indian activities. Ever since his stint in the Indian-controlled areas of Oklahoma's oil fields, Kevin had admired the rich Indian cultures and mourned the horrid treatment Native Americans had suffered down through the years. His Cheyenne bride, Marybeth, had been a part of that time, and she was lovingly remembered as godmother to two of John's children.

When Kevin reached John that afternoon, it was no surprise when he immediately launched into a description of his latest effort in Minnesota, and his need to trace some projects in IMM's huge corporation. "What I'm hoping we can locate, through some of the guys we've dealt with at IMM over the years, is an entrance to their Information Technology group. There ought to be a way to find a pattern, since those corporations keep such amazing records."

"Hold on a minute, Big Guy. Let's begin again with just what it is that you're trying to find up there. I'm not sure there is anyone that's going to let us go trolling through their electronic files on some kind of nondescript errand, without a pretty definitive objective. And besides that, you will recall that our past dealings with that bunch didn't work out that well"

Kevin ruefully recalled the heavy-handed management style that they had encountered when one of Christopher Valve's licensed manufacturers had been gobbled up in a round of IMM acquisitions. That relations spawned with IMM's new management group installed after the merger had resulted in the withdrawal of the manufacturing licensing agreement; a truly rancorous parting.

"Okay, you're right. Here's what we're trying to decipher. We're relatively certain that a division of IMM, a research group, has a reason for wanting to start a mining operation in the Pipestone National Monument. It's a truly holy place to some of the tribes, especially the Lakota Sioux, who believe that this was the place that their culture, their very people were made. Through their religious beliefs, they have used the mineral from there, catlinite, or pipestone as it's usually called, to make ceremonial pipes, amulets and so forth. For a change, our government has honored the agreements to keep everyone out of there except for the Indians, and there's a

137

complicated process of permitting even for them. My little group's objective is to stop the mining attempt before it gets started. Our problem is that we don't know why anyone *wants* the stuff! Our thought is that if we can discover that, then maybe the rest will fall into place. Unless we can somehow discover what's happening that makes catlinite essential to them, chances are good we won't be able to keep them out of there."

"And just how is IMM's IT group going to help? "

Kevin paused a minute to gather his thoughts, "It's my belief that the corporate IT group, somewhere, has records of who is at this facility, and the contracts or research projects they are working on now. With that information, we would at least have a start as to which project needs the catlinite, and then we should be able to make the product of that research indefensible from a cultural and political aspect by taking the whole thing public."

"Sounds a little thin to me, Kevin, but let me do a bit of checking with some guys over there and see if there is any way they can help. Don't you think it would make a better impression if you came down and met with them face to face, presented your theory directly?"

"Probably so...I've already done some checking with the airlines, and there's a flight I can still catch that would get me into Atlanta just before noon. If the traffic and the TSA cause me to miss it, I'll give you a call, otherwise, I'll see you for lunch."

He made the flight, and after takeoff, took some of the notes that he had gathered together out of the battered briefcase he used, and started over them one more time.

NORTHERN PLAINS - 1610

As he awaited the arrival of the youngsters, One Ear noticed that a number of the adults had found reason to be within earshot of the little group. He smile inwardly at this; everyone liked a well-told story! When the young ones had all gathered in a semi-circle in front of him, he resumed the tale where had left off without preamble.

"The bowl of the pipe is of the red stone. It represents the flesh and blood of the Buffalo People," and looking around the circle, The White Buffalo Calf Woman smiled at the people. 'It also represents the flesh and blood of those that have come before you, the Earth People, the Lakota. The wooden stem of the pipe is to remind you of the growing things on the Earth; trees and grass and all growing things.' Then she took willow bark and tobacco from her pouch, and filled the pipe and lighted it with a coal from the fire. And she took a draw on the pipe and passed to each, until all had smoked. 'The smoke of the Sacred Pipe is as the sacred wind, and carries your prayers to the Creator, Wakan Tanka. *I will serve you always, when you follow the Good Red Road. As you saw me first in smoke, you will always see me in smoke.'"*

One Ear paused, caught up in his own story, filled with emotion as he pictured the beautiful Wohpe *speaking to the people, instructing them in the Way. With a low cough, he cleared his throat, took a sip from the bark cup at his side, and went on. "After all these things were told to the people, White Buffalo Calf Woman told the shaman how to gather the bark and the tobacco, and how to prepare and care for it. Then she told the people how to hold the pipe and offer it to the Four Sacred Directions. When this was done, she remained with the people in the camp for many days. All the time she was there the people were happy, for she was so beautiful, and she went from tepee to tepee and spoke kind words to all. And so the People knew that all things were as joined as the different parts of the Sacred Pipe; were one, and that as long as the Pipe was kept, and handled, and smoked in the proper way, that Wohpe would take their prayers to Wakan Tanka, and plead for the prayers to be answered...*

CHAPTER 13

"...And so it was that the White Buffalo Calf woman brought the pipe to the Lakota, and so it is told."

Eyes wide, Michaela looked at her companion with a new feeling of respect. They had passed a pleasant afternoon on the bluff, and after they had come back from a walk through the woods, had rested at the picnic site. She had asked if he knew exactly what it was about the pipes that made them so very significant, and he had told her about the legend. At her urging he had recounted the entire story, unconsciously slipping into the measured cadence of speaking as that of a Teller. She had never questioned the depth of his intellect, but the way he had told the story had shown a whole new facet of this complex man. The telling of the story had been simply mesmerizing. She felt almost as if she should applaud, but on impulse stretched over and gave him a quick hard kiss. "That was marvelous! I never knew mythology could be so entertaining. Certainly not the courses I endured in school! Where ever did you learn to weave a tale like that?"

Matthew felt the heat rise in his neck in a combination of embarrassment and pleasure. "My grandfather was a great teller of stories, and I suppose I was fortunate enough to pick up some of his ways. Not a bad skill to have if you spend much of your time trying to gain people's attention. That, of course, is a Lakota story that I learned from some friends. I wish you could have heard my grandfather tell some of the old Chippewa legends; although like most of the old traditionals, he always referred to our tribe as 'The People', the *'Anishinabe'*."

141

"Well, wherever the skill came from, it's extraordinary. That kind of skill would do well in a courtroom, as well as a classroom. Now what would you prefer as a cap for the day? We've had that nice lunch, and the hike along the bluffs was a perfect way to work off all that food, so we've really done about all there is to do here, I think. And unless we want to watch a sunset from here, we need to pack up and get on our way." She paused, looking questioningly at him for his response.

"As far as I'm concerned, with a setting like this, a sunset would be hard to beat. Tell you what; since you didn't allow me to treat you to breakfast, let me make up for it with dinner somewhere along the way back. We can stop at the house to "wash our hands and powder our noses", as Momma Georgie used to say, and then get started back. We *could* make it a late dinner and catch the sunset here too. Very frankly, I've missed being able to be outside. Going on two weeks of poring over old reports and data sheets, preceded by a week of symposiums, and I'm turning into a complete slug. To paraphrase, 'You can take the Indian out of the woods, but you can't take the woods out of the Indian.' And I can't tell you how good it was to take that little hike. Beautiful woods, and just enough of a hill to make the effort worthwhile."

"Well, sure," said Michaela, with a soft punch to his shoulder, "but let's get this picnic residue back in the car anyway. It gets awfully dark out here with nothing around, and I don't want to be lugging anything back down there after sunset. And as far as dinner, sir, there are a couple of very nice, informal places along the way that would work very well. Maybe not the Blacksmith Shop, but quite nice. One in particular that I'm thinking about has a wonderful menu that specializes in locally grown food, and we wouldn't have to change clothes. Afterward, we can touch base with Kevin, if he's back, and see what he found out down in Atlanta. Sound good?"

"That sounds great, Michaela. I'll take care of getting the things down to the car, but we ought to keep the blanket here to sit on, OK?"

"You're right. That ground would get a bit cold, wouldn't it?"

The cryptic message, delivered in the familiar flat tones, informed George Benjamin of the "accident" on the Purcellville Bridge. There was no conversation, just a short sentence in response to his "Is it done?" Then the connection had been broken. Benjamin sat in the dimness of the room, pondering the future.

His press release, endorsing the mining of material from the Pipestone Quarry, had been composed and was ready to be issued once he was back in Washington. He had given his local staff a specific timetable, designed so that release would follow his own undisclosed announcement. His resignation from the Senate, being the much larger story, would effectively bury the local announcement. Having completed the necessary action to open Pipestone's materials to his clients, he could then depart the scene. Relying on the general lack of knowledge within the press corps of the significance of the Quarry, he was certain there would be little, if any, attention given that release.

He felt a sense of impending relief as he thought of leaving Washington and the Senate. That had stopped being enjoyable years ago, when the excesses of the mushrooming bureaucracy had placed each "special" program under ever increasing scrutiny. There was no longer the opportunity to pad obscure bills with pork barrel amendments catering to any particular segment of the constituency without some opposing special interest raising Cain over the neglect of *their* pet project. And all that prying by the press, eager to pander to the public's growing indignation over privileges of office he and his colleagues had taken for granted for so long, had made life trying at best. Yes, the excuse that he had "medical advice" that encouraged him to step down would read well. After all, he had consulted with the people at Mayo this trip, albeit for a minor stomach disorder. Mayo wouldn't say why he'd been there, and he was well skilled in saying just enough for people to think they knew something, when actually they knew nothing.

The exit had been very quietly planned for some time, but not just because the Senate wasn't fun anymore. There was the realization, born of an instinctive shrewdness that had brought him much political success, that his public days were numbered. It was not just the women, and the scent of personal scandal that was always with him, but deep, truly meaningful transgressions. IMM was not the only entity that had benefitted from his influence and inside knowledge, and had subsequently made "contributions"; not only acknowledged political contributions, but others, to certain overseas numbered accounts. Those were the kinds of things that could result in prison terms and loss, not only of position, but any future comfort. His instincts were good about these things; it was time to get out, and pleading unspecified health concerns an almost perfect reason. Careful leaks about digestive tract problems could easily infer cancer or some other such serious condition, and seeking help in clinics in Europe a reasonable cover for presence on the Continent while he cleared the Swiss accounts. His gradual retreat from the public spotlight would eventually allow for a quiet withdrawal to the Leewards. There, overlooking a secluded bay at an estate that he had already optioned, he envisioned a steady supply of nubile island girls anxious for his approval.

The girl stirring next to him had certainly been anxious enough to please, but he had found her lacking in many ways. The almost pathetic subservience, coupled with placid, predictable performance and lack of imagination had made the evening long, and, to his jaded tastes, dull.

Her deep breathing now bordered on a soft snore; he felt repulsed. He looked at the pale leg protruding from under the sheet, and wondered idly if her other lovers had been disappointed, or if they were merely ardent bumpkins content with a sweaty tumble in a loft or back seat.

Good wine and the subtle suggestion of favors-given-favors-returned had ultimately lured her here, although he knew she fought a straight-laced upbringing in doing so. It had probably been the idea of the heroic public servant seeking her "favors" as much as the inference of transfer that had landed her in his bed. *Well, it will be the last and only time, Deary, or maybe I should say "Dairy"; my God those things are huge!"*

Chuckling at his private crudity, he slipped from the bed, pulled on a long silk robe, and went into the sitting room of the bedroom suite. From there he called his administrative assistant. Joe would handle getting her out of here without notice, with the proper reassurances that "arrangements" would be made for the transfer. This was a task he'd handled for the Senator many times before, and he knew the drill well. Benjamin had no intention of ever laying eyes on her again, and was already forgetting her as he dressed for the day.

CHAPTER 14

Henry Genarro felt as if the weight of the Nike duffel would pull his arm out of its shoulder socket, but he walked through the parking lot of the laboratory with as little obvious effort as possible. He had decided that the safest way to get the weapons out of the lab would be to wait until after normal working times. Banking on the reduced traffic in and out of the building, he felt if he could make it to his car without someone stopping him, and on his previous trips it had been the case. This time he was certain that he would be gone before he was noticed. Even so, it was difficult to pretend the bag held nothing more than athletic gear. The combined weight of the weapons and ammunition had made it tough to even lift the thing; fifty pounds was more than he was accustomed to handling, and he worried that he would not make it the last hundred feet to where his car was parked. This was the last of the bags, and after that, it was just a question of getting the collection of bags into Jake's hands, and waiting for the act that would satisfy his requirement for vengeance.

The conversations with Monroe had been infrequent, and Henry felt far too lacking in information. He had repeatedly asked just what the intended action was, but all he had gotten back was a variety of lectures on outdated political subjects. He sensed that the obfuscation was deliberate, and it irritated him that his contribution wasn't being acknowledged with trust. Reaching the car at last, he placed the bag on the pavement, opened the trunk, and hoisted it over the bumper, carefully placing it in the compartment with the others. He closed the lid with care, and started for the front of the car. Starting, he heard the cheerful "Hi, Henry!" from somewhere behind. Turning, he was confronted by George Carson.

"What's all the athletics lately, Henry? Found some aerobics instructress with an interest in chemistry that you've been hiding from us, or did you just get a scary report from the doctor?" The man smiled in that open way he had, adding to Henry's nervousness.

"Neither, actually," he replied roughly, "just trying to keep from going completely to flab. Nothing in our work that's physically challenging is there?" He hoped his tone would be enough of a put-off that there would be no incentive for the conversation to continue. When George's mouth started to open, Henry rushed on, "And I have to hurry or I'll be late for an appointment. Goodbye, George." Without waiting for a response, he opened the door quickly, climbed in and started the car. Gunning the engine he pulled away, leaving the other man standing in the parking lot with a mildly puzzled expression on his face.

The drive through the outskirts of the town took nearly a quarter hour, slowed by the winding residential streets. Accelerating through the last of the housing developments he headed north on the Interstate in the direction of Minnesota. After a few miles he took an off ramp and stopped at a gas station-convenience store for a cup of coffee. He was only a few minutes from the meeting place, but nearly half an hour early. Jake had made it plain, over the past weeks, that he did not expect anyone to be at a meet before him, or late; that a time set was just that. In light of this recent behavior, Henry decided it was a good idea to simply play along, deal with the idiosyncrasies, and not test the limits of the relationship. Although he felt he had a secure position, he couldn't shake a small nagging concern that played at the back of his mind whenever he had to deal directly with Monroe. Here was a man who had eluded authorities for decades, all the while managing to keep his reputation and ideology intact. Obviously anyone that single minded for that length of time possessed an enormous source of inner strength and will power; and underlying it all a hatred of "the system" that had, so he said, betrayed him.

Sipping the steaming brew, Henry wished he could have found another means to extract his own retribution, but there had been none. He waited now for the minutes to pass until he could deliver the weapons, and learn the exact use to which they would be put to bring down the ire of society on those who had so cavalierly used him. Checking his watch, he tossed the Styrofoam cup into the trash can, restarted the car, and headed off toward what he felt was a rendezvous with destiny, redemption and retribution.

Slowing as he approached the turn-off, he flicked on the headlights as Monroe had instructed, even though it was early, and there was plenty of daylight left. It seemed a sensible signal, although he felt it a bit melodramatic. This was, after all, a little used dump for construction debris, and there was almost no traffic there after midday. Bouncing along the rutted dirt and gravel track leading to the actual landfill, he saw another vehicle parked alongside the massive earthmoving equipment that was used to maintain the dump. It was a nondescript van painted in the camouflage pattern popular with hunters in the region. *Good thinking, Jake. You'll fit in almost anywhere in this Godforsaken place in that heap. You'll look just like one of the good ole boys getting ready to go out and shoot up the countryside, killing things ostensibly for food that was not as good as what's available in any supermarket.*

Dust billowed around the car as he braked to a stop some ten feet from the van. He saw no one at first, but as the dust settled he spied Monroe squatting beside the van, lost in the shadow cast by the vehicle's boxy body. Stepping out of the car carefully to avoid stepping in anything that might have been left on the earthen bank at the edge of the disposal pit, he called out, "Hello there, Jake. Right on time again, huh?" He affected a slight smile that came off more like a grimace.

Monroe rose stiffly and approached with a blank unsmiling expression on his face. "Ya brought the things?"

"You bet Jake, and a bonus too!"

"What do you mean by bonus? I'm not wild about surprises, Genarro, you know that. What could you possibly have brought that I wouldn't expect?"

"Well, uh, I know how you like to keep with a plan, Jake, but this was just too good to pass up. Over the last few days we were able to make some additional things from the tooling residue…"

"Come on, out with it. I don't care about your work, just the results."

"What I'm trying to say is that we were able to make ammunition out of the compound as well as the weapons themselves. Not the explosive material, you understand, but the casings and projectiles. The projectile results are particularly gratifying. Something about the heat-altered properties of the material make it able to penetrate most types of body armor, almost as well as the Teflon coated bullets do. Isn't that a worthwhile extra, even if it wasn't in the original plan?"

"When will the loss be discovered, and what are the chances that someone will connect it with you?" Monroe was glaring, making it appear that there was indeed something wrong with the addition of the ammunition, although Henry couldn't understand what that could be.

"Uh, well, let's see now, uh…"

Goddamit, Genarro," Jake snarled, "Just spit it out."

'It's just that I d-d-d-don't quite know. It's hard to tell how long it will be before anything's missed. This is Thursday, and with our four-day schedule, it ought to be Monday before anyone goes back in there. It's possible that someone will have forgotten

149

something, or will go back to finish up some job that wasn't quite completed during normal hours" Henry hated himself for being reduced to such a stammering fool, but it was always that way with Monroe; in his way no better than those who held sway over him in the places he had worked. Although simply put, the raw menace of the man thoroughly intimidated him. He clutched his keys defensively to his chest and backed away toward his car. Unlocking the trunk, he watched the other man the whole while.

With a grunt of acknowledgement, Jake gestured to Henry to get the satchels out of the trunk. "Bring 'em over here, then, and let's see what you've got." Hefting the heavy bags over the edge of the trunk, Henry struggled over the rough ground, half carrying, half dragging the bags over to the van; Monroe watching the entire effort with that cold, blank stare that chilled Henry to the bone

His feeling of unease began to dissipate as he watched Monroe examine each of the weapons. He had fit four weapons into each of the bags; two assault rifles and two machine pistols in one, four rifles in two others, and the dismounted machine gun in the last. The dull red color somehow heightened the impression that they weren't real, but plastic replicas made for children's play. *But real they are, and I've seen what they can do!* The thought sprang unbidden in Henry's mind and he watched as Jake laid them out on an old blanket on the ground. *What's he going to do with them here? Surely he knows they work, and these are the ones he specifically asked for, all except the one that blew up when they tested it.*

Monroe stroked each weapon as he arranged them in a neat row on the blanket in front of him, feeling the smoothness of the composite material so carefully machined into the instruments of his trade. It had been a long time since he'd had such firepower available. He could sense the rise of the almost sensual feeling that weaponry aroused in him, and he waited, allowing it to seep through him as he squatted beside the deadly array. He felt a surge of resentment as Genarro spoke, breaking the ascent to euphoria.

"Well, what do you think, Jake? Aren't they just what I said they were? The ammunition is good for all except the machine gun; it takes standard fifty-caliber rounds, and you said you had plenty of that. There are a couple hundred rounds apiece for the others in the spare tire well of the car. I couldn't get it out with the guns; just too heavy all together." Henry realized that he was on the verge of babbling, but he couldn't help himself. The whole aura here was beginning to weigh on him; the vacant landscape, the smell of dust and decay from the pit, the feeling of danger that emanated from the man in front of him. He looked expectantly at Monroe for some indication of approval. After all, he had risked everything for the handful of weapons laid out on the ground, and he *needed* some recognition of his efforts. That's what this was all about anyway. No one had seen his contributions for what they were, and now it was beginning to feel as if the same thing was happening all over again. His intimidation was momentarily overcome with a feeling of anger and resentment, as quickly dashed by Jake's gravelly voice.

"Yeah, yeah, Henry. Ya did OK. The ammo is a good deal, and these are just what I've been looking for. You say they were all test fired at your lab? How'd they do that?" Relieved by the turn of the conversation, Henry explained how the test range had been set up, and that as far as he had been able to determine the only thing that not been checked with live ammunition was the grenade launcher. That had been fired, but only with dummy training grenades.

The two men then went over to the car, lifting the heavy ammunition cans out of the trunk, and carrying them over to the van. As they lifted the last one into the back of the truck, Jake looked casually around and asked Henry to hand him one of the assault rifles. Eager to be of help, Henry asked what the planned use for the weapons was as he handed the rifle over. "Getting these things through any sort of security should be a real breeze, Jake. When do you think your action will be? I have a statement all ready for the press that will once and for all condemn the fools at the lab that failed to recognize me; just telling the world that although I have contributed mightily to the cause of national reconstruction, my efforts were overlooked and demeaned by my superiors. While in college I was always faithful to the idea of rebuilding our society. Not so much as you, of course." Henry looked nervously at the other man who was apparently engrossed in loading cartridges into the rifle's magazine. "I thought when the group was assembled at the lab that at last our ideas would be given the proper exposure and the decadent institutions that have oppressed free thinking in our country would at last be brought down. I know the ideas have prevailed, but the conduct of those people, well really!"

Jake completed the loading, and smacked the magazine into the underside of the weapon with practiced ease. "Did I ever tell you, Henry, I worked for a time in Libya with the training groups there? We saw a lot of dedicated people come through those camps, and many went on to great things, although some gave up their lives in the process. The way those camps were set up, we had the ability to train with almost every type of conventional weapon in use in the major military groups in the world, and it was a pleasure to see the results our revolutionary brothers were able to bring about; Lebanon, Rome, Gaza, Ulster. I'll tell ya, Henry, we saw the cream of the heroic elements in the social struggle go through there, and the courage they showed when the Soviets betrayed the cause of the world order, well, I want to tell you, it was inspiring. It was the thing that brought me back to the States, because I could see that if those brave people could carry on in the face of such treachery, then I could continue my work to bring down the maggot-ridden institutions here. Really inspiring! Shall we see how your M-16 knock-off works? Good weapon considering it is American- made.

Not as much to my taste as the AK, but still good in a fire fight." Turning from the van he looked off across the scarred face of the pit, and raised the butt to his shoulder. "Just a short rapid-fire check, huh?"

Carefully squeezing off the shots, Jake blasted a plastic bucket to pieces with several well-aimed bursts. "Good job, Henry. This one even has well aligned sights. Just a bit to the left, but we'll adjust that; just so."

Henry notice an odd detachment in the way Jake was speaking but couldn't make anything of it. It seemed as if he were talking to himself, even though he had addressed him by name. *Strange man.*

One by one, Jake checked the weapons, sighting some odd piece of debris hanging out of the working face of the fill's pit, then making adjustments to the sights, or checking the grouping of a series of shots. He carried on the monologue through the process, speaking in a soft conversational tone, frequently calling Henry's attention to some detail in the process. Henry found himself fascinated far more than he had been while watching the armorers working in the lab. This was almost a passionate thing he was seeing, not the methodical work he had seen before, although certainly as thorough.

Feeling a need to somehow become more than a spectator, Henry tried again to find out to what use this was to be put. "So tell me now, Jake. What's the plan? Going to take over a government building, hold some hostages until some of our brothers are freed?"

Jake's reaction was almost as if he had been shaken from a deep sleep. He jerked around, eyes slightly out of focus, a confused look on his face. "What'd you say? What the hell you mean?"

Taken aback, Henry dissembled, almost fawning, all courage evaporating in the face of the man's threatening appearance.

Seemingly mollified, Monroe looked back at the deadly display and picked one of the M-16's from the row again. Turning it in his hands, he examined it as if seeing it for the first time, a dreamlike quality settling over his face. Then, as suddenly as he had seemed to retreat from reality he was back; the barrel of the gun swinging away from the pit, stock held against his hip. In a final moment of abject terror, Henry realized what was happening, but didn't have time to do more that throw up a hand to ward off the projectile. The first bullet hit the hand, shattering hand and arm, the next two from the three round burst struck him squarely in the chest, the tumbling bullets destroying the vital organs in the trunk of his body. With a gargled scream he was propelled backward, nearly lifted from his feet, falling with head and shoulders over the edge of the pit, blood spilling from his mangled torso, soaking into the loose dust.

"Press release, my ass, you stupid geek. What I choose to do with these beauties has nothing to do with your "revolution". This is business, not politics. I would have thought you would have figured that out by now. What you did was give me the means for mounting the finest terror for hire operation in history! We'll walk in and out of the airports and courtrooms all over the world, and nobody will know how we managed to get through in the first place. Yeah, we'll help the old causes along, some of them, but then there are some new ones that might need us too, like some of the environmental groups, maybe help their effort along with some well placed assassinations here and there among the power industry execs. No, I think there's far more we can do than tilt at the windmills we used to, and all for a nice fee! Think about that in hell, you jerk! Revolution, for Chrissake!"

CHAPTER 15

Malcolm Williamson, PhD, looked over at the group milling about in front of the small public library. Teachers herded their small charges in the general direction of the building's entrance, and he listened as the special quality of small voices filled the afternoon. They were apparently involved in one of the special program days the library had initiated for the elementary schools in town. It was, he felt, a worthy effort to instill some elements of independent thought in young minds already distracted with MTV. *Preaching, even to myself! I need to get a grip! It would be so much easier if I could just be honest about my feelings, not always hiding in this shell!*

He had some time to kill, waiting for Monroe. Jake had become edgier lately, and that could make him even more dangerous than Malcolm knew he already was. There had always been that feeling of danger surrounding Jake, even back in the university days when they had worked together with the Weather Underground. Those had been the best days Malcolm could remember; days when things they did seemed to have real meaning, days when society's outrageous actions made it so easy to enjoy the hate as it flowed through their bodies, riding the stream of idealism that came with youth. Shaking his head, he took a seat on a bench near the library entrance, and watched the squirrels hurrying back and forth, busy on mysterious errands. This meeting place had served them well, through the entire project. He mused as he waited, reviewing the project, its first phase now finally complete. He was sure that the long years of subterfuge had been worth it; their outlook evolving from the worthless idealism of the past for the more concrete, more rewarding business now open to them. It had taken more time than either had thought it would. Jake had trained in Lybia, worked with the Palestinians and some of the better European extremist groups, developing the network of contacts that could now become a far-flung clientele.

In the meanwhile, he had followed the undercover path. Malcolm, then Ronald Anderson, had befriended a young man, orphaned at birth, who had similar educational credentials. When he came to know young Malcolm, Ronald had been evading a conspiracy and unlawful flight warrant for his involvement in the destruction of a college administration building, and he badly needed a new identity. Malcolm was, at the time, traveling, seeking to "find himself", and working odd jobs for subsistence. His politics, as far as Ronald could determine, were non-existent. Constant striving, working his way through college, Malcolm had almost no friends, and those few were scattered widely in dead-end blue collar work. He was perfect for Ronald.

The "friendship" bloomed. Malcolm had been almost pathetic to think someone cared for him, and he had pressed a blessedly short homosexual affair; totally discreet, as was necessary in those times. So totally disgusting to Ronald that only the need for Malcolm's identity had gotten him through it. Then, late on a stormy summer night, a swift wrench of the neck, and that night Ronald Anderson ceased to exist, although the headless corpse bearing that identification was found in a quarry a year later by a pair of truant high-school students out for a swim. The skeletal remains afforded little more that the sodden contents of a wallet, and with no reason to think otherwise, the local sheriff had dutifully reported the location of the body of a missing student radical. Malcolm, nee Ronald, went on to assume ever more the identity of his deceased "lover". One by one, he located the few friends that had been mentioned, and eliminated them in "accidents" or seemingly random killings. Because of the disparate nature of the individuals and their locations, no link was ever established, and they became yet another statistical symptom of the unraveling of the nation's law and order.

The meager contents of Malcolm's knapsack yielded enough information that there was little trouble with anything else. There was the reliable old Communist in Berkley who contributed to the metamorphosis with driver's license and passport. Obtained with carefully forged letters, college transcripts, Social Security information and documents completed the make-over, and as far as the world at large was concerned, Ronald Anderson *became* Malcolm Williamson.

His new identity solidified, Malcolm re-surfaced in a smaller southwestern college, far from anything and anyone that the original may have touched. He applied himself diligently, and within three years had completed the academic requirements for his doctorate. Understanding his long-range mission, he repressed the impulse to obtain the appropriated documents by forgery, and worked through the awesomely difficult chemistry dissertation in another year.

Even he was surprised by his progress in the business world. A latent talent for administration was quickly noticed, surrounded as he was by brilliant, but fuzzy-headed, scientists. Working his way up through ever more responsible positions, he was soon lured away from the petro-chemical company that had hired him out of college. Promises of money, intellectual freedom, superlative research facilities, and a minimum of supervision heading a research group at IMM's Delvin Center led him away, but in his mind, these were merely fringe benefits. This was the opportunity he had waited so patiently to materialize; a chance to work within the system towards its eventual destruction!

Abiding by a code of rigid discipline known by all those who have evaded the law, contact with Jake during this period was restricted almost entirely to fourth- and fifth-hand messages passed back and forth through the remnants of the radical student movement and its current imitators. By those convoluted means, they had communicated the gradual change of philosophy that had ultimately led them here. From a point neither could specifically identify, they began to see themselves as agents for those groups who held grievances against a portion of society, and felt only a violent act could properly articulate their feelings. In order to finance their activity, they provided "eradication" services to these and even some quasi-official organizations for rather extraordinary fees. Malcolm furnished complex, undetectable chemicals that paralyzed or killed; Jake administered them through a variety of means and mechanisms. The cynicism was lost on them, but was now in full flower, and driving the two erstwhile revolutionaries in a tighten spiral of deceit, violence and self-delusion. They were undeniably successful. Malcolm, technically and scientifically accomplished, had achieved considerable stature in his field and among his peers; Jake had become an amazingly competent assassin, and a virtual chameleon, blending in anywhere he found himself. And both now knew the financial benefits of their "business ventures", with substantial fortunes cached in numbered accounts offshore.

With practiced grace, Malcolm rose from the bench to meet the nondescript car as it pulled into the lot, climbing into the passenger seat almost before the vehicle stopped. "How did it go?" he inquired.

"Not a hitch. All the weapons he was supposed to bring were there, they checked out, and he brought a few boxes of that ammo you mentioned. I still can't believe he bought that cockamamie story I fed him about embarrassing IMM! He must have been a real dumbo."

"Well, he wasn't the most balanced man I've ever worked with, but he brought some essential background in the ceramics engineering field that we really needed to get the job done. Speaking of which, is *yours* done?"

"Yes, of course! Think you're dealing with some amateur here?" Jake frowned at the implied questioning of his accomplishment. "I'll tell you one thing," he growled. That time I spent working out at the dump site was a real plus. After I got everything packed into the van, I walked that big D-9 Cat over the car to flatten it, scraped away the working face of the pit, and put the car and Genarro's corpse in there behind about a hundred tons of mixed construction crap. He's safely out of sight until some archaeologist excavates there in a jillion years or so. The guys that work the pit won't even know I was there!"

"Good job, Jake." Malcolm. "There was little doubt you'd get the job done, but we've got to be very careful! As we get down to the business at hand, we can't afford to let some curious cop screw everything. So far, our tracks are well covered, and we just need to keep it that way. I re-routed the notes on the composition so nobody at corporate knows what's going on. We've still got our dummy project number in place so we're good for the time being, and for about the next two years if we stay cautious and keep things off the IMM radar. The transmission of anything Genarro may have sent under his password code was assimilated into my personal database, so it's gone under. With that two year window, we can produce who knows how many weapons. I am almost certain that we will not be able to keep things as they are for more than that time, so we've got to be sure there are no surprises that come up out of nowhere. For the moment anyway, we only have to be sure our friend the Senator keeps to his end of the bargain and clears the way for extraction of the Catlinite material."

"You sure about all those geeks you got working in there? Makes me nervous thinking about how many people know about this stuff, and yet we're still trying to keep it a secret. Just too many people…"

Don't worry, Jake," Malcolm soothed. "There aren't any others like Genarro with personal axes to grind. You know as well as I do that those guys aren't all that different from you and me, dodging some kind of rap for the student movement crap, or just bummed out with the whole idea of what's going on outside the place. I frankly don't think there's a one that wouldn't happily join us in the field, so to speak."

"We both know that won't be necessary, my friend. This is a fine tuned little enterprise, and I don't see any reason to change that now. I have all the muscle help I need with the Indian Movement guys I string along…now there's a *truly* scary bunch!"

Laughing at the irony of any group being "scary" to them, they began to discuss their plans for demonstrating the capacity and special characteristics of the weapons in their new arsenal with potential clients.

CHAPTER 16

There seemed to be no end to days like this, thought Deputy Don Quesenberry. Ever since becoming a deputy in the Loudon County Sheriff's Department, he had despised working highway accidents. The methodical pursuit of criminals was the thing he loved. It was the tedious, plodding work most others in the Department found painfully boring, but to Quesenberry there was almost a beauty to it. Investigative work was the reason he had joined the Department, and it suited his mind; careful, steady, logical, and moderately inquisitive, and far sharper than his slow speech and easy going manner led people to believe. But dealing with the terrible and random violence done by hurtling machinery on the highways was something he would rather have left to someone else. This one was particularly distasteful, involving fire, and with the almost complete destruction of the identity of the car's lone passenger. But for a quirk that had put the victim's head in a shallow pool in the rocky river bed, there would have been no hope of identity other than dental records, but at least this way, there was something to show someone. Aside from the horror of individual tragedy, it would mean long hours with the medical examiner, and piles of paperwork trying to find out who this poor soul had been before closing the file. Shrugging into his lightweight uniform jacket, he stepped from the patrol car, and signaled the approaching tow truck to pull in ahead of him. "Put it right there, Jerry," he called out to the driver. "We'll need to take a look at this thing and see how you want to handle getting it out of there. This'll be no cushy job, that's for certain. Gonna test ya this time, yes sir!"

"Now Donny-boy, you know you're talking to the master of the hook! No such thing as a job too tough for Jerry and "Tatum's Towing Titan"! Let's see whatcha got."

The jocularity of their exchange was almost a ritual with the two men, cloaking the fact that each respected the other's role in the often grisly circumstances that brought them together. Jerry Tatum leaned over the bridge rail, studying the steep bank for a route down to the blackened hulk resting on the bottom of the ravine. "Great Gawdamighty damn! What a helluva mess! Guess it was only a matter of time before one of those city folks that been movin' out here got goin' too fast and went through that bend, but Jesus, that sucker coulda been shot out of a gun! Folk inside taken out already, I 'spose? He arched a brow at Quesenberry, and at his nod, returned to his consideration of the mangled metal at the base of the cliff. "Maybe you right this time, Donny-boy. This gonna be a tester."

It took almost an hour to bring the burned out hulk up from the river gorge and dragged over onto the shoulder of the road. Jockeying the truck and its burden, Jerry shouted profanity-laced instructions to his helper over the roar of the truck and shriek of overused machinery as they winched the charred tangle of metal onto the bed of the hauler. At last the sweating operators and deputy sagged against the fender of the huge vehicle, taking turns at the spout of the water can. "Lord love us, Donny-boy! You sure called that one. Wasn't sure we were goin' to be able to get it over that last rock ledge, but, by God, here we are! Whatcha want me to do with it? Take it to the county impound yard?"

"We'll need to do that," Quesenberry agreed. "Right now we don't even know who owned the car or who was in it when it went over the edge. Guess we'll be out here again tomorrow when we have better light. Something about the way it went over; goin' like a bat, it looks like, but absolutely straight. It's like he didn't even try to make the turn. "Anyway, let's get out of here, and I'll see if I can catch the ME in his office." He turned away, then back. "Good job Jerry. I told Dispatch we'd need you for this one. Ole Gordon Delaplane woulda been out here a week! See ya'." Quesenberry climbed back in his cruiser, and contacting the dispatcher on the radio, announced his intention to go by the ME office and then he'd be off for the day. After passing a few pleasantries, he switched the transceiver off and turned for town. Whether he managed to meet the ME tonight or not, he knew he would get the ME's formal report tomorrow and he could go back out to the Purcellville Bridge to see if he could figure out what had happened. He knew it was probably a waste of time, but there was something not quite right about that whole scene. Putting those thoughts out of his mind, he wondered what his wife might have for his supper; she usually made something special for him after an accident day.

The small restaurant was tucked into a corner of an intersection on the main road back towards the City, and its appearance belied the wonderful smells emanating from the rear of the building where the open kitchen buzzed with early evening activity. Matthew and Michaela were shown a seat that looked towards the back of the property, where a well tended garden filled the slope down to a wide stream. They were still mellow after the pleasant evening and rather special sunset, although there had been one awkward moment as they closed up the house following their "washing of hands and powdering of noses".

Mickey had asked Mathew to go down in the cellar and shut off the water well pump. After an uncharacteristic hesitation, accompanying a shuffle from foot to foot, he had said that he would prefer not, actually could not do that. When Mickey, surprised, raised her eyebrows in question, he confessed a problem with claustrophobia, and said that places underground, especially cellars, with their low ceilings and closeness were something he could hardly tolerate. With a quick "No problem", and offhand dismissal of the whole thing, she had scampered down the stair, and thrown the switch. Now, they conversed quietly as they awaited their meals, a sense of comfort enhancing their enjoyment of the view, and the low-key atmosphere of the place.

When the dinner arrived, they roused from their reverie and, surprised at their appetites, attacked the food with vigor. "I didn't think I'd need to eat for days after that lunch," laughed Michaela "but it seems I can't shovel it in fast enough. How's yours?"

"I'm afraid I'm suffering from the same problem as you; this is wonderful, but decorum prevents me from picking it up and shoving the whole thing into my face! It must have been the fresh air after all that time indoors. Whatever it was, I think we've found another place to add to our list of dinner places, headed of course by the Blacksmith Shop! It's a shame Kevin can't be here to enjoy this as well. He would love this trout."

"That reminds me; we should call and see if he's back from Atlanta." The call was answered by Kevin's machine, and they left a message that if he had exciting news to call Mickey's cell phone, or the service would pick up and they wouldn't get the message until the next morning. That obligation met, they resumed their dinner and relaxed conversation.

As they left, engrossed in each other's company, and feeling relaxed from the day, they again took no notice of the older blue Suburban pulling into traffic a car behind them as they left the parking lot.

A single lighted window shown from the stark façade of the large angular building that housed Malcolm Williamson's office at the research laboratory; a space adjacent to the larger developmental area with its jury-rigged test range. Williamson, with frequent references to a Department of Defense contract preparation manual, worked intently at the computer terminal, characters flashing over the glowing screen as he typed. Jake and Malcolm had decided that in order to solidify sales negotiations for the new weapons, some special, noteworthy event needed to be staged. Jake had suggested something overseas, but as they had talked, it seemed a better approach to have something right here in the States. It would be an indication that there was nowhere that would be safe. They had considered and discarded several options, finally leaving that particular issue unresolved, but deciding that Malcolm would immediately begin processing more of the ceramic catlinite-based material in order to be able to meet orders for the weapons, as they were sure to come. Malcolm was now involved in the generation of a false contract and work orders for the effort. He knew it was something that couldn't be done during the normal work day, so had invented an authorization for afterhours lab work; a simple matter in a place where half the staff worked odd times of the day and night. "Work in an environment completely free of the normal restrictive constraints of time and discipline...." Malcolm laughed as he thought of the seductive effect that wording had upon prospective scientists during the recruiting days; especially on those he had sought for his special group. All disciplines at the lab were represented in that group, and Genarro's insertion into the group had been unique. Not that any of the others had a real idea of what they were involved with, or for that matter cared. All they wanted was a place where they could work in the kind of obscurity that certain past acts had made desirable. He'd managed to compartmentalize the work well enough that nobody knew what anyone else was doing, exactly, but Genarro had been a true outsider. *Good to be rid of him, though. It always made me nervous to think what he might be able to do it he caught on to the overall picture. It was an amazing stroke of luck that he had developed such a hard on for the company as a whole. Really amazing!*

Concentrating on his keyboard he continued with the fabrication of the DOD contract authorizing development of "special weapons" so that he could be out of the lab before someone found it curious that one at his level was putting in so much late time.

CHAPTER 17

Deputy Donald Quesenberry glared through the windshield of his cruiser, unspoken obscenities racing through his mind. When he had arrived at the Medical Examiner's office, he had expected to endure a few minutes of the ME's grisly humor, listen to a lectures on the advantages of various testing techniques for the detection of some chemical in the bodily fluids of a victim and then be given the report and other information he had come for. But instead, he had been brusquely ordered, *"Ordered?!"* out of the small autopsy room and instructed like a schoolboy that the report would be forwarded when ready, not a minute before, and good-bye!

"There is no way in hell that miserable old reprobate is goin' to get away with this," he finally muttered, slamming the unoffending car into gear and accelerating with a spray of loose gravel on to the county road. "That report is goin' to be in my hands this morning, or I'll eat my hat!"

He was still operating under a "full head of steam", as an old railroader-uncle used to say, when he strode through the corridors of the courthouse and into the Dispatcher's room. "Where's the Boss, Cheryl?"

The Dispatcher looked up from the arced console in front of her, regarding him with an unfriendly look. She had long considered Donald Quesenberry as ill suited for the Sheriff's Department. In her opinion, "he's just downright uppity, puttin' on airs all the time." She had made a life-long practice of categorizing people, and that this particular opinion was not shared by others mattered to her not at all.

"Come on, Cheryl. Where's the Sheriff?"

"Oh, is that who you were referring to, Deputy?" She tried her very best haughty voice, somewhat unsuccessfully. "The *Sheriff*," she said with emphasis on the title, "is testifying in court this morning, as you would know if you bothered to check the posted schedule."

"C'mon, now Cheryl. I've not got time for that. The Sheriff ain't in court, and I know 'cause I was just there. Now where is he? Just straight talk, now."

Taken aback, the Dispatcher shuffled some papers in front of her as she thought about what to say. It wasn't like Don Quesenberry to be pushy like this unless there was something going on. She didn't like him, but she knew him as a man who paid attention to his job and went about it with, she grudgingly admitted, a good level of success. The Sheriff liked him, no doubt about that. "I'm not supposed to tell…" She held up a hand to cut off the protest that had begun to form in Quesenberry's throat, "But I'll tell you if you swear you won't tell anyone else." She looked up from under heavily penciled brows, waiting for his acknowledgement; at his nod she continued, "He'd just kill me if he knew I'd told, and don't you get all red in the face, now, Don Quesenberry," she hurried on. "I'm going to tell you, I just want you to know the kind of grief I'll catch."

"So help me Hannah…"

"All right now! Just you stop." Looking furtively around to see that no one else was within earshot, she leaned toward him, voluminous bosom perilously close to several alarm switches. "He's at the health spa place over on Old Harper's Ferry Road. There's a program there for older guys to help them lose weight; and you know how the Sheriff, well, he's kinda porked up a bit of late, ya' know? Well, anyways, he found out about this special program, and thought he could do it without anyone knowing if he went in the middle of the morning. That part's workin' out, too; not so sure about the weight. He hasn't seen a soul over there. His car isn't marked at all, and he always changes out of his uniform at a service station or someplace like that so's nobody'd figure out who he was."

"You mean to tell me he's hidin' out in some gym, tryin' to lose weight, and thinking nobody'd catch on? Well bless my boots! If that don't get all." He smiled broadly at the thought of the portly Sheriff on an exercise bike, with sweat rolling down his face. "Thanks, and I'll never let on how I found him. Just say I recognized his car, waited for him to come out. So long," he said swinging out through the heavy door leading to the parking area.

Quesenberry's "happenstance" meeting with the Sheriff, a full mile beyond the spa, went better than he had hoped. The Sheriff, in civilian clothes ("coming from a meeting with my grandkid's teachers; didn't want them to think I was trying to impress them with my office."), sweat dampening the collar of the blue oxford shirt, was obviously anxious to shorten the conversation, and said quickly that he'd "handle that arrogant sumbitch". Confident the Sheriff would be good to his word, and that the Medical Examiner's report would be forthcoming, Quesenberry set out for the County's impounded vehicle yard, to see what he could determine from an examination of the wreck Jerry Tatum had pulled from the riverbed.

Standing Bear emerged from the sweat lodge and greeted the rising sun in the prescribed Way. He felt, as he always did, the uplifting sensation of being in complete accord with the universe, the spirits that ruled it and the creatures that inhabited it. He had never understood those who had rejected this most satisfying of the old ways. The *inipi*, the sweat lodge ritual, created a balance between man and all that was around him.

Standing Bear found his thinking clear now. It would be possible to relate his feelings about a number of questions to the Council, including the uncertainty surrounding the troublesome Jake Monroe. *"The Council"*, he thought wryly, *is rather a grand name for a collection of aging rebels.* The membership represented a loose confederation of the few surviving militant groups that dated back to the Second Wounded Knee; men from several diverse Midwestern tribes with little in common but anger with the whites. *If the truth be known*, he mused, *most on the Council can barely remember the true ways of their people.* Most were clinging to vestiges of their cultures, hoping that in some way there could be a rebirth of sorts; something that would allow their balanced, natural ways to continue, restoring a sense of continuity that had been wrung from their people by the despised white men. *And yet, it is a white man who now occupies much of our thought. Could Jake Monroe possibly hold a key to the future course of our people?*

He pulled himself from his reverie, and after washing in the clear water of the lake, dressed and prepared to make the journey back into the city to grapple, again, with the question of Jake Monroe. He was already forming the words he would use to present his declaration. There would be little discussion this time on the principles involved; this was a decision made. All that remained was to lay out the desired end, and then the means of dealing with it, in detail. Young John Wolf was a good man, and this would be the occasion for elevating his status. It was too bad about the troubles of the Moore lad. The two had made a good team and could have gone a long way together. Now it would be only Wolf, and Moore would slip back into the squalor that engulfed those stricken, directly or indirectly, with the alcohol-poison. *Just another example of the evil that had befallen The People from their contact with the whites.*

170

There was very little of the car that was recognizable. Impact and fire had reduced the machine to a twisted tangle of melted plastic and charred metal. Don Quesenberry wondered if there would ever be any resolution to what had caused the lonely death of its driver. He had always felt that everyone should have an explainable end, and it bothered him to think that this would be any different. Following his visit to the impound yard, he had faxed the vehicle identification number off the wreck to the State's Division of Motor Vehicles, and departed for the scene of the accident. Pulling off to the side of the road, he parked just beyond the ragged gap in the guard railing, and walked thoughtfully about the area where the car had gone through. Standing with this back to the hole, he looked back down the roadway towards Purcellville, trying to create an image of the car coming toward him.

Here the road was straight, sloping gently up a long rise and cresting about a quarter mile away. He knew the grade flattened after that, running virtually level as it wound through the countryside. *This isn't a high-speed road*, he thought, *but on the other hand it's not a real twister either. If you take it that anyone on the road that time of day would most likely be a local, then they'd know this hard turn was coming up. They might have been bookin' it pretty good before they hit that little grade, but they'd have known to slow for the bridge. They would've been going pretty slow, almost creepin' along. Judging from the distance the car must've traveled through the air, it hit that rail at a good clip...more than a reasonable guy would even if he's late for work. Someone chasing, or being chased?*

As he walked along the shoulder of the road, he caught a glimpse of something, just a glint off a shiny object. Lengthening his stride, he walked to the spot, bent and picked it up. Turning it over in his hand, he examined the chromed metal letter, a stylized "E". Lost part of the trim package, he mused, sharply focusing again on the letter. *Something ending with a special-looking "E"*...

He shoved the small piece of metal into his shirt pocket, and trotted back to the police cruiser, and keyed the microphone, confidence growing that he had found something significant. Following a short exchange with the impound yard custodian, he walked quickly back to the place where the letter had been leaning against a stone, and began a careful, methodical search of the shoulders and roadway.

The sun-glow from light shining through the loosely closed blinds of the Huntsman's Tack Room Suite infused the room with a warm, soft feel. As Matthew slipped back into the bed from the bathroom, he was reminded of other mornings. Mornings with the first light filtering down through the thick branches of the trees outside his grandfather's dwelling. His well-conditioned mind had awakened early, as usual, and he experienced a split second of unease, until he recalled where he was and the sensed the presence of another...

After their dinner, Michaela had driven him back to the Huntsman, their conversation continuing in a most relaxed, familiar way. As they had approached the hotel, her message service had called, asking her to return a call to another attorney. Her conversation with him was short, a postponed meeting for the following day, and coincided with their arrival outside his cottage-suite. A friendly parting touch became an embrace, a kiss, then another, and suddenly a need; a longing with unexpected urgency. Unexpected, yet no less compelling in its passion. By unspoken mutual consent, they had left the car and gone into the little suite in a half-embrace; Matthew's arm tight around her shoulders, pulling her close to him, her arm around his waist. Pushing the door closed, they embraced tightly, feeling the electricity of the contact of hips and mouths. The kiss was long and deep, Mickey shuddering with the passion that had begun to course through her body. As they grasped and pulled at the other's clothing there was a searching of hands, seeking to explore the other's body in every aspect. As their clothes dropped away, they fell to the sofa, still moving constantly against each other. Matthew drew back and gazed at her through half-closed eyes, taking in the high, firm breasts, now partially hidden with beige lace of her bra, hip-hugging panties showing just a hint of auburn hair, and that beautiful face! The full lips now parted, seeming anxious for their next kiss, the deep blue eyes hooded with passion. He bent to her, yielded to the need for another kiss, deep, drinking her in, then rose, with arms at knees and shoulder, lifted her and carried her into the bedroom, her head laid against his throat. Laying her gently on the turned-down bed, he unhooked the bra, tenderly pulled the panties away from her hips, down the legs. Quickly removing his own underwear, he stretched out full-length beside her, and softly touched her cheek and ran the back of his finger down her jaw line, across her throat, and down between her breasts. She moaned as he caressed her and moved his hand down through the dark curls and between her legs. She partly turned, and felt for his erection, grasping and stroking, feeling the need that matched her own. Stroking and caressing, they kissed and moved together, their arousal growing at each touch. He parted her legs further, and found her special place with his fingers, and slowly stroked her there as he kissed her eyes, her throat, and then took an erect nipple. Massaging it with his tongue in rhythm with his fingers, she began to move with ever-increasing tension in time with his hand and mouth. Now moaning together, he moved over her, as she widened her thighs to receive him. She shifted her hips as she positioned him to enter her, lifting her body to meet him as he pushed against, and then into her

173

passion. They moved together in a rhythm as old as humanity, and crying out as they reached climax, clung damply together as they descended from that peak.

They rested, dozed in each other's arms, and later came together again in a slow, easy coupling, finding pleasure in the other's body, and learning the taste and feel of their togetherness. A tender, smooth coming together, and afterward, spent, they slept for a time, rousing again in early morning hours to once again find that ultimate pleasure they could now know.

Rubbing his free hand across his eyes, Matthew rolled to his side, and found himself looking into her wide blue eyes, gazing steadily at him. He reached out to touch her cheek, "How are you, love?"

"Well served, good sir. A bit sore, but blissfully happy and content. You?"

"The same, and not wanting this to end; not at all…"

Michaela moved to him and took his face in her hands. "Nor do I want this to end, but I need for you to stay right where you are while I answer a call of nature, and then we can see what the morning will bring." She rolled to the side of the bed and stood, looked back at him briefly, smiling, and went into the bathroom.

What now, Grandfather? This is something we never discussed much. It seems and feels the most natural thing to be with her this way. Not like it was with those young women at the university, or the few around the reservation in the summers. Altogether different, Grandfather.

As she returned to the bed, she stood for a moment, looking down at him. *My God, but he's beautiful! I'm not sure how I could have been so slow, so unwilling to get close to him , but now I don't believe I want to ever be away from him again!* She sprawled on her belly next to him, and ran her hands over his chest and down to his waist. He took her hand in his and stretched, pulling her over to him, bending up to kiss her. They talked softly, lightly, still stroking and caressing as they did. Then, as with one mind, she moved over him, and guided him into her again, moving slowly, then with urgency as once again, they reacted to one another's desires and passions.

CHAPTER 18

Jake watched with fascination as the newscaster described the record of the Senator in terms that were gushingly, fawningly respectful. He was constantly amused at the manner in which the press found ways to forgive the most outrageous behavior of those they favored, and how they become so righteously solemn over trivial gaffes by ones held in disdain.

Hell, I know at least a dozen of those pompous bastards on the take; they can't hold a candle to this Bozo, and yet they talk about him as if he's God's gift to the country! What the hell are they thinking? He shook his head in disgust and clicked the television's remote off, dropping it with a clatter on the scarred coffee table, glaring agitatedly around the cramped little room. The queasy, flu-like feeling swept over him again as he fumbled for a cigarette from the pack on the table, and slumped back into his seat, staring angrily at the television screen. At one time he had held the press in very high esteem, as they filled the pages and screens with the screaming antics of his and other activists' demonstrations against anyone that didn't agree with them. Since then, he and his causes had been neglected and condemned in turn by those same cretins that once had been his allies. They had forgotten him, but he vowed inwardly that things would not stay that way. He had abandoned the causes that were once dear, embraced a palette of others as it suited him, never sensing the hypocrisy in the course he had taken. The selfish cynicism always there had become the guiding force in his life; no principal too radical to be embraced when it suited him, none too important to be abandoned at his whim, allegiances shifting as the dollars were found.

Too frustrated to sit still, he clambered to his fee, and, lapsing into deep thought, began pacing with the shuffling, rolling steps he had affected over the years; it seemed from a casual glance that he was just another alcohol-soaked street bum. He thought about the broadcast. They had said the Senator was leaving for Washington in a few days, but had remained in his home state for a press conference at which a major jobs-producing announcement would be made. The press conference, so the tele-journalist had oozed, had been called to take place at the airport, from which he would depart for Washington, where he would resume "the decades-long battle for the downtrodden souls of the country, and especially for those in his beloved home state." *That's enough to make me puke! That sonofabitch never gave a damn about anybody that couldn't do something for him. Downtrodden souls, my ass! But maybe, just maybe...could be there's a way to use that stage show for something worthwhile...*

The strangely gaited pacing continued for several minutes, gestures and grimaces punctuating the silent arguments he held with himself. When at last he had reached a conclusion, he sank again onto the worn cushions of the sagging sofa and reached for the phone beside it on the floor.

The process for reaching Malcolm was complicated and required call-backs from a series of phones, each covered by a voice mail system. Jake knew that his crony would be irritated by the midday call, and its interruption of his routine, but here was an opportunity that didn't often present itself. After placing the initial call, he pulled on the slouch hat and shapeless sweater that completed the illusion of street person, and shambled out into the cool day, his mind whirling with plans to relate to Malcolm.

177

Standing Bear looked from one worried face to another, seeing the consternation he had anticipated; ready for the next flurry of discussion as the Council considered his decision. They would be here for some time, he was sure, and in the course of all the talk, he would be able to influence the more reluctant members with a word here, a pointed question there. In the customary way, every man would have his opportunity to speak, and rebuttals, sometimes heated, could be expected. This rare session during the day, when they could not take comfort in the darkness to conceal their coming and going had already gone on for almost half a day and no real resolution could be expected until the sun was well on its way down the sky. He enjoyed this! He could picture the fire-lit gatherings of the past, with blanketed elders wrangling over the various issues of the day; composition of war and hunting parties, sites for encampments, the disposition of the spoils from raids. It was a most gratifying tradition and he was elated to see it happening again! There might never be a new uprising, but he would do everything in his power to see to it that the world of the white man learned of this Council, and respected its wishes.

Listening subconsciously to the discussion, he caught from the tone of the words that those in favor of his proposal were beginning to feel the acceptance rising in the others. Soon it would be time for him to once again take control of the discussion, and summarize the points made for and against to this point. This would prepare them for the next rounds of discussion which would lead to the inevitable decision. He was completely unaware of the parallels between his actions and those involved in the workings of hundreds of political caucuses going on in halls of government all over the country.

John Wolf stood to the rear of the room, watching the discussion, arguments, go back and forth. He had never been in a council meeting for more than a short time previously, and he was absorbed in the way the debate ranged thorough the group. He had been asked specifically by Standing Bear himself to come and be

178

available for questions; a signal honor, and one that filled him with pride and pleasure. As with the others, he had been astonished by the proposition laid before the group. This type of behavior was foreign to most of them and the totality of departure from what they had come to think of as a cultural given was radical in the extreme. This type of thing was the stuff of whites, and not easily accepted even to deal with one of them. Most of the discussion had centered on whether the dissembling proposed would be too great a breach of honor for them to even consider endorsing. True, many of The People had become so irretrievably entwined with the ways of whites that they easily deceived and cheated without regret; not the ways of this group in the past, for certain, but could it be now? Should it be now?

Such journeys into the esoteric world of cultural philosophy were not part of Wolf's makeup. He simply acted as The Red Way indicated he should; it was as simple as that. He let his mind wander, back to the time earlier in the day when Standing Bear, in that distant-thunder voice of his had stated that the Council and its work were soon, if not now, compromised by their contact with Jake Monroe. He knew this as fact; the revelation coming to him during the *inipi*, the sweat lodge ceremony.

He had paused then, anticipating the shocked grunts of disbelief, the murmur of anxious comments. As the group had once again grown quiet, as decorum dictated, he continued, "And now we are, as John Wolf has told us, expected to join again with Monroe on some vague venture. Monroe came to us filled with talk of joining the cause of his red brothers. He is not our brother! He is *washicu*, a white man!" he had said with a sneer. "That is something we must never forget. *Washicu* ways are not Our Way, and are filled with lies and deceit. Since they first came to the People, there has been nothing but broken promises. They brought their diseases and the alcohol-poison; they stole our lands and killed our women and children; they divided our people and took away our way of life,

179

killing the *tatonka*, the buffalo! The way of the *washicu* brings nothing but death and dishonor to The People, and now this Monroe, this *washicu* calls us his red brothers? We must not continue with this man! Aside from some money and the few weapons, he has done nothing for us, and I say that he will bring nothing but harm to us, to our cause, and dishonor to what we stand for. I say he must not only be rejected, he must be stopped! We must not do this with risk to our young men, our warriors, as *washicu* would do." Standing Bear had paused here, a sly smile creasing his face before he continued. "We will let Monroe answer to the *washicu* law instead. Then we can be truly rid of him, and his ways." This last had been said with such strength, such force and finality that there were long moments of silence while the entirety, the enormity of the proposal had sunk in.

John smiled inwardly as he remembered the speech, each utterance of the Lakota word *"washicu"* coming closer to a true expletive, the last leaving no doubt the disgust it was meant to bring. Yes, a stirring delivery of a rather simple idea. Now came the discussion of how to deal with Jake Monroe. And here was where the most troubling aspect of the proposition came; they would do this through the same deceitful ways that had marked the relationship with the whites, but from the other side. In this instance *they* would be the deceivers! It had been suggested by none other than Standing Bear himself that in order to assure the downfall of Monroe they should go along with him until such time as they had complete knowledge of his plans, and then relay the information to the authorities. These same authorities were ever looking for the members of the Council and their followers, and no level of trust existed for them. How the betrayal of Jake Monroe would actually be done was only a part of the overall plan that caused such consternation, and even anger among the men in the old room. Marion Three Dogs had just finished an impassioned dissertation on the evils of dealing with whites, bringing up the injustices of Leonard

180

Peltiere and Second Wounded Knee, and seemed ready to go back through the complete catalog of broken treaties and land grabs that had afflicted the various Nations when the oldest man in the room, George Lame Horse, rose stiffly to his feet. He did not interrupt, which would have been a gross violation of good behavior, but merely stood and looked solemnly at Three Dogs. But his simple act of standing had brought complete silence to the gathering. Three Dogs stopped in mid-sentence.

Lame Horse's very age commanded deep respect from those on the Council, as did his thoughtful contributions to all matters which were discussed. But it was his feelings towards whites that were unique and special. Lame Horse harbored perhaps the deepest hatred of whites of any of the Council members. His two daughters had been raped and murdered by three drunken white hooligans who, although their act was known, were never tried for the offense. He had properly, patiently, waited for the white man's justice to deal with the criminals. Eventually realizing that it would not, he abruptly left the reservation. No one knew where he had gone, but when he returned months later he told the remaining members of his family that he had been with the Sun Dancers, and had taken part in the *hanbleceya,* the vision quest ritual. This spiritual odyssey had brought him great peace of mind and strength of purpose. After telling his family of his journey, he bid each of them farewell, asking that they not speak of his return. Later that week, the emasculated bodies of the three rapists were found staked to the ground in a wooded area, heads severed and each affixed on a tall stake.

Marion Three dogs, recovering his composure, returned Lame Horse's look and asked, "You wish to speak, Lame Horse?"

"Yes, my friend. I wish to offer my thinking to the Council on this matter. Because of the hour, I wish to say these things before it is much later, and my old bones do not allow me to rise with dignity." This last brought a low chuckle from the men, and a smile

181

from Three Dogs. This small self-deprecating remark allowed the breach of courtesy to be allowed with grace.

"Then please speak, my uncle, and share with us your thoughts on this matter. I would not bring discomfort or loss of dignity to such a warrior." With a sweep of his arm, he seated himself, and with the others looked expectantly at Lame Horse's creased face.

"My Brothers, I have heard the talk here of the need to preserve our dignity and honor. I have heard the talk of the wickedness of a departure from the Red Way, and the consequences this could bring to our people and our cause. And I have heard much about the need to rid ourselves of any connection with this Jake Monroe. All that I have heard is good and true, my Brothers, and we must always listen to our hearts when we deal in matters of honor, but there are other voices to which we must listen." The old man paused, seeming to gather himself up, and went on with the strength in his voice that none in that room had heard before. "Those are the voices of all those who have gone before, from the ancient ones whose blood colored the sacred pipestone, who lived and died with great honor; the voices of those who died to preserve the *tatanka* and the only way of life they and their people had ever known; the voices from a hundred encampments, a thousand villages destroyed and burned by *washicu* soldiers after they had raped and murdered the women and children; the voices of the hundreds trapped in *washicu* prisons and the thousands on reservations. It is these voices, my Brothers, and yes, the voices of my two daughters. I found my vengeance for those two voices, and the songs I hear from them now are sweet in my mind." He paused again, and in the minds of those gathered there were the voices of the ghosts of those who had been wronged, calling out to demand *washicu* blood.

"So many of the others have never been avenged, and it is to them we must now listen! We are given a chance to still more of the voices! And in the same way that we have so many times been

182

betrayed; by the twisting of their law to meet the needs of those who wield it. We do this, and we bring no dishonor to ourselves, to our people or to our cause. It is the same as seizing the weapon of your enemy and killing him with it. The *washicu* use their law like a knife, and cut the life from our people. We can now use that same knife to be rid of one, maybe more of them. And by doing that we do not place the very lives of our young men in danger, as Standing Bear has reminded us. By doing this thing, we do not follow in the ways of the *washicu*, we turn them in upon themselves like the serpents that they are. I say this is the honorable thing to do, and I say that we should do whatever we can to bring as many of them to face their law as we can!"

Finished, he turned from the rest, and looked out the window toward the sinking sun, straight and rigid as a war lance. In the silence following this impassioned statement, it was obvious the depth of the impression that had been made. Standing Bear took the opportunity to move from his position to one side, and seek the consensus he knew was now there.

With Council's concurrence, it was decided to proceed with John Wolf's connection with Monroe, and he was instructed to make every effort to find out who else might be involved that they could also be brought into the snare being arranged for Monroe himself. That decided, the *chanunpa* was carefully removed from its pouch, and with appropriate ceremony was filled, lighted and passed around the circle. Later they quietly dispersed, and slipped away into the gathering darkness.

"Goddamit, Jake,"

Malcolm Williamson began, to be interrupted gruffly by his cohort.

"Look, Mal, I feel like shit, and don't have the time to listen to you bullshit about how you can't be disturbed. I've come up with a real barn burner for a demo to show off our "pretties", and I need some info on just what you can have for me in the next three days. This is a big one, and will make all the headlines, all the networks. It's exactly the kind of thing we were talking about, all we could ever want. Now what have you got ready, in addition to the stuff I got from Genarro the other night?"

"It's been a lot slower than I'd hoped. For some reason there's a flu going around that has really laid the armorers low. They seem to be the only ones really affected; guess it's because they are all living in such close proximity in that motel, but the long and short of it is that there are only a couple of guys left on the team that can work all day. Some of the others part time, but they give out at about noon, and that's put a real crimp in the production. All I have ready now are a couple of additional M-16's, and a replacement for the 9mm that broke apart when we tested it. We still don't know why that one failed, and I'm a little reluctant to say that it's ready, but guess you could count on it in a pinch. Other than that, I think, and emphasize think, that we can put together another M-60 machine gun, and that's about it. Oh, and maybe another several hundred, maybe a thousand rounds of the special ammo, and that is all there'll be for a while until these guys get over whatever the hell it is they've got. Think it'll be enough?"

Jake shook his head at his partner's ability to switch so quickly from stuffy scientific administrator to knowledgeable, precise planner. Jake had never been one for quick attitude adjustments; he stayed hot a long time once aroused. And he well knew that on a number of occasions, especially when dealing with their Middle Eastern customers, it had been Malcolm's quiet intervention that had defused the situation and allowed profitable deals to be made. "Yeah, that'll be OK. Not quite as strong as I'd have liked, and the variety is a bit slim, but the gig doesn't really demand a lot. The 9mm is actually good; won't have to use it, just leave it so the Feds, or whoever, can find it, analyze it, talk about it, and do our 'advertising' for us! When we get together tomorrow, I'll fill you in on all the details, but this is going to be the 'Greatest Show on Earth', just you wait and see."

Malcolm, ever more conservative than his volatile partner, grunted in acknowledgement and hung up. The mention of "the Feds" made him uneasy. Unlike Jake, he harbored a deep respect for the skill and persistence of the Federal law enforcement agencies. There were times when Jake's imagination had stood them in good stead, others when he simply went off the deep end and had to be reined back. Williamson only hoped this was not one of those times, given the high level of excitement in Jake's voice. It would be hard to stop him when he was up at such a level. Sighing, and automatically checking the people around him, he turned away and went back to the table in the restaurant to finish his noon meal.

CHAPTER 19

George Benjamin was in a fine mood. The parade of constituents that had made its way through his office during the course of the day had been not at all troublesome. For the most part, they had come in adoring pairs or small family groups, all properly respectful, thrilled at just being in his august presence. Two special things about the day set it apart from most others; no one had asked more than the most trivial favor (a photograph, signing a copy of his book, consideration of a kid for one of the service academies), and a truly spectacular brunette, administrative assistant to an environmental lobbyist, had agreed to meet him later for cocktails and dinner. Her warm smile when accepting his invitation had filled his mind with hopeful anticipation of much more than dinner. *Yes, a good day altogether, and unless I miss my bet, a better night yet! I just wish the last few appointments were behind me and I could get ready.* He turned back to his desk and fingered the intercom switch. "Are there any more folks out there, Janice, or do we call it a day?"

"Just one more group, Senator. There's a delegation here from the Native American Council of Elders. They have a plaque to present to you."

"Well, what do you think of that? Send the Council representatives, in, and call that new photographer back. We'll want to commemorate the occasion!" He rose, and effusively greeted the solemn trio of aged men as they came in from the anteroom. The photographer, a frazzled- looking young man with stringy hair and bizarre tie bustled in with a clatter of equipment, and began to arrange everyone in front of an array of books, all unread, in antique glass-front cases. By ironic coincidence a good print in a heroic Indian theme hung above the bookcases, a mocking counterpoint to its owner's actual intentions. With even a small smile from one of the elders, the plaque was presented for what were described as "Services on behalf of the Native America people of Minnesota". Two photographs, *just to be sure,* were taken and hands shaken all around. The entire occasion had taken less than ten minutes, and yet Benjamin was chafing to be rid of the men and resume his lascivious meditations about the evening to come.

Gently herding the last of them out the door to his office, he walked quickly to the desk and informed his secretary that he was no longer available, should some latecomer arrive. His earlier mood had been dampened somewhat by the intrusion of the old men, and as he shoved the award into one of the drawers in his credenza he swore under his breath.

Another, underlying, factor contributed to his declining mood; the change in the plan for issuing the two press releases. He had been persuaded that the announcement of the opening of the Pipestone Quarry to industrial mining would carry considerable political weight if, and only if, he personally announced it. This new plan would note that a scientific breakthrough had found a use for a plentiful, environmentally safe material found in the state, and also that, taking the initiative, Senator Benjamin had negotiated jobs-creation agreements with selected corporations to mine this material on public land. Someone had even come up with a ploy that avoided the use of any mention of the Quarry as such, just vague references to "southwest corner", and "below Marshall" locations. He had bought into that part of the idea entirely, but was still uneasy with making the announcement here. He had prevailed in insisting that it be made at the airport just before he left. That way any deeper investigation that showed the only source of this mined material would be the Pipestone Quarry would come to light after he had left and was

187

safely distanced, possibly even on his way to Europe if they took long enough to make the connection.

Not normally one to remain in a poor humor for long, he began to anticipate the evening ahead as he stuffed some correspondence into his briefcase, thinking as he did so that it would make good "set decoration" when the brunette (*I need to check on her name again; wouldn't do to call her by the wrong one!*) arrived for cocktails. No thought of a striking blonde that he had left in Virginia crossed his mind in the course of his ruminations.

Kevin studied the list of names, and the quickly drawn relational chart he and John Washington had made, with mixed feelings. He couldn't help but admire the care and audacity of the organizing mind behind this; yet he was chilled by the fact that it had been done, and done inside a heavily scrutinized facility endowed with every security check imaginable. It was brilliant in the same way that many criminal ventures were brilliant. He was saddened to think that such fine planning and subterfuge had been utilized to create an organization that was so totally hostile to the country and its aims.

But there it was. Somehow a very fine scientific team had been assembled that was made up almost entirely of student radicals; some from earlier organizations, some more current, and at least one with definite radical Muslim connections. He was now certain that there was a sort of Underground Railroad that had been established to help these individuals. An operation that had been set up to allow them to lose themselves in the populace as a whole, and go on with their lives, evading the efforts of the various law enforcement agencies that looked to put them away. The astonishing thing to Kevin was that they had chosen to hide in such a place. The need to shield identities from the investigative efforts needed for the security clearances would have been a very delicate undertaking; one not possible without collusion at various points within the security community! So if this was yet another piece of the puzzle, the exact nature of the ties, the real mission of the group, and the link to Benjamin were all still out there waiting to be resolved.

Checking his watch, he was astonished to see that it was still only mid-morning. He put his cigar in the ashtray, stood and stretched. Shoving his hands deep in his pockets he left the study and went out to the terrace. Standing there, he let the beauty of the day wash over him, taking in a deep breath of the cool, sweet-smelling air. There was just a hint of summer now; when it came fully it would carry with it the often oppressive heat. Days of that sort were nearly always followed by afternoon or evening thunder storms; a delight to him since he was a child. Then, he had sat on the wide front porch with his father, watching the flash and roar of nature. They would talk then, just father and son. He then recalled an occasion when his father had talked about money, and how some worshiped it and others ruined their lives yearning for it. He had even mentioned a quote from the boxing great Joe Lewis, who was supposed to have said at one time that he really didn't like money, but found great comfort in knowing it was there. And there it was! In the words of his father, it was the one more and perhaps the most elusive piece of the puzzle. Turning agitatedly about on the flagstones, he smacked fist into palm over and over, punctuating the words as he muttered to himself. *"Why in thunder didn't that come to me before? It is just too simple! Surely a United States Senator wouldn't throw away all that power and ego-feeding just for money? But of course he would, if the money was good enough. And if the times were changing to a point that he needed to get out and away from it before the scandals just became too much, then it would make a sort of perverse sense... Or maybe he had always been there, been in play. Not just quiet stock tips, or resort vacations, but real money, heavy money just flowing under the table. This isn't just influence peddling, it is influence in wholesale lots to the highest bidder! My God, what the man must have done! And imagine the amount he must have stashed away somewhere. Undoubtedly offshore, probably Caribbean, maybe Europe..."*

Kevin spun towards the house, grabbing the phone as he came into the study again. Calling John Washington, he filled him in on what he'd gleaned from the records, and related his conclusion as to why Benjamin was involved. John, flabbergasted at this probable revelation, asked to be kept involved, and made Kevin promise to include him in any way that he could to bring the whole affair to light. How much he had sorted out in just the past few hours! Never again would he decry the inhumanity of computers! Without those guys up at IMM headquarters, and that massive main frame, he knew they would still just be guessing. Continuing, he placed a call to Mickey's cell phone and then her office. Reaching her service, he asked that she call him on an urgent matter, and then dialed the Huntsman. He glanced at his watch as the operator rang him through to Matthew's room, thinking that at ten o'clock he would be lucky to locate him there. *"Crazy guy,"* he thought, *"he's probably been up for hours, with that Indian-way teaching from his Grandfather. I'd like to have known that old man..."*

"I'm sorry, Mr. Christopher," the operator interrupted his thoughts, "but Mr. Little Crow doesn't seem to be answering. May I take a message, and have him call when he returns?"

"Thanks, no. I'll locate him, but thanks anyway." Hanging up, he felt a twinge of frustration at reaching neither of his colleagues. Not wanting to let that sort of mood overtake him, he went back to his work table, and began to list the points he wanted to go over with Michaela and Matthew when they surfaced; lists about both the scientific team and the possible involvement-link to Senator Benjamin.

At that moment, the two missing colleagues were smiling at each other over coffee at Michaela's kitchen table; both were content to be in the company of the other. When eventually they had decided they really *must* leave the bed, they had showered together, involving more kissing, and stroking, and ultimately another joining.

With Mickey muttering good naturedly about wearing yesterday's clothes, they had left through the private entrance to the suite, and each in their own cars had gone directly to her apartment. Quickly changing into a more business-like outfit while Matthew attended to an offended Lucille (fresh food and water, a check of the litter box) they had prepared breakfast, and chatted amiably about what to do next on the Quarry matter, then had lapsed into long moments of simply smiling at one another.

It had been decided that when their morning meal was finished, they would go on to her office, calling Kevin from there. That they had nothing to tell him, and in fact were hardly thinking about the joint effort they had been so wrapped up in for the past fortnight did not even enter their thoughts. For now the only thing that mattered was that they were together, and could conceive of being together indefinitely.

The faint chirp of the cellular phone roused Charlie from his wool gathering, and he pulled the cell phone from the Suburban's console. "Yeah," he growled. In response came the beeping of a fax machine, so he turned on the portable device under the phone. It was not as common to have instructions this way. No one had wanted to have any hard records, but sometimes it was better if they weren't sure of the security of the voice line. He read the message as it scrolled out of the machine:

"From Controller. Your surveillance is ended. Christopher, lawyer and activist can't hurt us. Data from wire-tap taps show none of that group are close to us. However it is considered necessary to make a close pass at lawyer and Indian and make them worry about what they are involved with. No terminations authorized, but bring fear to their lives. Your discretion as to how that is done, but soon. Christopher's line protected; no info there at all, but other conversations as analyzed seem indicative of low probability of trouble. The termination was good work, each of you will receive earned bonus. It will be forwarded to Cayman accounts as usual. It has been decided to end the watch entirely; new approach will meet our needs. Return vehicle to long term parking at Dulles, dispose of the keys in another city. Equipment to remain with vehicle. Do not return to HQ location. Take time out of the country, minimum one month. Advise location on arrival."

"Well, I'll be damned, Mac. Would ya' look at that. After all that work in getting the taps set and they're going to pull us out and end the whole thing! What a waste! Guess we could jerk the taps off tonight, then hit for the airport. You have that phony credit card still, don't you? We can charge the tickets on that; then dump it somewhere."

"Yeah, I got it. What sort of scare tactic should we use for the lawyer and her Indian pal? We could watch 'em and use the car to push them into a ditch, or something like that...What's your take?"

"That would probably work, but don't know it's so good to have two car-linked 'accidents' so close together. What do you think about maybe a Molotov cocktail through the window of her office? That would make for a really bad scare, and we could even leave some sort of message at the same time."

"That's a good idea! What we need to do now is come up with some crude warning message that won't be too specific, but

192

clear enough they'll know where it came from. Why don't you think something up, and I'll see about getting us out of here."

"OK, but this whole change is strange; seems a lot of trouble for so little. Wonder what kind of 'new approach' they've come up with up there. Can't be anything too slick, or we'd still be in on it. 'Spose they were able to turn somebody so far that it'll come off without that Senator? Don't seem possible, but those guys can be good. Whaddaya say, since we got almost all day to do nothing while we wait to jerk the taps, we go over to one of the tracks in Maryland. I haven't been to a good horse race in a long time. OK with you?"

"Sure, that'll suit me, but let's get all our ducks in a row for our little "barbecue" I'll get the tickets; then we go to the track. We could dump the card there, maybe even pass it to some joker, let him use it, confuse the hell outta the cops if this ever does come down. Then we can go on up to maybe Pimlico before we take off?"

Agreed on the course of the day, the two IMM operatives pulled out of the drive where they had been watching "the lawyer's" carriage house, and went off in the direction of her office.

Back in Iowa, Jake Monroe, sometimes know as Controller, sometimes, as when he spoke to Senator Benjamin, as Security Headquarters, tore the typed instructions into small pieces, and dropped the pieces into the trash can adjacent to the public fax machine. *That ought to handle that end of the deal. Now all we got to do is to wait for the 'Distinguished Gentleman from Minnesota' to make his announcement and we're on our way,* he said to himself. There was a time when he had enjoyed working with these two mercenaries, and the others that had comprised the "Internal Security

Force – IMM" (an element unknown in the offices of the corporation) but he had tired of their steady stream of tales of various wars. That brought to mind too many times he would have rather forgotten. Lately he simply spoke or faxed them instructions. None had ever connected him with the distant voice, and he preferred that. As he made his way out of the bus station, he was again swept with a wave of nausea, almost doubling over as cramping knotted the muscles in his abdomen. Gasping with the pain, he straightened, and continued on to his meeting with his Indian ally, John Wolf. He regretted the loss of the other one, Moore as he remembered, but maybe if the guy's head was somewhere else, it was better. Wolf was a good one, though. Hated the "White Treachery" from the past, would do anything that involved hurting anything of value to white society. His recruitment, into a basically white operation was, Jake thought, one of his better moves. *Yes a good move,* Jake mused, a*nd now is the time when that will really pay off. The inclusion of these guys will make the whole affair seem to be racially driven, and cause one hell of a backlash! People'll be screaming to dig the damn place up!* A muttered chuckle in his throat at the thought of the double cross, he shambled off down the street in the direction of the restaurant, to all appearances just one more homeless soul seeking comfort in a bottle of cheap wine or shelter in a dingy doorway.

CHAPTER 20

Hiram Clancy had been the sheriff of Loudoun County for more years than he liked to think about any more, and even the occasional boost he got from the campaigning and re-election was beginning to pale. He knew that with the growth of the county it would not be long before some young hot shot who wanted the job would get it; simply by saying that it was time for a change, etc., etc. He looked steadily at the man across the desk from him, realizing that Don Quesenberry was, of all the others, the individual he would pick as his successor if he could. But then, maybe he *could*...But that was for another time. For now he would have to deal with the situation at hand, which was to decide whether this apparently straightforward highway accident should be investigated as such, or under the entirely different auspices of murder, undoubtedly premeditated. As usual, Quesenberry's reporting of the incident and the follow-up were complete, succinct, and without embellishment. It was apparent, though, from the bare facts of the case that it was at least probable that the car had gone over the bluff due to some third party's actions, not simply the "hurried commuter" scenario it seemed on the surface. He looked at the diagram of the scene again, then addressed his deputy, "Don, are you sure of these distances? If this picture is correct, then that little car was rear-ended some 400 feet or more from the turn onto the bridge. That's a long ways to push another vehicle, even if it's not a very big one."

"I'm sure, Sheriff. I measured that scene myself, and took it from the guard rail back to the point where I picked up that piece of trim. There is some question as to whether the trim came off that specific car, but it would be a strange coincidence if it didn't. Our accident records for the past nine months don't show any occurrences on that particular stretch of road involving vehicles that could have produced that trim. There's no way, given the condition of the wreck, that we can say absolutely this was the accident that produced that particular piece, but that's the way I see it, personally."

"Have you been able to get a VIN that can be traced off the wreck?"

Quesenberry smiled grimly, "We did, in fact, Sheriff. The plate was badly bent, but we were able to pull all the digits when we got it straightened out. It was a Virginia-registered car and we found the license plates in the riverbed, so that helped. We'll have some word on who to contact before the end of the day, anyway. May be done now, for all I know…"

Sheriff Clancy punched the intercom on the phone and listened while the connection was made with the communications desk. "When the dispatcher answered, he said,

"I need to know if you've been able to reach the owner of that car that went over the bluff at the Purcellville Bridge. Deputy Quesenberry tells me you were working on that."

"Yessir, I've been working on it. I haven't been able to reach the owner by phone, and was about to ask you if you thought it would be okay to try and locate an employer, or some other person who might know where the owner is."

"Yes, you do that. And get back to me as soon as you can, when you've located someone. There's a real need to know just who was in that car, so get on with it now, and call me as soon as you have that information." Turning back to Quesenberry, he said, "the ME's report sure wasn't out of the ordinary. You have a chance to go over it yet?"

"Yes, sir, I have. Like you say, there's nothing unusual about it. Obvious cause of death was massive trauma. I suppose that going over a sixty foot bluff and landing upside down in a river bed would cause that." He paused, considering the grim humor of his statement, then went on, "It did say that it would be a few days before all the toxicology and blood-tissue work was done, but there was no reason to believe that there would be an indication of anything other than the obvious. Body was pretty badly burned, besides the other damage, and it's only a fluke the head was essentially untouched. If we can find someone who knew her, we could probably get a positive visual ID." Knowing the Sheriff was going to appear in court in a short while, he rose, and asked, "Anything else you want me to take care of before I start my patrol today?"

"Yeah, there is, Don. I want you to stick with this thing, until we've been able to find somebody to take a look at that poor girl's body, so we can get on with our investigation. I'm going to call this probable homicide, and I'll want you to coordinate with the State Police when they start their look at it. You stay around here; be ready to meet whoever it is that we're able to come up with for that ID. That'll pretty well close out our involvement, but it needs to be done. And Don, just in case I forgot to say so earlier, this is good work. Putting all this together is what this job is all about. Good job, good job." With that he turned his attention to the papers on the side of his desk, and Don Quesenberry left, closing the door behind him, smiling at the rare praise.

Kevin reached for the phone, answering on the first ring. As he raised the receiver, he checked his watch again, startled that nearly three hours had passed since he'd started to work on the listing analysis. Upon hearing the voice of Michaela's admin assistant, *"Would you please hold for Ms Campbell?"* he delightedly started speaking when he heard the extension picked up, "Hey! Glad you called! When can we get together? You'll be amazed what we've found since we last talked. That trip to Atlanta was just the ticket; gave us the break we've lacked, and in addition to that, I think I've finally puzzled out just what it is that'll make the Benjamin connection more understandable."

There was a protracted pause, and Kevin thought for a moment that the connection had been broken. Then he heard Matthew's voice, oddly subdued, "Kevin we've got trouble on a couple of fronts here! Just before the office opened this morning, someone threw a makeshift Molotov cocktail through the window in the back of the building. Thankfully it wasn't all that big, but with the fire from it, and the results of the sprinkler system going off, it's made an unholy mess out of the library back there."

"Is everyone all right? Nobody hurt or anything/", Kevin asked anxiously.

"No injuries, just fire, smoke and water damage. Mickey's admin has already called the insurance people, so that's being taken care of. To add to the strangeness of that, there was a message on the general voice mailbox warning her to stay the hell out of business in Minnesota that wasn't in any way her business, and that she should take her 'redskin friend' away from there too, or this little fire would be nothing compared to what they are willing to do. It really spooked her badly. Guess she doesn't work the side of the law that deals in violence and mayhem much anymore. The other and probably more worrisome problem is that Mickey just took a call from the Loudon County Sheriff's Department. Seems they have a Jane Doe traffic fatality in the Medical Examiner's office over there that was pulled from the wreckage of Laura Atkinson's car. The people where she worked had suggested that Michaela might know where she was; she hasn't been in for work for a couple of days, and they thought maybe she was ill. They were, in fact, on the verge of calling Mickey to look in on her anyway. She is, as you might suspect, extremely anxious. We'd just arrived at the office and begun dealing with the fire mess when the Sheriff's call came."

Without hesitation, Kevin broke in with "I'm on my way. Don't leave without me, and don't let Michaela start to extrapolate from that call. It'll take me ten minutes." With that he hung up and raced out to his car, slamming the door behind him.

There was a small room adjacent to the viewing area at the Medical Examiner's office. The chemical smell of the place had penetrated this area too, and the plainly finished pale green walls reinforced the room's institutional nature. The stark furnishings seemed to emphasize the notion that this was not a place for lingering. Matthew and Kevin stood slightly behind and on either side of Michaela, as she listened with rigid attention to the low-spoken comments from the Assistant ME who had brought them here from the general waiting room. A bulky deputy sheriff, Quesenberry from his brass name tag, was just inside the door, hat in hand. His expression was, so Kevin thought, curiously compassionate. His experience had always been that those often exposed to death became habitually callous in its face, and tended to disregard the feelings of those most directly involved. He unconsciously registered the deputy's name for future reference.

"Miss Campbell," the Assistant ME was saying, "since the cause of death was as it was, we will present the, uh, remains, uh, on, or rather in the storage device. Only the face will be visible."

Thank God for that, Quesenberry thought.

"We can pull these drapes at any time that you feel ready," he continued, "and when you feel that you have, uh, seen enough, or rather, well you know what I mean, uh…"

199

"Yes," Michaela replied, "I understand. Please open the drapes and let's get this over with." The dread that she had felt was not apparent in her steady voice, but she felt at any moment that she might scream with the tension. *This is, maybe, a good friend. I will never be ready for this, and no matter how little time, it will be too much.* It occurred to her as the drape parted that the last time she had been called upon to view a body of someone she could have possibly known, it was for other victims of the crash that had taken her parents' lives. That thought further heightened the feeling of somehow knowing the face she would see.

Kevin and Matthew responded together, each taking an elbow as Michaela gasped, nodded, and then sagged against them. The wonderful yellow-gold hair was splayed against the shroud, tangled and darkly matted in places. Purplish bruises marred her cheeks and forehead and her nose was smashed. Although not the face she *knew*, it was, indeed, the face of Laura Atkinson.

Quesenberry quietly turned and left the room. He had seen enough that, although no words had been spoken aloud, there was no doubt as to the identity of the corpse. Setting his jaw as he remembered the hurt and pain he had just witnessed, he jammed his hat on his head and descended the steps of the building towards his car. Settling into the seat, he keyed the radio. "Seven two Charlie to Base, seven two Charlie to Base."

"Seven two Charlie, go ahead."

"Base, please advise Sheriff Clancy that a positive ID has been made regarding case F4725. Victim was registered owner of the vehicle. Disposition of remains not determined at this time. Seven two Charlie now en route your location. Out here." Reporting over with, Quesenberry turned out into traffic and headed back towards Department headquarters, reflecting sadly on some of the things he witnessed in the course of his work. As he drove, he dismissed those thoughts, and mentally began to go over the parts of his report that he would share with the State Police investigators.

The malodorous surroundings made John Wolf reflect, as he had so many times, on the strange attitudes of the white man. Here they were, near some of the finest open country imaginable, and they were instead meeting in this stinking café again. *Don't they even see where they are, know that a man can think better when he is in the open, and way from all this?* He frowned, knowing that the answer to that question was buried, somehow, in their makeup, and that he would never understand them; not that he really cared to anyway. He listened as Jake outlined the plan he had for their involvement in a holdup. It seemed to be rather straightforward, although he didn't like the idea of being out in the open in a public place. There seemed to be little that had not had Jake's attention, though, and he was now going into the role John and his men would play.

"When we get to the airport, I'll have a package for each of you, containing…well, you know what will be in them. I won't have to worry about what you will do with the *packages*, just be sure that you make your way to the positions we talked about, and be sure that you're there at least five minutes early. I don't want to have to wonder where everyone is when we take the loot."

"Just what is it, Jake, that we'll be taking. You never got around to saying?" John's question caused Jake's eyes to narrow, a sure sign of anger, but Wolf looked steadily at him, and waited for an answer.

"John, John. You know that I can't tell you that. Have I ever let out all the details of an operation? Well, have I?" The response had an edge to it, and it was obvious that Monroe was having difficulty curbing his rather legendary temper.

Not deterred, John pressed the issue. "No you haven't, but you've never neglected to tell us what we're after, either. I don't really care, just like to know what I'm in for. We do get something from this other than just practice, right?" He knew this was pressing it, but he also knew that he needed more information before he could bring a reasonable report back to Standing Bear. That they knew when and where the operation was taking place was good, but it would be necessary to know the specific objective before they really could form their own counter-plan. He continued to look straight at Monroe, hoping the other man would open up, be uncomfortable with the unremitting stare.

"Well, now, you're right about that, but in this instance you're just going to have to take me at my word that it's a good show; and yes you people will get an appropriate cut from the take. I need to get out of here! I've had a stomach flu that just won't give up, so now I'm going to drink about a quart of Pepto and hit the sack." Rising, he looked piercingly at Wolf and the other two men that had come with him. "You guys just make sure you are on time, and leave all the rest to me. Your involvement here is mostly back-up anyway. I'm gone." And with that, he strode out of the place into the night, immediately settling into the shuffling gait of his street persona.

John looked at the other two men, who had spoken hardly at all after introductions had been made at the beginning of the session. "Well, that was Jake Monroe," he said, with a small smile. "We'll need to be careful, and more than usual." He considered the two, both acquaintances of long standing. They were a good pair, and John was pleased to be working with them on this unusual operation. They didn't know the whole plan that the Council had approved, but were more than willing to take the word of Standing Bear at face value; that they should follow John Wolf's instructions without questions. John knew that each would arrive at the designated point with his small contingent of men as agreed, and that there would be no trouble in carrying out the instructions that he gave them.

"I think you are right, John," one commented, "This is not a man I would want to know well. Even to work for him does not sit well with me, but I understand we must do things like that sometimes. But we must be very, very careful; he has loyalty to nobody but himself." Nodding his agreement, John rose and said, "Let's leave this stink hole. I can barely breathe in here!"

Nodding their agreement the other two also rose, and the three men drifted out into the night at irregular, predetermined intervals. Their rendezvous a half hour later to discuss their actions within Jake's plan was approached in the same manner. Watching Federal agents would not have noticed any connection of the three.

Monroe, gulping antacids to ameliorate his continuing discomfort, had started the tedious process of contacting Malcolm Williamson to set the time for the weapons pickup. While waiting for the message to work its way through their shielding system, he criss-crossed the small city, stopping at second hand shops and discount stores where he accumulated a number of cheap pieces of luggage to be handed out to the Indians. In addition to some odds and ends of clothing that he also purchased in the stores, each would contain one of the special weapons and its ammunition.

CHAPTER 21

Kevin absently stirred his coffee, waiting with Matthew in the kitchen of Michaela's apartment. They had returned there after identifying Laura's body and Michaela had retired to her bedroom to regain her composure and rest for a bit. Thinking back to the experience at the Medical Examiner's office, Kevin found his irritation rising again. There had been a number of papers to sign, and affidavits regarding the intended "disposal of the remains."

"What an awful way to refer to someone," he had snapped at the clerk. "This was a friend, someone's daughter!"

With the bland expression of the entrenched bureaucrat, the clerk had merely shrugged and asked what they wanted done, responding in no way to their collective distress. In the end, Michaela had asked that Laura be held at the ME until she could arrange for a local funeral establishment to pick her up. On the way back in the car, she had apologized to both for her emotional outburst, tearfully relating that it was the first time she had gone through anything like that since her parents' death, and that it had brought all those memories back. Kevin and Matthew both did what they could to lend support and a level of sympathy in keeping with her outlook and felt that she was much better when they reached the carriage house. Now the two men simply waited, each lost in his thoughts.

Rousing himself, Kevin said, "Before all of this, I had wanted to share with you two the things I have either found out, or suspect. I would think that Mickey's mind will be on other things for a time; maybe we should carry forward, letting her deal with the things she needs to while we keep after the situation at the Quarry, and let her re-join, so to speak, when she feels she can. What do you think?"

"I think you're right about Mickey, and there are possibly some other factors there". Matthew paused, then continued, "This whole fire bomb and warning call thing puts this whole thing in a different light. The police and the insurance company will deal with the damage at the office, but that phone message had an edge to it that raised the hair on the back of *my* neck, and I believe Mickey's genuinely frightened. Basically, I believe we need to work the Quarry issue, as hard as we can, to a conclusion that will expose the kind of people that could do things like we have seen today! And I agree with what you said the other day, that there is a sense of urgency to it, especially now. Something is happening, and it is happening as we speak. We simply can't afford to allow more time to pass. The people behind this are prepared and indeed have already resorted to the worst kinds of criminal behavior, and even more than the cultural damage we could witness, these people need to be stopped because of who and what they are! Aside from the personal danger that we see, there is still the original question; will the Quarry continue as it was intended, or it will be lost forever? *That* we can't allow; we just can't!"

"Okay, then. I thought, *knew* actually, you'd feel that way. Here's where we are…"

Matthew listened intently as Kevin related the discovery of the bogus DOD contracts, and the peculiar makeup of the scientific team. "You're saying that all these people are not just scientists, but re-cycled radicals! Who in the name of conscience was doing the background checks? You'd think those kind of guys couldn't get a clearance to go into a high school chemistry lab, much less a place like that, and to become a part of a classified development team! It's just incredible!"

205

"Oh, but it gets better. Not only do we have this ghost DOD research program, but the facilitator for the material from the Quarry is none other than the good Senator Benjamin!" Kevin couldn't help but smile at the incredulous look on Matthew's face. "I don't have any solid proof at this point, but I firmly believe there is an element in the IMM organization, somewhere, that has pushed money at Benjamin over the years. Not all that unusual on the surface; campaigns always find money with local corporations, but in this case it looks like big, big money under the table. And the purpose recently is the access to the Quarry. Basically the simple greed factor is what bought Benjamin's involvement."

"That is almost too much, but then, we *are* dealing with a politician not well known for his high moral or ethical standards. But the suggestion of escalating violence and the arson at Mickey's office don't seem to fit the man. He's for sure a slimy creature, but this doesn't seem to be the kind of thing he'd want to be connected with. Have you found any other facets to this that could point in that direction?"

"Not yet, and that's fueling this feeling of concern that I have that time is our enemy. We could speculate until the cows come home and not get any closer to real motives, much less come up with proof. Another worrisome thing is that if these guys get away with whatever it is they are doing now, who knows what horrific schemes they could come up with if left in place. Just think about a group of way out radicals with access to the best in scientific equipment, and notions of anarchy...would make the Tokyo subway attack look like a kindergarten picnic!" Kevin smacked his fist into his palm, scowling at the image in his mind.

"Then maybe the only way to bring this thing out of the shadows is to confront those involved. We don't know who the right people are at this Iowa facility, but we sure as hell know where to find George Benjamin. Why don't we get up to wherever he is these days, march into his office and…"

They both turned at once, as Michaela emerged from the back rooms, and paused in the kitchen doorway. "I'm glad you've been able to carry on with what we started, and again I want thank you both for just being there for me today. Aside from the day my parents died, I believe this has to be the worst day of my life. We all wonder how we will react to threats and violence and the death of friends…let me tell you that now that I have, I don't ever want to endure it again! We need to find these… animals…and put them away, preferably forever! I'm OK now, I think, and I'd like to join in whatever it is you have been talking about and help come up with a means to put a stop to whatever they are trying to do. It'll be good to get the mind out of this trough and do some genuine thinking again."

"Are you sure, Mickey?" asked Kevin. "You look more than a little peaked, and we don't want to add to your stress in any way; right, Matthew?"

"Of course not! Are you really up to it?"

"Look guys, I'm not some magnolia-mouth swooner. This has been horrible, and I've been really shaken, but I'll be all right. Right now, there's nothing I need more than to have something productive to do, and I sense that since ya'll seem to be on to something, that is exactly what I need."

After a pause, Kevin broke in with, "All right! Then let's get on with it, Miss Campbell, Mr. Little Crow! To bring you up to speed, Mickey, here's where we are…"

At the Loudon County Sheriff's Department, the meeting with investigators from the State Police Criminal Investigation Unit was coming to a close. Sheriff Clancy and Deputy Quesenberry had briefed the two State Police detectives for just under an hour, laying out the known facts of the incident, the indications there may have been another vehicle, the broken piece of trim, and then sharing their observations and gut feelings. These men had worked together before, and trusted in the professional judgments and opinions that had been expressed. Given that, there was little doubt in any of their minds that a crime had been committed. Considering the tiny bits of information available, they were just as sure that this was a crime that would probably never be resolved and closed.

After a few minutes of silence, one of the State Troopers said, "Well, Don, you did your usual fine job of gathering information; just a cryin' shame there's so damned little of it! From what you say, I think you're dead on about some other vehicle being present, but I'm afraid we'll just have to wait 'til God smiles on us, and drops the thing on our heads. No tire marks, nothing?"

"Nope, afraid not. I found an indication of rubber on the road not far from the location of that piece of trim, but it was nothing that could be identified, and what marks there might have been around the bridge itself would have been so comingled with the hundreds of others from people taking the corner too fast that it wasn't even worth the trouble to look."

"Ya'll let us know," Clancy said, "if you do find anything? If God does smile, won't you?"

"You bet Sheriff. I guess we better be on our way. Ya'll run across anything else, give us a call, you hear, now?"

"Right, boys. Take it easy!"

And with those parting words the case involving the death of Laura Atkinson at the Purcellville Bridge began its long slide into official oblivion.

With little information to pass on, John Wolf had toyed with the idea of omitting any report today, but in the end decided he would tell Standing Bear the whole story of the meeting with Monroe, and see what he wanted to do. Keeping to the arrangements for meeting that they had agreed upon at the Council meeting, Wolf, called, left the coded message, and sat back to await the set time.

Pondering his situation, he reflected on how honored he was to have been taken into the workings of the Council. It was not unknown, of course, for younger men to be asked to perform a specific task, but most uncommon for them to be given a contributory role, and even more unusual for an individual to relate directly to the head of the Council personally. He felt honored, but was concerned about his failure to gain more information from Jake. But then again, that was why Standing Bear was who he was, and why John Wolf reported to him; knowledge and experience would guide the younger warrior, that was the Red Way. He would listen to the wisdom of his elder, and deal with the situation as he was advised. This was a time for him to learn much, and he resolved to make the most of the chance. Patiently biding his time, he sat cross-legged on the floor, facing the window, clearing his mind for what lay ahead.

When at last it was time to leave, he glanced around the small efficiency apartment. There was little character to the place, but it had provided a shelter for him for several weeks. Unlike many of the places in which had had resided, this one was fairly clean, and the landlord had made a genuine effort to maintain the old building. But, like so many of the other places, it was simply shelter, and held no attachment for him. He had decided to spend some time away from cities and the white men's ways when this thing was over, living in the woods near the Lake, the beloved *Gitchegoume*. This, then, was the last time he would be here, and he automatically checked for things that could connect him to the place. He felt some regret about leaving while still owing for rent, but then the landlord was a white man, so it really didn't matter. Noting nothing that might identify who had lived there, he hefted the rucksack that held his belongings to one shoulder, closed the door softly behind him, and silently descended the back stairs. In his mind, he was already reviewing what he would say when he talked with Standing Bear.

Matthew's idea of going directly to George Benjamin and confronting him with their suspicions found little support from Kevin, although Mickey found some merit in the approach as it would certainly catch Benjamin off guard. "You know, it might even be better if we could approach him while he's still up in Minnesota, she said. "He won't have the array of support up there that he does here, and I can't help but believe that he would be more relaxed, less in self-defense mode."

"Yes, but the problem," Kevin growled, "is that we don't have a shred of actual *proof* that he has anything going with some secretive branch of IMM, much less any solid connection to the Quarry."

Matthew looked blandly at his old friend, "But that's the beauty of it, Kev. We don't need to *prove* anything yet; we're not in court! All we have to do is make him *think* we can bring some proof, make him believe that we know what's going on. He wouldn't chance that sort of thing, especially the money part, coming out…too much to lose!"

Knotting his forehead, Kevin leaned toward the others. "I don't know why you can't see what I'm trying to tell you! This is not just some jerk from the local School Board that we're talking about here. This is a real, by God, all-powerful, sitting senior Senator with who knows how much time making back room deals; bluffing and being bluffed by the best in the Senate Cloakrooms. He has more allies in this town than you can shake a stick at! It would almost take black magic to imagine him falling for some empty threat of exposure without *some* concrete fact to wave in his face and make him hesitate." He spoke with some heat in his voice, and the silence when he had finished was palpable.

Answering heat with calm, Matthew relaxed against the back of his chair and said, "Kevin, all you've said is right, and facts and connections would put us in charge of any meeting with the Senator." Kevin smiled grimly at this concession to his logic. "But the one thing you're not taking into account is something we all agree on; time is running out. Not sure how we know, but we all think so. The worst thing we could do now is retreat back into research that might just turn up those lacking facts in a week or so, but by then the track-hoes would already be in the Quarry stripping off the quartz to get to the pipestone. We just can't wait!"

So the conversation continued for several hours. Kevin opposed to the confrontation plan, Matthew its champion, Mickey the arbiter, trying to maintain the train of discussion and avoid the distracting tangents brought on by the strong opinions. As the afternoon turned to dusk, the men's rhetoric began to soften, and eventually they reached accord; time was the dominant factor, and they would have to do something to sidetrack the Senator's participation. Without it, the Quarry's status would remain as a National Monument under the Park Service protection.

"Look guys," said Mickey, "Since we agree that we need the Senator out of the picture, and soon, now we're stuck with deciding how that gets done. No matter where we do it, we need to present our 'case' firmly and with all the confidence in the world. What we say needs to be stated in such a manner that the Senator will be led to believe that proof of his complicity with a mining scheme *is* available, and further, that information regarding other, past occasions when he had accepted bribes for his influence and vote is also in our hands. That no actual proof is available is beside the point. Lawyers go into courts all over the world with inference and innuendo their only weapons, and often they are successful. As for me, I still think we stand a better chance of catching him off guard and possibly feeling a bit vulnerable away from his power base here in DC if we arrange our meeting for his Minnesota office. What's everyone's opinion on that tack?"

Looking from one to the other, they nodded agreement, and with Kevin's reluctance to make such a bold bluff finally overcome, he became fully committed, and being the consummate planner that he was, began to sort out the details for the trip. "Matthew, I think it would be best if we all went, there being a certain intimidation factor in sheer numbers. Mickey, you could even present certain things in the appropriate legal jargon, enhancing the impression that we are more than ready to press the matter in the courts, while Matthew plays the outraged minority representative countering that the best place to disclose our 'proof' is in the press and electronic media."

"I don't think I can go now, Kev," Michaela stated slowly. "There are a number of things that have to be dealt with regarding Laura's funeral, and with no family, I'm really the only one available to do that. I couldn't let something like that be handled altogether by strangers, could I? And, of course, there will be all sorts of issues I can already see with the insurance company when they come to look at the office..." She looked from one to the other, seeking the approval that she knew was sure to come.

"Of course, Mickey," Kevin said quickly. "It was thoughtless of me to suggest that you come. Please, don't think I'm uncaring about Laura; simply caught up in the planning for a quarrel that now I'm already looking forward to. Please, forgive me."

"Don't be silly! Of course I know you didn't mean to be uncaring. After all, you hardly knew Laura, and besides, there's plenty I could help with here if the situation demanded. All the files, the contacts we have are much more easily reached from here. Let's say no more about it, okay? And I can still gin up some pretty heavy-looking documents that you can wave in his face for effect."

"I wish that you could come," Matthew said, looking directly into Michaela's eyes, "But it's best that you stay and attend to Laura. That will be your first priority, I know, and as for the office, your partner and the admin can handle that; take that off your plate. Kevin and I will 'beard the lion', and we can always be reached by phone if you need us, or we can call you should the occasion arise where some detail in the file has to be looked up. We'll miss your support, though…"

"Then that's settled and done," said a relieved Kevin. "Mickey will stay here and hold the fort, attend to what she has to, and we will keep her updated throughout the whole show."

"Good, then we have at least that settled, said Michaela, "But something we haven't thought or said anything about is that it is long since past my dinnertime, and as surprising as it is even for me to hear myself say it, I'm starved! How do you guys feel about ordering in a pizza? I can make a salad, and we can continue our discussions here, or maybe just relax and clear our minds a little. As I recall I even have a half-way decent bottle of Merlot."

"My Lord, but it is late," exclaimed Kevin. "By all means, let's do that. Pizza sounds good. How about you, Matthew?"

"Couldn't think of a better idea!"

"Absolutely. Now what do we want on that pizza…pepperoni certainly, and some mushrooms and extra cheese?"

With the call to Dominos made, they all moved then to the kitchen to kibitz as Michaela made the salad and they awaited the delivery man, chatting animatedly about the prospect of doing something proactive, and not just searching.

CHAPTER 22

Arranging the trip to the small town where George Benjamin kept his home state offices had been rapid and enormously efficient. Kevin had contacted a close friend in the oil business and arranged for the loan of one of their corporate Gulfstreams. As things began to accelerate in their planning, it now became apparent that the press of time was becoming even more significant. John Washington had called to report that computer flags placed on the bogus contract numbers by his IT contacts inside IMM had started to show activity.

Washington had also raised questions about notification of authorities inside and outside the company. He understood Kevin's concern about moving too soon, and jeopardizing their inquiries, but on the other hand he felt it was imperative that the fraudulent operation be halted. He noted that if he had been able to gain access to information as he had, it was possible, even likely, that there was a counter-check program in place that would alert the perpetrators of the fraud. After a short conversation from the sumptuous cabin of the Gulfstream they concluded that the optimum time to bring in the authorities would be shortly after the meeting with Senator Benjamin. The link between Benjamin and the IMM research facility remained extremely tenuous, and they all agreed that one of their objectives would be to reveal the Senator's conduct to the press, and thus the country at large. Laura's death had left them with no way to prove any contact or involvement. From the legal perspective, as Michaela reminded them, there was nothing but the rankest kind of hearsay and speculation, leaving them with virtually no chance of challenging the Senator in court. Their best chance to discredit the man with what they had to work with was through the glare of publicity, letting the media take on the investigative burden of uncovering other nefarious activities in his past.

As the sleek craft swooped down towards the little airport, Kevin looked over at Matthew and asked, "Have you ever figured out what the Quarry can yield that would interest anyone engaged in the design and production of weapons?"

"I haven't been able to come up with anything at all that could interest the R&D people at the Pentagon. The catlinite material is very soft, and although special to Native Americans, and has some limited commercial value, it's certainly not so unique that someone would go to the effort that seems to have been utilized here. I even toyed with the idea that maybe it wasn't the catlinite, but the quartz that overlays the catlinite strata, but that didn't make sense either. That stuff is as hard as the catlinite is soft. Certainly not really adaptable to weaponry...unless you would count dropping it on someone's head."

Kevin chuckled at the small joke, and said, "There's no doubt that the Senator, along with his associates at the Research Center have come up with something, and I'm anxious to know just what. Whatever it is, if they can find something, then someone else could too, and we need to take steps to see that no one is allowed to desecrate the place."

Matthew's expression hardened with resolve as he spoke, "I'm glad to see that you feel that way, because I think you're absolutely right. This is just one group. We need to get them out of the way, and then turn towards strengthening the agreements that restrict the access to the Quarry.

"But first things first; I think we have about a ten minute drive to the offices of the 'Honorable Senator', and I can hardly wait to see how he reacts to what we're going to tell him."

Standing Bear had listened to Wolf's recitation of the meetings with Jake Monroe and had pondered the course of action the Indian group should take under the circumstances. He was especially concerned that whatever it was that Jake had in mind, it was to be done in a public place, with little chance under normal conditions that there would be any level of anonymity. Troubling also was the number of firearms involved. This was something that could turn into an ugly bloodbath, and one that would bring the full extent of the law, through a variety of enforcement agencies, on all who were involved. Monroe apparently didn't seem to be bothered by that prospect, but Standing Bear was *greatly* bothered. In the end, he decided that even given the risks, it was necessary that they continue to go along with Monroe's plan, and that Wolf would have the decision to make when the entire operation was revealed. John was stunned by this revelation, but felt his heart swell with pride. *This is so much more than I could have expected when this all began!*

Acknowledging his instructions, John left the small house and joined the others in a pair of dilapidated cars. They had a two-hour trip to the assembly point Jake had designated. If they encountered no trouble with the cars or the highway patrol, they should be there in the late afternoon. John Wolf was already anticipating his intended journey to the woodlands, but remained keyed up and anxious to hear the objective of Jake's plan.

When his secretary had ushered the two into the office, he was taken aback with their appearance. The first to come in was a tall older man, lean and straight, followed by a very large man who appeared, and likely was, Native American. From their serious demeanor he knew right way this was not a social call.

"Welcome, gentlemen. I am George Benjamin, and you are..."

"Kevin Christopher," the older man started, "and this is my associate, Mr. Matthew Little Crow of the University of Minnesota, and the Mississippi Band of the Ojibwa nation. We have come to discuss with you a serious situation that has come to light regarding the basic culture of the Native Americans in your state, and for that matter, in any state."

"My goodness, but that does sound as if it might be of concern. Would you care for some coffee, water while we talk?"

"Thank you Senator, but no, Kevin demurred. "We wish to go straight to the point. It has come to our attention that despite National Park Service mandates, and other protections, a plan is being formed to displace the Park Service and conduct a commercial mining operation in the a place known as the Pipestone Quarry, located in the southwest corner of your state. It is an extremely significant element in the Native American cultures, and especially the Lakota Sioux. Our reason for coming here today is to ask you to confront the situation and lend your assistance not only as the Senator from the state, but particularly in your role as Sub-Chairman of the Select Committee for Native American Affairs."

Seeing the blank look from the Senator, Matthew spoke, in the measured cadence that of the storyteller, "This place, Senator, is thought by most to be the origin of our people, their very blood colored the sacred stone, and it must not be taken from us!"

Before Benjamin could respond, Kevin spoke again, "The most important thing to remember, Senator, is that although there are many places where the catlinite can be found, none are within the control of the government, in this case the National Park Service. Your perspective, from your position on the Senate committees must be brought to bear in preserving this place, sacred to so many. It is well known that you favor the people of your state. Here is a chance to speak out for one of those constituencies that has not had much of a voice."

"Your point is well made, but I haven't any knowledge of this sort of a plan, and only faintly familiar with the place at all.

"With all due respect, Senator, we can possibly accept that you are not knowledgeable about a plan for exploitation of the place, but it is well known that you regularly and consistently campaigned, and where your campaign staff established an office during the last election cycle. It is hardly credible that you are not aware of the place, as it is so much a part of the commerce and cultural fabric of that region. In addition, there are indications that someone within your office has established a dialogue with mining and manufacturing interests; and to what end? Your efforts to assist us in this effort to save the Quarry could relieve any perception of misuse of your office in assisting in the destruction of an important symbol of our multi-cultural nation", Kevin said with fervor.

Again with the storyteller speech pattern that they had agreed was best in the circumstances, Matthew intoned "We must take every means possible to prevent this desecration. Your assistance is an element of our plan, as is the enlistment of the local and national media. There are ample indications that this conspiracy is being put forth to enrich those involved, and it will be our goal to uncover them and have them brought to justice as well as halt the mining operation. A young woman, Laura Atkinson, mysteriously lost her life as she attempted to aid us with our inquiries. We cannot let her death have been in vain."

"I am sorry about your colleague's death, and would ask that you convey my condolences, but can't imagine how it could have to do with this Quarry matter. And your inferences are alarming, Mr. Christopher! I could easily take offense at your statement that would link this office with any sort of nefarious scheme to usurp an iconic cultural site, and can assure you that nothing is further from the case. I will take your revelations under consideration, study the situation in detail, and work through the committees. As those discussions move forward, I will make it a point to include your concerns, and will keep you advised of any progress.

"If that is all, then I must take your leave for another appointment. Good afternoon, gentlemen." With that he rose, did not offer to shake their hands, and exited the room through a side door.

As they walked back to their rental car, Kevin said, "Well, Matthew, that was short and *not* very sweet. I can't tell how that went. If I had to guess, I would say we pricked his ego, if nothing else and possibly caused him some discomfort. Not at all sure we made up any ground, or if we even made much of an impression."

"I'm not so sure, Kev. That was a pretty strong statement there, saying he "could take offense". The sort of thing I would think spoken by someone with a guilty conscience or something to hide. And I have to tell you, that mention of the media and "bringing to justice" made him decidedly uncomfortable. We've stirred up the hornet's nest, and now we have to see where they fly. There doesn't seem to be anything further we can do here, so what do you think about getting on back to the airport and heading for home."

"Good idea. Maybe we've jarred something loose that would have them make a mistake, or move before they are really ready. Under any circumstances, there will be some maneuvering in DC before anything goes forward. We just need to be ready to put everything out in the public eye, and rely on the eventual force of those knowing that they need to do the right thing…"

George Benjamin was a shaken man. Although he felt he had managed to put off the two men who had been in his office earlier, it was obvious that they were on to something. *This should have been a very simple thing; commercial use of an obscure piece of ground that's under the control of the Park Service, for Christ's sake! Most people have never even heard of it, and those that have don't amount to a hill of beans. Bunch of Indians and 'wannabe' whites, not even all from around here, just a scattering across the country. Damn it all to hell! What with all these guys* could *know, or at least I* think *they know, it'll be almost impossible to make anyone buy into the idea that this 'job creation' proposal is what I say it is, and if they can make any kind of splash it'll bring the whole house crashing down around my ears!. By the time they float all this stuff they say they've found out to the press, nobody will think there isn't some sort of hidden agenda. Maybe I ought to get in touch with those IMM guys; pull the plug on this mining thing for the time being. Let them figure out how to do whatever they want without the Pipestone Quarry. Let them know the long-range risks are too great to do that now. No need to let them know I don't have a long-range plan that will do them any good or that includes them or their plans at all. What I'll do, I'll put off the 'jobs creation' thing, let the reporters know that something urgent has come up in Washington that won't allow time for a press conference here, then I can just endorse some other generic jobs plan from DC…Yes, that's it.*

Pacing as he debated with himself, he finally went to the phone on his desk and dialed the number he'd been given for times like this. *Now to call them. No, they said not to do that except in the case of a genuine emergency…I'll wait until I get back to DC, then call. Christopher and that Indian guy, Little Bird? Anyway, they won't be able to do anything in the little bit of time it'll take me to get back. Then we can sort out just how we move forward without giving ammunition to those do-gooders.*

Kevin was discouraged. When he and Matthew had confronted the Senator with their suspicions, he had been at first curiously impassive, then had puffed himself up with all the dignity of his office that he could muster, and had strongly denied any connection with the Quarry or any part of any mining operation. He chuckled wryly, "I thought for a minute there he was going to deny that he was even a Senator

"I have to agree, Kevin," said Matthew, "that the way he started out was almost simple-minded. But what bothered me was the way he came around. After berating us and taking offense, he did a big deal about Committees and discussions! He actually tried to make us think he wanted to help find out what was going on; no mind he had just denied he knew anything meaningful about the Quarry in the first place."

"The man has something up his sleeve," agreed Kevin. "Although I am afraid we may not have made the headway we wanted, we just may have shaken him up a bit. If we're just the least bit lucky we've probably bought ourselves some time. He'll likely, if we get that bit of luck, put off any overt action to free the Quarry for mining...just maybe." After musing a few minutes, he roused himself, "Matthew, what we need to do on the way back is decide just what we want to put out for the reporters to chew on. If we don't do that part of this just right, not only will we not help the Quarry, we're apt to get our butts in a crack for saying things about a Senator without foundation; slander, libel, that sort of thing. Don't know about you, but I don't want to have us in that position at the end of the day!

"Absolutely, Kev. We need to be judicious in what we say, and let the inferences carry the message that the media types will bite on. No need to confuse them with facts! But I'll tell you, Kev, as slippery as and as sure of himself as he is, and in my book much more than your average politician, something we said shook him. Problem is I'm not sure what it was. That turn-about at the end of the conversation was strange, didn't you think?"

"Very strange; almost as if there was something in the works, and he thought he might get the first jump. I'm just not sure."

"One thing for certain though," said Matthew, "And I'm very sure of this. When we mentioned Laura I thought he'd swallow his tongue. I'd bet he knew what happened to her, and I would also bet he knew it before we did. Not entirely sure why I'm so convinced of that; just something in the way he looked when her name came up. Maybe that's the opening we should try to exploit. Mickey mentioned that she had heard from some guys in the State Police Felony Investigation Unit, and they would not have been involved if Laura's death had been considered a genuine accident. She found it most peculiar, and if that's the case, that the police think they're dealing with a crime, then couldn't it be just possible that 'dear ole George' could have at least been party to a conspiracy? This wouldn't be just another illicit affair that we're dealing with. Heaven knows there've been plenty of those, and he wouldn't flinch over another allegation in that regard, but to tie him to a crime, a murder? That's a horse of an entirely different color!"

Re-energized by Matthew's ruminations, Kevin sat up and pounded the dash with his first. "You've got it Matthew! That'll be the angle we use when we get back. I think we can get that fella over at the Times to meet with us…maybe even dig around for someone at the State Police to make a statement for him. Yes, by George, and isn't that an interesting play on words, that's it! I couldn't see it myself. Thank God for different perspectives!"

After dropping the car at the rental lot, they walked out to the plane, animatedly discussing the new slant on the situation.

The drive up from Iowa had taken much longer than anticipated, the aged automobiles balky with a trip of that length, and the small group of Ojibwa was relieved to see the abandoned farm implement dealership ahead. They were about an hour behind the time they had thought they would arrive, and John Wolf anticipated that Jake would be furious. For all his shabby appearances, Jake was a very precise planner, and hated to see his schedules go awry. When they finally pulled up at the rear of the place however, Monroe seemed to be in an almost disinterested mood. Maybe he's just psyching himself up for whatever is ahead, thought Wolf, or maybe he's just becoming more and more lost from reality. *Guess we'll know soon enough.*

"Hello there. Trouble along the way? Thought you'd be here a lot sooner." Jake's tone was level, inquisitive but not irate.

"Yeah, one of the cars has a bad carburetor, transmission acting up on the other, had to coax them along a little, but we finally made it. So, what's the plan?" John knew he would have no opportunity to discuss the eventual plan with anyone, and wanted as much time as possible to consider his options once Jake laid out the whole scheme.

"Come on in here, and I'll show you what we're going to do. While I was waiting I had the time to make a diagram that'll show you how we're going to get away with it." Turning he disappeared through the sagging back door into the dim interior of the place.

A Coleman lantern had been set up on a shelf over a dusty work bench, it's hissing the only sound. They gathered in a rough semicircle in the harsh glare, Jake at one corner. Drawn in the dust of the bench was a rectangle with several openings in the sides, an arc across the long face of one side, and several "X's" in and out of the box. Speaking carefully and with the extra attention to diction common with people speaking to those they think may not know the language, Jake launched into an explanation of their mission. "This box represents the airport terminal in Marshall, not much as you can see. The purpose of this effort is to take out an enemy of your people, and an insult to mine. He will be coming through this terminal to pick up a plane he's had donated for his use. He will also speak to the press and reveal this latest betrayal of all Native Americans. In order to protect the culture of your people and to provide some salve to the conscience of my people, I will personally kill Senator George Benjamin." Jake paused here, for effect. *No need telling them that I'll be waiting until after the Senator has announced that the Quarry will be opened for his "jobs initiative" before he is hit. Those lemmings in the Senate will then feel morally obliged to carry forward with the "Benjamin Employment Initiative" in his memory. What a bunch of nitwits!!*

Jake knew that he had to convince only John Wolf, the nominal head of the group. In the fashion of many Indian groups, they would have selected a leader among themselves, and Wolf was the apparent choice, and Jake knew that this was where they would look for direction, not to him. It was one of the more aggravating things about working with the Indians, but he had learned to accept it, and even to look upon the advantages of dealing essentially with

225

an individual and not a divergent gang, as had been the case when he had worked the LA riots a while back.

"This is very serious business, Jake," Wolf said in amazement. Nothing that had gone before had prepared him for something as momentous as this.

"Yes, extremely; but this is a matter of some necessity, and your participation will show the whites that there are limits to what they may do."

"And what is it then; that this man, this Senator Benjamin, has in mind that is so significant that he must be killed for it?" John didn't want this situation to get completely out of hand without knowing what the stakes were going to be. Killing a United States Senator would bring down the law such as they had never seen; and he was certain that Standing Bear and The Council were not thinking of anything of this magnitude.

"This man, this maker of laws, intends to turn the Pipestone Quarry over to mining interests! They would bar your people from gathering the material for your sacred uses, and dig it all out with machines. It would be worse, much worse than when the pipestone was destroyed when they took the quartz for buildings, or when just a few men took pipestone for making trinkets and bogus artifacts. It would be almost as bad as the carving of president's faces on the holy mountain they now call Rushmore!"

Stunned into silence, the men gaped at the revelations made, and John Wolf felt his face growing hot with rage. As he contemplated the enormity of the desecration he felt a flash of inspiration. This was a way to not only prevent the Senator from completing his betrayal, but would also bring about the downfall of Jake Monroe at the same time. Senses sharp, he focused on the outlined plan that Jake laid out.

226

It was simple, really. Jake and one other man would take up a station near the departure area the Senator would go through to board his plane. In a widened section of that space, a backdrop had been hung, and lights and a flag erected so that the news briefing could be held just before his departure. This was where the attack would take place, and in the ensuing panic and disarray, the two would escape out the terminal door, turning around the building where their vehicles, newly stolen from a long-term parking area. Others in the group would hold the security guards at bay, and contribute to the pandemonium by firing the weapons randomly, even at the ceiling if they chose not to take additional white lives. Under this withdrawing cover, they would easily make their escape from such a small building. Given the level of confusion, probably no accurate eye witness accounts or descriptions would be available to the police. Anyone who had gotten too close a look would simply be eliminated on the spot.

Jake had scouted the terminal, and said that except for a few extra security guards, there was little in the way of special preparations. Metal detectors and X-ray equipment had been put in place as might have been expected with the Senator making his departure, but should not prove any trouble. John thought this comment curious, but was enlightened when Jake showed them one of the special weapons that he said were undetectable by x-ray machines or metal detectors. Although skeptical of this last, the men observed that since Jake was going to use one as well, maybe there was something to what he said. When Jake had finished his lecture on the plan of action, he looked at Wolf. Using the Ojibwa language, John told his half dozen compatriots that he would give them their final instructions, and then indicated to Jake there would be no questions.

Eyes narrowing with suspicion, Jake turned on Wolf, "What the hell did you say just now? I want to hear everything you tell those guys, and in English, ya' hear? No more of this Indian talk!"

"Sure, Jake," Wolf said in a placating tone. "I just told them to be on their toes when we went in there. Some of these guys don't understand all they hear in English, and it comforts them to know their instructions will be coming in a language they fully understand. But I'll be sure and interpret if I need to do that again."

"Just be sure that you do," Monroe growled. Then he walked over to a stack of mismatched satchels on the floor, and handed one to each man. Looking over at John, he asked, "Do these guys know anything about assault rifles?"

Gesturing to a young man standing at the forefront of the group, John said, "He does. He spent some time in the Army. He'll be able to show the others that aren't all that familiar." They both watched the bag was opened and the odd looking weapon revealed.

With questioning eyes, the man, Justin Walking Bear, turned about and said, "This thing ain't right John. It's all kinda red, not black like the ones I've used. Looks almost like a kid's toy."

"No, no," Jake pushed through the group and took the weapon. "This is just a new material that it's made out of, why the detection machines won't see it. And believe me, I've use it and it is no toy. You use it just the same way as one of the ones you had in the Army. Here, let me show you…"

There's a way to make this work, John thought. *This.is really going to work! All I'm going to need is a little time to pass on the word to them…Know how to do that…"*

"Billy, hey man! Come on out here and let's see if we can get this car running better. I don't want to have to walk to this thing", he called out to one of the others.

Jake looked at him with a scowl, but continued to pass the weapons out to the men, giving each man spare ammunition, and spending a few minutes explaining the particular characteristics of each type.

Wolf and Billy Elkhorn walked casually to one of the cars and raised the hood. "What're you talking about, John? There's nothing wrong with either of these cars now, except they're old and may want to break down again."

"I now that, but I needed some time away from Monroe. He's going to want me to ride over there with him, put one of the other guys in his van as a driver, so I wouldn't have time to tell you what I want you to do. Start the engine, I'll hold the carburetor open so it sounds bad, then we can talk while it looks like we're fixing the thing. And remember; speak only in Ojibwa when you're giving the guys these instructions. Don't want to take the chance Monroe will overhear. Now here goes..."

Jake felt completely pumped up as he sauntered into the small air terminal, John Wolf and two of the other Indians trailing behind a few paces, seeming not to be with him. Glancing casually about, he saw other Indians strolling, looking at magazines in the newsstand. That many Indians might have caused an eyebrow to rise in some places, but he knew that it wasn't all that unusual around here; just one more little detail he savored as having been covered with his planning. He walked over to an isolated alcove that had once held a now-defunct car rental desk, and placed a final call to Williamson, leaving the service with a coded message that all was in place and working.

That done, he walked with some added purpose towards the departure area, passed through the security checkpoint, with a seemingly nonchalant. Wolf followed shortly behind, and took up his position near the fire exit door. Jake stood out of the main concourse walkway but with a clear view of the draped area. As he stood there, he wished that he felt better physically. After this was over, maybe he'd see about getting to one of the doctors that he knew to be safe, and see if maybe he had an ulcer starting or something.

John Wolf stood back and to one side of Jake, slipped on a pair of thin leather gloves, and felt again for the nine-millimeter pistol inside the carry-on duffel bag. True to Jake's word, they had passed through the metal detectors, and had the bags x-rayed with no problems. Jake had brought both a machine pistol secreted in a worn briefcase and a folding-stock assault rifle, which he now had concealed in the folds of his grimy overcoat, having removed it from the battered suitcase he had used to get it through the security checkpoint. John thought it odd that he carried both rifle and pistol, but then, Jake Monroe was an odd man.

CHAPTER 23

There was a commotion at the entranceway to the terminal, and the Senator swept in, reporters darting in from each side with microphones, and members of his entourage forming a wedge through the crowd as he made this way across the terminal and into the departure area. Moving behind the small podium, he smiled broadly at the gathering as the reporters arranged themselves in irregular rows in front of him. Cameramen checked focus and lens openings and both print and electronic reporters readied notepads. Benjamin joked with those he knew, smiled willingly for pictures.

Altogether maybe fifteen, eighteen, mused Jake. *That's good. Coverage in some of the major markets, and then worldwide from there. What a sales presentation this will be!* He chuckled softly to himself; the Senator having made a joke, the gaffe wasn't noticed.

Raising both hands, palms down, George Benjamin quieted the small crowd and, beaming with apparent pleasure asked needlessly for quiet. Then, with a small frown of concern, he addressed the microphones and cameras, "Ladies and gentlemen, I know that when you were notified of this conference, you were advised that I would be announcing a job creation program that would have significant economic impact on the nation, the state, and especially the southwest region of our great state. Unfortunately, as I worked with my staff to complete the details of the program, I received a most urgent call from Washington, and find that I must return there immediately, in order to confer with party leaders on a vital civil rights measure coming up for vote very soon. Since my program was not completed, I feel it would be an injustice to it to

231

present even an outline to you with the essence only partially done, and…"

As the Senator continued, Jake's eyes widened in disbelief. *That son of a bitch isn't going to do it! By God, he's led us down the garden path, taken our money, and now he's weaseling out! I can't believe it, but I know what to do about. The bastard!* Thoughts churning with rage and frustration, he swung the assault rifle up through the folds of his coat. With a surreptitious glance around, he saw that all eyes were fixed on the illuminated face of the speaker. Having chosen his spot carefully, he slowly raised the weapon, his clear line of fire to the Senator widening a bit as reporters leaned forward in anticipation of a question and answer period.

John Wolf had also chosen a line that gave him a clear shot, and he had extracted the blocky automatic from the carry-on and was holding it pointed straight down, ready in an instant to fire. As he listened, he realized that the announcement Jake had said would be made was not to be forthcoming. Relaxing a bit, listening to the words that had come to have no meaning for him, he looked over at Monroe, seeking an indication of his reaction As he watched, he saw the shabby coat move, and the barrel of the assault rifle emerge from the voluminous folds. He thought, briefly, *Given the choice of two, I wonder why he's using that instead of the more compact machine pistol…doesn't make any sense…* Then as the movement's significance registered, *My God, he's going to do it anyway! Without the Quarry announcement, he's still going ahead…Well, then, we'll have the same outcome, just the bonus…*

George Benjamin had begun breaking off the briefing when the first burst of gunfire shattered the podium and his left hand. In shock, he looked down at the blood and splintered bone. The second burst, almost instantly following the first, plowed through his chest, and a single bullet from the third entered his brain through his right eye and tore out the back of his skull. His standing corpse was flung against the draped wall, and slid slowly to a sitting position on the floor.

At the sound of the first shots, reporters and admirers dropped instinctively to the ground, or stood in stunned confusion, depending on whether or not they had ever heard the sound of a semi-automatic weapon. The security force, such as it was, looked about wildly for the source, echoes in the building rendering sound a useless locator.

After the third burst, Jake, a maniacal smile fixed on his lips, began to turn towards the exit door to his right, dropping the machine pistol, anticipating the sound of the covering fire from the Indians. In that strange aftermath of extremely violent episodes, everything seemed to move in slow motion, and as the echoes from the rifle fire died, there was an almost overwhelming silence. Taking his first steps toward the exit door, the silence registered in Jake's racing mind. Where the hell are they? Why aren't they covering? He looked to where Wolf should have been waiting by the door, ready to take out any following security and saw only the door, slowly closing.

Having called from the plane to tell John Washington that it was probably time to notify the authorities, Kevin and Mathew had settled back in their seats and waited while the plane made its way to the runway and took off. They began to discuss the manner in which they would apply political and media pressure to restrain Benjamin from releasing the Quarry's resources, and puzzled over how to launch the campaign to raise public awareness of the history and continuing desecration of sacred Native American sites. Although they had not been able to gain any specific promises from the Senator regarding the Quarry they contented themselves with the thought that they would be able to allude to non-specific action, and then hold him to it through a series of expectantly worded press releases. It was something of a surprise when the phone was brought to them by the cabin attendant, saying there was a call from a Ms. Campbell.

"Mickey, how are you?" Kevin responded to her greeting. "What a pleasant surprise to hear from you. Is everything all right there?"

"Kevin, you are not going to believe this. Is there a TV on that flying palace, or are you guys roughing it?"

"Well, yes, there is one, but why would we be watching television?"

"You'll want to watch this," she said. "Turn it on, and I'll stay on the line. And it doesn't really make any difference what channel; it's on all of them."

Catching the urgency in her voice, Kevin covered the mouthpiece and, turning to Matthew said, "It's Mickey. She says there's something important on the television. Turn that on and let's see what she's talking about."

Matthew switched on the small flat-screen set into the bulkhead and was confronted with a scene that looked like a gangland shooting. Blood spattered cloth and walls, mass confusion, a huddle of medical technicians over a body, police holding a mingled crowd of reporters and the curious at bay. "Kevin, you know what we're supposed to be looking at?"

"No, but I'm sure we'll find out pretty soon. News people can never *not* say anything. Mickey, are you still there; want to give us a hint?"

234

"Kev, what you're looking at is the departure area at the Marshall, Minnesota airport. Someone just assassinated George Benjamin!"

"You must be kidding! But no, I hear now that you're not! My Lord! Are there any details? Did they catch the killer? Any motive?"

"Not a lot being said, except that a suspect is in custody. You can bet there's going to be a fairly tight lid kept on this so one of my tricky defense-lawyer colleagues can't say that pre-trial publicity made a fair trial impossible. Ya'll need to come on over as soon as you get in. Do you know when that will be?"

"Not really sure. Why don't you talk to Matthew for a minute, and I'll check with the crew." Handing the phone to Matthew, Kevin gestured to the attendant, who said she would be back in a second. Kevin watched as Matthew's expression changed from a grave frown to a gentle smile. He unconsciously turned slightly away, and spoke softly into the handset.

Tapping him on the shoulder, Kevin said, "Tell Mickey that we'll be in around ten, and that we can meet her at the Blacksmith Shop about a half hour later, if that's okay with her."

John Wolf sat easily opposite Standing Bear in the semi-dark room. He had related the entire incident from the time he had left for Minnesota until now. He was comfortable with his actions, and waited for Standing Bear to speak. His only uneasiness came from the lengthening moments since he had presented the facts to his mentor. The silence, with which he usually had no problem, had lengthened to a point where he began to feel like a small a boy called

235

to discipline before a classroom. Still, he calmed himself, and waited for the great man's words.

"You tell me that the plan Monroe presented was for the killing of this Senator in order to sooth the conscience of his people over the proposed desecration of the sacred quarry. Before going to the airport you felt this would be a chance to rid our people not only of Monroe, but the danger to the quarry at the same time, and that your intent was to kill the Senator yourself, saving the honor for one of us, then allowing Monroe to be taken by the police. Why, again, did this not happen?"

"What the Senator said when he came to the airport had nothing to do with the Pipestone Quarry. He said things about a job creation program he had not finished, and some sort of civil rights meeting in Washington. Monroe just opened fire. As it happened, the others in our group did not know who fired the shots but had acted as I instructed. They simply walked out of the terminal before the firing began. I was close to a door and left as soon as Monroe began to shoot. He was left with no distraction, no cover, and the security police were able to take him right away. I do not believe anyone in or around the airport even knew we were there. On the way back, we filled the bags with stones and dropped them and the weapons in the river as we crossed. The weapons were very strange, and could have linked us with Monroe."

"So we have accomplished our task of ridding ourselves of Monroe, and you have committed no crime other than to associate with him; a thing easily overlooked." Standing Bear paused, and looked out the window at the moon hanging over the trees of the wooded area near the house. Turning with a grunt, he pulled the decorated deerskin pouch to him and began to remove its contents. "You have done extremely well, John Wolf. It is through young men such as you that the message of the Red Way will be carried forward. You will go from here a respected and soon widely known warrior in our fight to retain what is ours. The People will know the name of John Wolf. I will see to that. You planned well, and knew when not to do certain things. That is the lesson many of our brothers must learn. The whites are too many for us to go all the way back to the way things were, but we may hold them where they are, and keep them from taking more. The war days in the best way have finished. We are left to fight this new kind of war. And now we will smoke. I will prepare the *chanunpa*. We will thank *Tunkashila* for his support in our success. I apologize now for using the Lakota words. You know their meaning, but think them in your Ojibwa. Then you will be on your way. You are right; it is good to go to the wilderness. It reminds us of our oneness with the earth. We will make a small fire here now, and smoke..."

Newscasts had been filled with little other than the assassination, and the three friends had taken a break from the constant repetition of essentially the same facts. Kevin looked over at his companions, at the way they seemed to always touch, and smiled at this reaffirmation that normality would return. The blossoming of their love had been something of a surprise, having known them both for so long, he would never have put them together, but then that was the way of such things. He returned to the terrace, where they had moved from watching Fox News, and offered the tray of coffee refills to each before seating himself on a bench. "It seems almost impossible that this has happened. I heard one newscaster say that the man who did the shooting was raving something about being betrayed by Indians."

"Yes, I heard that too," said Michaela. "I also heard earlier while you two were still in the air that he had been tentatively identified as a Jake Monroe. The name meant nothing to me, but they said he was one of those Weather Underground terrorists from the sixties and seventies, and has been wanted for years in connection with some sort of bombing incident."

"Interesting," Kevin nodded. "I've heard of the organization, of course, and I vaguely remember the name. He was never as notorious as some of them, such as Bill Ayers, but guess there were more than we thought that eluded capture back then; still around to haunt us."

He was interrupted by the insistent chirping of the telephone. Going quickly to the instrument just inside in the greenhouse, he heard John Washington's excited voice on the other end. Listening intently he mouthed John's name to Mathew and Michaela, then continued listening as the other man went on. After several minutes, he thanked him for calling and walked back to the terrace, shaking his head. "It's incredible. When a team from IMM reached the research lab, they found that the chief of the division, a man named Williamson, had attempted to run, and had fallen on some stairs. He's now in serious condition in a hospital there. He's expected to remain in a coma for a time, but at this point is under guard as the state of his recovery is established. The computer records that Williamson had kept were hidden behind a dual password access code, but the team was able to get in, and the findings are astonishing. Apparently Williamson, in league with the researchers he had recruited from the student left, had been developing weapons that would be invisible in metal detectors and, I emphasize this, x-ray as well. The ingredients were unusual, but included in the list was catlinite. Can you believe it? Anyway, the IMM internal auditors are going through all of the contract files now. They've already found enough to put the whole bunch away almost forever. One other thing, though, they found a notation, apparently the last made, that one member of the team had found that the weapons material gave up an oily residue when it became hot, as in when the weapons were fired. That residue is suspected to be a toxic compound, and is absorbed through the skin. It's not certain which component was the

238

culprit, as none are on their own, but in combination they produced this poisonous substance when heated. They discovered this when the armorers that made and tested the things all came down sick, and then two of them died. A real shame there, as they were true innocent bystanders, so to speak. They'd just been hired to do a job. The only one that wasn't affected was a guy who had an artificial arm, and used it quite by coincidence, to handle the hot weapons. Needless to say, there won't be any more research done with that particular compound!"

"Do you think someone won't pick up on that though, Kevin, and try to rearrange the components a little to achieve the same thing? I would think they would, and that means that despite all that's happened in the last few days, the Quarry is still in danger." Matthew's concern came through in the tone of his voice, and it was obvious that he thought the "battle" might be over, but the "war" continued.

"I think Matt has something there," Mickey chimed in.

"And I agree with you both. We've a lot of work ahead of us, and I'm afraid the Quarry is just one of many sacred places that are in danger. But along the lines of doing something about it, I think we could all do with some rest. It's been one helluva couple of days, and I, for one, am completely bushed. Let's call this a night and talk again in the morning about how we'll carry this forward."

EPiLOGUE

Mickey smiled as she tucked her legs under her and curled closer to Matthew. They had moved from dinner in the little resort cabin to the deep porch; looking down the mountains to the Shenandoah Valley. The summer sun was beginning to set as they swayed on the creaky swing suspended by chains from the porch roof rafters.

"I never thought we would find things again this peaceful after the past month," she said.

"My thought exactly, my love. These past weeks have been frenetic as I can ever recall, but the last few days have made it all right," he said with a grin

"Well there was that wedding thing, and meeting your parents. After the total circus the press created with Benjamin's funeral, I would have bet there wouldn't be a chance that anything crazier could have happened, but the way things played out in Iowa really topped it all... but the wedding of course!"

"Amazing..."

Although the EMT crew had moved swiftly from their pre-positioned spot outside the terminal, there was no doubt that the damage caused by the bullets at such close range made their haste fruitless. Benjamin was quickly placed on a gurney and pushed into the ambulance, with the grim faced medics pushing past the crowd of the curious. During the race to the local hospital, John Gilliam, the lead medic, leaned back and placed a gloved hand on his fellow medic's arm. "Jimmy, no matter how quick we'd been, it didn't make a bit of difference. I saw enough of shot up men in Afghanistan to know a corpse when I see one. I'd be surprised if he had hardly *any* blood left, not to mention the back of his head is gone. The docs will call it when we hit the hospital, but this guy is gonzo. Do you know who he is?"

"I'd forgotten you were new here. This is the one and only Senator George Benjamin, Senior Senator from our beloved state," Jimmy Middleton's sarcasm evident not only in what he said, but the sneering tone of his voice. "That old tom cat didn't do squat for anybody but his donor-buddies, and if half the rumors was true, he screwed a good portion of the females over twenty and under sixty from here to Washington, DC. My Daddy said that he not only talked out of both sides of his mouth, but that he had all the morals of a goat."

"Geeze, I had no idea he was who he was, and hadn't heard enough about him to know what he might have been like. A Senator, huh? All that gone now, though. Let's see about cleaning him up a bit, cover him and then let the docs take it from there. We ought to be at the hospital in just a few minutes now."

Gilliam's observations were true. After a speedy but thorough examination in the ER, the doctors pronounced George Benjamin dead, and proceeded to a small covered porch outside the emergency room, now surrounded by members of the press who had followed the ambulance to the Hospital. In a low, solemn voice, the lead surgeon, flanked by two other doctors that had been in the room, he said "I must inform you that at 2:57 this afternoon, after receiving gunshot wounds to his upper body and head, Senator George Benjamin was pronounced dead, although he was technically dead on arrival at our facility. Inasmuch as this is a crime, we will issue no further statements, and advise you to pursue your questioning with the police and other authorities that might be involved." With a swirl of his white lab coat he stalked away from the shouting reporters, with his fellow physicians following back through the emergency room doors.

The furor in the press began almost immediately, with a mad rush of network anchors racing to airports in the frantic drive to be the first on the scene of what one termed "a scene of utmost horror in the Heartland". The onsite reporters, frustrated with a lack of information, or even someone to talk to at the hospital, returned to the airport to see if there was anyone there that could make a story. Each vying with the other to present the most dramatic account of the day's happenings, interspersed with faux-heartfelt tributes to "the great son of Minnesota". The complete lack of factual information deterred them not one bit, as some them saw the assassination a possible rung up the ladder to the "Big Time" in New York or Washington.

Little information was made public about the actual crime, and soon the press corps moved en masse to Washington for the beginning of the funereal spectacle. Being the first sitting Senator to be assassinated, they spewed the considerable back-story of the history of the Senate, and the various characters that had reigned there over the years. After three days of lying state at the Capital, and a seemingly endless succession of speeches, a near-weeping President delivered a eulogy decrying the loss of "this noble servant of the people of his state, and of the nation".

A funeral train had been nixed when it was discovered that the trip would entail changes of railroads, crews and engines along the way, and would eventually take almost four days to make the trip. At the last minute the President allowed the use of one of the planes in the Air Force VIP fleet. The final trip started from Andrews Air Force Base outside Washington and ended with a military escort cobbled together from personnel of the 934th Airlift Wing located adjacent to the Minneapolis – St. Paul International Airport. After the arrival ceremony, George Benjamin was loaded in a hearse, taken to the Fort Snelling National Cemetery nearby, and after a few more speeches by various local dignitaries, finally laid to rest. The entire proceedings, from Andrews to Snelling was conducted under the ever vigilant eyes of the entire spectrum of media, engaging in their own eulogizing before turning, finally, to other topics.

One of those topics swirled around a man named Jake Monroe, found to be a long-sought fugitive for his participation in what were essentially terrorist activities in the seventies. He had been arrested, with some furious resistance, at the airport where Benjamin was murdered, and awaited arraignment on the formal charges. While incarcerated in the local jail, he had complained repeatedly about illness, but found no sympathy from the prison staff. On the third day following his arrest, he was found dead in his cell from causes unknown. An autopsy revealed a remarkably high level of inorganic toxins in his system from some unknown source. A full-scale investigation by the Federal Bureau of prisons, activated due to the high profile nature of the basic crime, revealed no contaminants that could have been the source of the poisonous substances in either food, water or furnishings in the prison. Nonetheless environmental groups and inmate advocacy groups joined forces and petitioned the Governor and the President to have the prison closed until it could be proven that it was safe for habitation by prisoners, and that those within be granted immediate parole on the grounds that incarceration in a possibly toxic environment was "cruel and unusual punishment"

243

forbidden by the Constitution. Offices of both the Governor and the President stated that they would take the matter under study, in the meantime transferring the prisoners to other facilities to quiet the strident voices, and then they quietly returned them to their original place of confinement after a few days.

In addition to that little tempest, it was widely reported that documents found in the IMM Research Center in Northern Iowa implicated seventeen individuals in the fraudulent execution of government contracts and tax evasion. Sixteen of the seventeen were found to be fugitives from various radical groups and they were promptly taken into custody. A nationwide bulletin was issued for the arrest of the last, one Henry Genarro, who had not been found with the others at the facility. All of those arrested knew him, but none knew his whereabouts, noting that he had not been around for several days.

A Justice Department spokesman stated that indictments would be handed down shortly for the named individuals on a wide range of charges beyond the fraud, contract, and tax crimes. Most notable among those named was Dr. Malcolm Williamson, who had headed the Pure Research Department. Found in his computer by FBI experts were hundreds of files that laid out the scheme to produce special weapons, as well as numbers of several accounts in Switzerland and the Cayman Islands, apparently with staggering sums in each. Privately the prosecutors assigned to the case felt it was doubtful that anything would come of the indictment of Williamson. In his haste to escape from the Center when he received news of Monroe's arrest, he had fallen on the stairs from his office, and was eventually found to have suffered significant brain damage. He was moved to the Western Iowa State Hospital for the Mentally Disadvantaged, and placed in a secure section of the institution in the event he ever recovered sufficiently to stand trial.

In a short announcement of the disposition of Federal grant funds for bridge improvements, the Virginia Department of Transportation announced that several older bridges in northern Virginia counties would be earmarked for replacement. Located in Fairfax, Clarke, Loudon and Fauquier Counties, the group of spans included in the work was the Purcellville Bridge.

"Mickey?"

"Hmmm?"

"Do you suppose we could delay our return for a few more days? I'm thinking we could let your associates cover for you in your office, and I don't have to be at my new position at Georgetown for another couple of weeks. We could take our time getting back, stop at one of those Bed and Breakfast places we saw on the way up here. We wouldn't need to be back until Kevin's presentation ceremony up in Minnesota... How about it?"

"I like the idea a lot, but don't believe it would be right to take *that* much time out of my office, and with your new appointment to Georgetown's faculty you must want to get settled in your office before the new term begins. I can't wait to see the presentation ceremony, though! Kevin seems so pleased by the whole idea of the thing!"

"You can't fault him for his pleasure. It is a fine testimonial to his attention to the Indian issues; can't imagine why that recognition hasn't come sooner. He's going to be made an honorary member of the Lakota tribe, and he told me that they were going to present him with one of the old, antique pipes, a true *chanunpa,* complete with an equally antique carrying pouch. But you're right as usual, we can't, don't want to be away that much, either of us. We'll just have to find a way to extend our little honeymoon other ways," he said with a smile.

"I believe we could start on that right away. Have any ideas, big fella?"

As they left the little porch, they took one last look over the beautiful vista and embraced in the lowering shadows.

George Catlin   (1796 – 1892)

"I have seen him shrinking from civilized approach, which came with all its vices, like the dead of night upon him. I have seen him gaze and then retreat like the frightened deer ... seen him shrinking from the soil and haunts of his boyhood, bursting the strongest ties which bound him to the earth and its pleasures. I have seen him set fire to his wigwam and smooth over the graves of his fathers ... clap his hand in silence over his mouth, and take the last look over his fair hunting ground, and turn his face in sadness to the setting sun. All this I have seen performed in nature's silent dignity ... and I have seen as often the approach of the bustling, busy, talking, whistling, hopping, elated and exulting white man, with the first dip of the ploughshare, making sacrilegious trespass on the bones of the valiant dead. I have seen the grand and irresistible march of civilization. I have seen this splendid juggernaut rolling on and beheld its sweeping desolation, and held converse with the happy thousands, living as yet beyond its influence, who have not been crushed, nor yet have dreamed of its approach."

"They waste us, aye, like April snow,
In the warm noon we shrink away;
And fast they follow as we go
Towards the setting day,
Till they shall fill the land, and we
Are driven into the Western sea. "

"Gleaming with the setting sun
One burning sheet of living gold,
The mountain Lake beneath him rolled;
In all her length far winding lay,
With promontory, creek, and bay,
And islands that, empurpled bright,
Floated amid the livelier lights
To sentinel enchanted land."

ACKNOWLEDGEMENTS

As with any creative work, nothing stands as a totally singular effort, and this book is no exception. Aside from the unrelenting support from my wife Barbara, I want to acknowledge those who have helped bring a full cycle to the story of Pipestone. Carl Linke, twice published in his own right, was the hero that made the first read, and his comments and ongoing support through the entire process have been greatly appreciated. Lois Gilbert lent the touch of a professional to the first content edit, and my hope is that the finished product is one that she would admire. Susan Stroh added some very helpful comments dealing with context that made the end result better. Daughter Beth Garriques lent the eye of a well-schooled English major, and her suggestions regarding grammar and content have to be recalled. And finally, I wish to extend my gratitude and admiration to the National Park Service and the Lakota Sioux nation for their persistence and diligence in the preservation of the Pipestone Quarry for the cultural welfare of future generations.

www.ingramcontent.com/pod-product-compliance
Lightning Source LLC
Chambersburg PA
CBHW030136180626
46812CB00002B/709